HEALER'S TOUCH

HEALER'S
TOUCH

by

ANNE GRAY

SUMACH
PRESS

Library and Archives Canada Cataloguing in Publication

Gray, Anne (Anne Elizabeth)
Healer's touch : a young adult novel / Anne Gray.

ISBN 978-1-894549-77-6

I. Title.

PS8613.R386H42 2008   jC813'.6   C2008-902966-6

Edited by Jennifer Day
Copy-edited by Emily Schultz
Designed by Liz Martin
Cover art by Charmaine Lurch

*Sumach Press acknowledges the support of the Canada Council
for the Arts and the Ontario Arts Council for our publishing program.
We acknowledge the financial support of the Government of Canada through
the Book Publishing Industry Development Program (BPIDP)
for our publishing activities.*

ONTARIO ARTS COUNCIL
CONSEIL DES ARTS DE L'ONTARIO

Printed and bound in Canada

Published by

SUMACH PRESS
1415 Bathurst Street #202
Toronto ON Canada M5R 3H8

*info@sumachpress.com
www.sumachpress.com*

For my husband
David A. H. Newman

Acknowledgements

There are many people I would like to thank
for their help over the years, but I'm especially grateful
to my friend and first reader, Gillian Chan, for her
encouragement since the beginning, and also
to Ann Fedak and Nairn Galvin for their many
helpful comments and suggestions on this and other
manuscripts. I am also grateful to my publishers at
Sumach Press for their continued support, to my
editor, Jennifer Day, for her guidance in shaping the
manuscript and to the copy editor, Emily Schultz.
I would also like to thank my husband,
David A. H. Newman, for his unfailing
faith and encouragement.

When our forefathers came to this world, they received gifts from Machia, each according to his merits. Those of Technol became great makers, carving tunnels through the mountains, harnessing the might of the lakes and rivers to provide water and power to their Villages, erecting buildings that would last through the ages.

The navigators received gifts that allowed them to sing the winds and tides, enchant the creatures of the sea and, with their singing and music, enchant others. But early these Fisher Folk turned to the Sea, and we know nothing more of them.

Others went to dwell in the Hills where they worked with plants and animals, using their gifts to make these strong and plentiful, and they learned the many mysteries of healing.

To us, The Blessed, was given the greatest gift, the gift of Mind. Some of us were destined to roam our world, exploring the unknown regions, often going separate ways, yet once we had mapped those far places, we always returned to our first home and kindred and, through our gift, we remained as One People.

But the Giants of the land were envious of our great gift and refused to teach us as was our due. When we would compel the Giants, those of Technol, the Villagers, joined our battle, but the treacherous Hill Folk refused to take up arms and stood apart. To thwart our just cause, the Giants raised a great Shield against us.

Then came the second wave of Technol's children to the Village and led their brothers there into false worship of the unnamed gods, causing them to forsake the Goddess Machia. Then they turned against us as well, condemning our ways of worship, and thus were we doomed to abandon our homes and flee to the far ends of our world.

Yet, we have been promised that there will rise One who will lead us to reclaim our rightful home and heritage, and when the many gifted ones are united, the Shield of the Giants will be brought down by us, the People of the Plains, Machia's Blessed Ones.

From *The Chronicles of the Blessed*

One

A T THE TOP OF THE HILL DOVELLA REINED IN THE GREY
mare and gazed at the fields spread out below, a few
patches of yellow and grey amidst the dusty brown of
drought-stricken land. Farmers were busy in the fields, a sign
they had found hope that there would be a good crop this
year, after all. And indeed there was hope, now. More than
hope. There was promise, she thought, noting a few sprigs of
green pushing through the soil beside the road.

And she had brought that promise. It was she who had
journeyed to find out why the waters flowing to her Village
had diminished; she who had found the source of that water;
and she who had restored power and water to her people —
with help from the Hill Folk. She glanced over her shoulder
at her retreating companions. She had urged them to go with
her all the way to the Village, but on reflection they had left
her here, afraid that their presence would cause trouble in the
already divided Village. Even though she would tell everyone
how she could not have succeeded without these people of
the hills, enmity between Hill Folk and Villagers had lasted
too long to be wiped out so easily. Such ways of thinking
would take time to change.

Dovella kneed her mount forward and continued down
the road. A few farmers paused in their labour and waved

even though they couldn't know who she was or what she had done. She smiled and waved back. That new hope had also brought new friendliness, she thought; or restoration of the old friendliness that had been lost in the troubles of the past few years. She rode on toward the Village, the sunshine warming her face, until she crested the last hill. Home, she thought. She was almost home! Sensing Dovella's excitement, perhaps, the horse broke into a trot and then cantered the final stretch to the gates.

The ostler came to greet her, a broad grin breaking out when he saw who it was. Clearly he was one who did know who she was and what she had done. He whispered something to one of the stable boys who threw a respectful look over his shoulder at Dovella and then raced off down the main road. Favouring his left leg, the ostler hobbled forward and took hold of the reins. As Dovella dismounted, he stroked the mare's neck.

"I'll see to your horse and pack," he said. "You go on. Your parents will want to see you. Everybody will want to see you." He shook his head with a solemn air. "You can't know just what you achieved in getting our power and water back to capacity." Then he grinned. "The timing could not have been better! But ... well, you just run along. That story is not for me to tell."

"Thank you," she said, returning his smile. "You can't know how good it is to be home." Dovella smoothed her dark braid and slapped at her dusty tunic, wondering what he meant about timing. Well, she'd find out soon enough. She glanced around, her own energy renewed as she breathed in the Village air. Everything seemed newly washed and fresh.

The streets were more astir than usual as small clumps

of people gathered here and there waving. Shouts rang out. "Welcome home!" she heard, and "Thank you!" and "Good job!" as more people fell into step around her. She could feel her cheeks redden at the unexpected tributes, and smiled in embarrassment as she wiped damp palms on the legs of her trews. A black dog under a tree looked up as she passed, and even he seemed to be panting a welcome.

Workmen, their tunics laid aside, were busy repairing the roads and painting store fronts in preparation for the up-coming festivities. The fresh paint glistened in the afternoon sunlight. I'll be home for Festival after all, Dovella thought. She smiled and waved when one of the workmen took off his cap and gave a half bow, grinning through his bristly beard.

Behind one group of welcoming Villagers, she saw three men scowling in her direction as they whispered among themselves. She'd seen several such groups along the way. Not everyone was happy with what she'd achieved. As she had discovered on her journey, the breakdown of the machine at the source had been no accident.

A little girl ran up and thrust a scraggly clump of flowers into Dovella's hands then raced back and buried her face in her mother's apron. The woman beamed at Dovella. Tears filled Dovella's eyes and the bystanders became a blur of col-our. Dovella heard an excited shout up ahead: "She's home!"

She paused outside the building where her family lived. Much as she desired to go up and wash off the dust of the journey, it could wait. She was anxious to find her parents, who would be at work.

As she neared the park across from the Engineering Building, she noted that the leaves still drooped, but again there was new growth in the grass. A window opened above her and one of the Engineering apprentices stuck out his head. "You're home!" He turned and shouted over his shoulder, "It's true! Dovella's home!"

She was about to enter the building to see her mother, when she heard shouts and a great clatter coming from a distance. Her mouth gone suddenly dry, she checked her steps to listen more closely. The sounds of violence came from the direction of Healer's Hall where her father would be working. *No!* Dovella's mind screamed as she broke into a run.

Guided by the yells and clamour, she rounded the corner of Healer's Hall and came upon a rioting mob. Dovella stopped short in amazement at the sight of her father, the gentle Healer Safir, flailing away with a stave at the New School fanatics who attacked him from every side. Seeing her peace-loving father forced to violence, she rushed to his defence, turning back the rioters with kicks and blocks and punches. The drought-seared grass crunched under her feet as she lashed out at those nearest Safir. With a quick glance, he acknowledged her presence, relief and welcome lighting up his eyes, but there was no time for Safir to express either aloud for they were hard-pressed to protect themselves against their attackers.

One of them came at her now and she had to bring to bear all the training she'd received from Security Master Pandil. Dovella dodged the man's attack, whirled and kicked the back of his knee. He faltered, but recovered quickly and swung at her again. She ducked, kicked again and whirled away. Finally, her attacker made too hasty a turn. He lost his balance, allowing her to kick him so hard that he dropped his cudgel and screamed curses at her.

She grabbed up the cudgel and gave her opponent a blow

that sent him tumbling. She leapt over his still form to her father's side. Taller than most of his assailants, Safir had the advantage of reach, but there were too many for him and the few Villagers fighting beside him to fend off on their own. Safir's hair, dark as blackwood, blew in the arid wind that also whipped his blue robe around his ankles. A ragged brute waved his stave — a distraction, Dovella saw, that allowed another to come at Safir from behind. Her anger refuelled at this ruse, Dovella slammed the attacker with her cudgel. They fouled everything, she thought, these New Schoolers with their intimidation and violence.

Assuming fighting stance at her father's side, Dovella marvelled at the skill with which he wielded the stave, keeping those before him at bay and clearing space for Dovella to position herself so they could fight as a team.

As they struggled in the tumult of crashing staves and the constant clang of knife against knife, a roar of triumphant voices rose from the other side of the courtyard. Dovella grinned at her father as the mob shrank away from a strong phalanx of Villagers that had arrived to move against the rioters. These foulheads might not know it yet, but their battle was surely lost. Among the reinforcements Dovella recognized two councillors, one of them old though he moved as if he thought he was still a young man. Amidst the yells, grunts and curses, the fresh fighters moved forward, staves and cudgels and blades cutting down and pushing back the throng.

To clinch the victory, Security Master Pandil and several of her apprentices, supported by still more Villagers, moved up behind the mob. Seeing themselves surrounded, most of the belligerents put down their weapons, though a few foulheads fought on. No longer beleaguered, Dovella watched in awe as Pandil moved among the remaining fighters. In three successive movements, she disabled one, cracked another's jaw with her fist and knocked a knife from the hand of a third. Flushed with triumph and panting from the exertion, Pandil looked over at Dovella and raised a salute. After the New School prisoners had been secured, Pandil pushed her way through the milling crowd toward Dovella.

Tall and wiry, Pandil had the same coppery skin as Dovella and her father, but her eyes — like Safir's — were black while Dovella's were the brilliant blue of her mother's.

Pandil and Safir hugged Dovella at the same time, squeezing her until she was almost smothered. The smoothness of Safir's robe soothed one cheek while the rough weave of Pandil's uniform chafed the other.

"Thank the gods you're home," Safir said, pulling her tighter into his embrace. "Oh, Dovella, we've been so worried."

"I'm fine," she said. "I've got so much to tell you, I don't know where to start."

"I'm glad to see you too, but you shouldn't be here," Pandil scolded. "You should be home resting after such a journey."

"I wanted to see everyone," Dovella said, "and when I got here and saw what was happening, I had to help."

"Well, it was more than welcome," her father said, "but I'd rather you didn't have to be part of this."

And you, she thought. Why should you be part of this? He was a healer; dealing injuries such as this distressed him.

Safir stepped back and took hold of the medallion Dovella wore, his dark eyes filled with confusion. "Dovella, this is a Healer's Medallion. How did you come by this?"

"I got it in Hill Country." Her voice swelled with pride as

she added, "I got it from their great healer, herself."

"Well done!" Pandil said. "That's a story I'm eager to hear. I wish I could ..."

"I know. You've work to do. I'll tell you about it later," Dovella said. "Besides, we have to help the people who have been injured." She glanced toward the figure of Master Healer Plais, who knelt by a fallen Villager. He had not yet seen the healer's medallion that Dovella wore and she wondered how he would react when he caught sight of it.

Thin as a withered reed, the Master Healer gently touched the brow of the injured man. Master Plais was a dedicated healer, Dovella knew, but still she could not like him. She didn't know why he was so set against having women in Healer's Hall, but he was, so she had not been able to apprentice as a healer. Most of what she knew about the healing herbs and oils, and the techniques for preparing and using them, she had learned by working with Safir.

She nudged her father. "Will he let me help?" she asked.

"He'd better," Pandil said, "or he'll have me to deal with." Pandil gave Dovella another quick hug. "I'll see you at home later. Now, I'd best go deal with these foulheads we've captured."

"He's too busy to notice right now," Safir said. "Later ... well, no doubt he'll have words about you wearing that medallion after having missed the Rites, but he won't deny anyone help whatever his feelings about that may be."

Dovella touched the medallion around her neck, identical to the one her father wore. While she had been in Hill Country, she had come to know and work with the Khanti-Lafta herself, the Great Healer of the Hill people. It was she who had awarded Dovella the coveted medallion in recognition of her extraordinary gift for healing.

Dreading the confrontation with Master Plais she knew was to come, Dovella shook her head to clear her angry thoughts and knelt beside her father to help the wounded. As a somapath, Dovella took into her own body the hurts and ills of others and transmuted them to healing energy, which she then transmitted to her patients. It was a rare gift and Safir had cautioned her from childhood to keep it a secret for fear that it would be misunderstood. She had always wondered about that; now she understood only too well it was because others would think it was magic. Village teachings denied that magic existed ... but condemned it as evil anyway.

When all the injured had been tended and the most seriously wounded taken into Healer's Hall, Master Healer Plais looked toward Dovella. She tensed herself for the explosion and, as she had feared, when he saw the medallion he frowned and turned deep red.

"How dare you?" he roared as he strode toward her, his outstretched hand closed into a fist. He might look weak, but his voice was strong. "You have no right to wear that medallion!"

He reached out as if he would yank the chain from around her neck, and she stepped back, appalled at how close she had come to slapping away his hand — an instinctive action that would have been unforgivable. She took another step back, and grasped the medallion in her hands to protect it. "It was given to me by the Khanti-Lafta, herself," Dovella said. "She told me I had earned it."

He glowered at her. "The *Khanti-Lafta,* if indeed she exists, does not determine for the Village who earns the medallion and who not. That is a matter for our Guild. You missed the

Rites so you can not claim the right to admission."

Angered now, Dovella snorted. "Is it the Guild, or you? Nothing in the rules says ..."

"You will *not* claim a place you have not been granted by the Guild. It may be that I cannot take that cursed medallion from around your neck but I *can* exclude you from Healer's Hall." Clenching his hands into fists, Master Plais glared. "And you'd best take good care if you practise healing here in the Village without Guild sanction." Without waiting for her reply, he stalked away.

Dovella turned to her father. "That's not fair!"

Safir gathered her into his arms. "I know. But, Dovella, you missed the Rites and ... those are the rules." He stroked her cheek the way he had done whenever she was distressed since she was a child.

"Well, they are poor rules! Other Guilds offer more than one chance for going through *their* Rites." Dovella knew she sounded like a whining child but she couldn't stop. "It's only Plais who holds to the old ways that allow only the one opportunity." She could tell that Safir was torn. As a member of the Healer's Guild and subordinate of Master Healer Plais, he could hardly raise objections, especially since it would be on behalf of his own daughter.

"And anyway," she continued, "I *have* been through something like the Rites. The Khanti-Lafta herself opened my sight so I can see the energy patterns in a person." Then she crossed her arms and glared. "How dare Master Plais question whether or not she exists!"

"I've no doubt that Master Plais believes a great healer still exists in Hill Country, but he resents seeing you wear that medallion. And he resents all the more that she gave you something he would have withheld."

"So he'll deny me further training, deny me the chance to heal."

"I'm afraid he will. Of course, I'll try ..."

"He won't listen. He was glad I missed the Rites. Why is he so set against women healers? He supports Mother and Master Pandil in their positions."

"Truly, I don't know, Dovella." Safir gripped Dovella's hand. "We'll talk later," her father whispered, then he hurried away toward Healer's Hall.

As Dovella stomped along the cobblestone road, she paid scant attention to her surroundings. Stalls had been set up to sell pies, sweets and trinkets, small stages prepared for the musicians and the Doll Masters, but even these ever increasing preparations for Festival, usually her favourite season, got little more than a glance. She just couldn't stop thinking about Master Plais and the way he had treated her. The Villagers who had welcomed her home saw her as a hero, but he acted as though she were nothing. Even if she didn't want public praise, she'd thought that when Master Plais learned why she'd missed the Rites, when he saw the medallion she'd been given while she was in Hill Country that he ... She let out a little snort. Well, no. In truth, Plais had reacted exactly as she had expected. Foolishly, she had only hoped it would be different.

She tramped up the stairs to the apartment fuming, the memory of her triumphant return shadowed by Plais's behaviour. Flinging open the door, Dovella saw her mother and Master Pandil sitting together drinking tea. Petite and fair of hair, Avella shared only one physical trait with her daughter — her blue eyes, which now opened wide with welcome. Surprised to find her mother at home, Dovella halted for a moment in the doorway, then threw out her arms and rushed to Avella's side. As Dovella knelt beside her mother's chair, she noticed bruises on Avella's pale cheeks. "What happened to you?"

"I was hurt in an earlier riot," Avella said, "but never mind that now, I'm fine. Really, I am." She pulled Dovella into an embrace and held her for a long moment, then pushed away and studied her daughter's face. "But let me have a look at you! Oh, it's good to have you home. I've been so worried ... and I'm so proud of you. I want to hear all about your journey, but we'll wait for your father." She reached out to touch Dovella's medallion. "Pandil told me about this. What wonderful news!" She stroked Dovella's cheek and smiled, her eyes moist. "I was distressed that you and Safir were caught up in the fighting." She poured a cup of tea and handed it to her daughter.

Dovella sniffed. Collitflower. That was good for relaxation, and they all needed that.

"But now I see that you are uninjured after this riot, I can rest easier. Your father, though ..." Avella fell back into the red-cushioned chair.

"He too is uninjured."

"In body," Avella murmured. "But this fighting ... what it does to him goes deeper than physical hurt."

Putting aside her cup, Dovella dropped down to the floor by her mother's chair and took hold of her hand. Looking at Pandil, she asked, "What brought this riot on? I thought that with the restoration of water and power, the Villagers would settle down."

"Most of the Villagers, yes, but the New School fanatics don't give up their aims so easily. And they were angry about Havkad being in prison. This attack was merely a diversion to free him from custody."

Dovella gasped. "Havkad didn't escape!" Just the thought of the squat New School leader with his malicious smirk and hard eyes made Dovella squirm.

"I fear he did."

"But when they learned that he was responsible for the loss of power and water, how could they not turn against him?"

"Some of them did," Pandil said. "But the more rabid ones follow him all the more fervently. Because of the injury he took when he attacked me with his sorcery, he was taken to Healer's Hall and was not as heavily guarded there as he should have been."

"Havkad attacked you? With sorcery?" Dovella couldn't believe he had such power.

"Not successfully," Pandil replied.

"But you, child," Avella interrupted, "you seemed disturbed when you came in. Was there further fighting?"

"Only with Plais," Dovella snapped.

"*Master* Plais," Pandil corrected. "He deserves respect."

Dovella shot her an angry glance. "So does the Khanti-Lafta, but he questions whether she even exists, and denies my right to the medallion." She fingered the medallion, but instead of soothing her, the touch inflamed her further. She'd been so proud when the Khanti-Lafta had placed the chain around her neck. "He told me to leave Healer's Hall and not to return."

About to launch into a tirade against Master Plais, she

paused when Safir strode into the room. He gave a quick nod to Pandil, kissed his wife on the forehead, knelt down beside Dovella and hugged her again.

"He had no right to speak to me that way," she said.

"He's the Master Healer," Safir said softly. "He shouldn't have done so, I agree, but the right to give or deny access to Healer's Hall is his."

Dovella snorted. "And the right to deny me teaching." She turned to her mother. "You should have heard what he said when I told him how I got the medallion."

"I fear that only made it worse," Safir said. "He resents that fact that you received it from the Khanti-Lafta rather than from him."

"He would never have given it to me," Dovella said, "and well you know it."

"No," Safir said softly, "he would not."

"Well, I don't need him," Dovella said. "I don't need anything from him. The Khanti-Lafta said that if he refused to teach me, I could come back and she would teach me herself. So that's what I'll do."

She almost choked on the words. She'd just returned home, and had no wish to leave again so soon. But if that was what it took to receive training for her healing gift, that was what she would do.

Safir took her hand, rubbed it against his cheek. "I understand your anger," he said, "but if you do not receive your training from a Village healer, you'll never truly be accepted in Healer's Hall, nor in the Village."

"I'll never be accepted anyway." Dovella could feel her voice was strangled as she tried to hold back the tears. "As long as Plais lives ..." She glared at Pandil as if daring her to correct Dovella's naming of him without his title. "So what does it matter? At least I'll have training."

"There is another way." Pandil leaned forward and they all turned their attention to her. "Elder Master Faris would not refuse to teach Dovella, and if he acknowledged her right to the medallion, it would be hard for *Master* Plais to deny her." She looked pointedly at Dovella when she once again stressed the healer's title.

"Plais wouldn't like it," Safir said.

"In truth, he would not, but Dovella shouldn't be denied training. And she shouldn't be forced to receive it elsewhere. It would be an honour for her to study with the Khanti-Lafta, but you are right. Even if we make peace with the Hill Folk, which I fervently hope we will, there will always be the feeling that Dovella demeaned Village healers by taking her training elsewhere." She held up a hand when Dovella started to break in. "I know, I know. But no one said they were rational."

Dovella knew the Elder Master, of course, though she had never studied with him. But if Pandil thought he'd teach her, Dovella was prepared to accept. And she could stay with her family after all. She looked up at her father, who was nodding.

"Yes," he said. "Much as Plais will dislike it, he won't be able to gainsay the Elder Master's approval."

"When can I start?" Dovella asked.

"Ah," said Pandil. "That's the problem. You'd have to leave the Village again."

"Why? Surely *Master* Plais couldn't interfere." As she emphasized his title, she smirked at Pandil, who only smiled.

"No, but Elder Master Faris has gone to Jael's village." Pandil looked away for a moment when she said Jael's name and Dovella drew in a sharp breath. Did this mean that Jael had been hurt? Killed, maybe, and the Elder Master was returning his body? Ever since Jael first arrived in the Village, Dovella had held secret feelings for the apprentice, and recently she had begun to hope that he felt the same way about her.

"He and Jael became friends, and Jael invited him for an extended visit," Pandil continued, seeming not to notice Dovella's concern.

Dovella let out the breath she hadn't realized she'd been holding.

"Faris wanted to study with some of the *shagines* in Jael's village," Pandil explained, "and also to share with them his own knowledge."

"When will he get back?" Avella asked.

"Not for a while, I'm afraid. If you wish to study with him," she said, looking at Dovella, "you'll have to go to Jael's village and study there. This would also be a good opportunity for you to learn some of what the *shagines* can teach about healing."

Even as she felt a touch of excitement about going to Jael's village and seeing him, even as she hungered for what the Elder Master could teach her, Dovella felt a tightening around her eyes at the thought of leaving her parents again so soon.

"I've just got her back," Avella cried, reaching out to touch Dovella's cheek.

Dovella glanced up at her mother. "Of course, I could take up my duties as engineering apprentice again ..."

Dovella knew now that she had a gift for that as well. Magic: that's what the Hill Folk called her work with the machine. She knew now that there were things she didn't understand, and clearly sorcery did exist whether she wanted to admit it or not. But surely that was completely different from her healing gift and her understanding of the machine.

"I would welcome you," Avella said. "I've missed your help with the machine. You know it as no one else does. It seems to recognize your touch."

Dovella knew she felt something when she worked with machines. Still, she also knew that, before anything else, she was a healer.

"But," Avella went on, smiling though her voice was unsteady, "dearly as I would love to have your help, you have been given the Medallion of the Healer. That gift is too great to be neglected."

Safir took Avella's other hand. "Yes, and she needs training now."

Dovella looked at him questioningly. What was the hurry? Surely she could at least stay for Festival. Safir returned her look with an even gaze, and Dovella understood that he didn't want to say any more in front of the others. When she'd been touched by the Khanti-Lafta's hand, Dovella's senses had been opened so that the workings of the body had become visible to her in a new way. That opening of one's sight was a probably a healer secret, not to be shared with outsiders. Dovella understood too that having the ability to *see* workings of the body didn't mean understanding how to use that sight. For that she needed special training.

"Besides, if Elder Master Faris agrees to teach her," he went on, "he may be able to sponsor her when the full Guild next meets. The sooner she is presented, the better her chances of being accepted over Master Plais's objections."

"I know," Avella said, but though she agreed, her eyes filled with tears.

Dovella looked down at her hands so the others would not see her face. She felt pulled in all directions. She didn't want to leave her family again and Festival was coming soon. Still, she didn't think Festival would hold anything for her this year, not with the bitterness she felt toward the Village. Not fair, she knew, to blame the entire Village for Plais's treatment, but he had soured her beautiful homecoming. And who knew, perhaps Festival in Jael's village would be an interesting experience. She had never celebrated Festival away from the Village before. And Jael would be there ...

"But how will she get there?" her mother asked. "Travelling alone is too dangerous. Despite our gains, New School renegades are still active in the Outlands."

"I'll arrange for the guide Drase to go with her," Pandil promised. "She'll be safe with him." She turned to Dovella. "Why don't you go and see what supplies you will need for the journey?"

Safir accompanied Dovella to the door of her room. "What —" she started to ask, but he put his fingers to her lips and said softly, "I am not sure, but whatever is on Pandil's mind, she will explain to you."

Dovella kissed him on the cheek and went into her small room, which contained only a desk and chair, a narrow bed, and a cabinet for her clothes. In an alcove, she had made a small work space, for Safir insisted that she prepare her own herbs, and the room was redolent with their scents. On the bed, she found her pack, which must have been brought there by the ostler's boy, and began to lay aside things that needed to be washed. She paused to finger an unusual knife with a hilt of carved blackwood. This had been a gift from Pandil. Pandil had also given her the pair of grey boots she wore, and they had served her well. The intricate designs on the boots concealed a compartment with a smaller knife, to be hidden away for use in times of danger. Dovella laid the big knife aside; she wouldn't need it for this journey. She would take her sling, though, in case she got a chance to hunt. Dovella was proud of her skill with that weapon. She went to the cabinet that held clean clothes and examined its contents. Her visit to Jael's village would likely last some time, but she'd still need to choose carefully so as not to have too much to carry.

There was a familiar rap on the door.

"Come in, Pandil," she called.

Pandil entered and closed the door softly behind her. "I am sorry to see you go away again so soon," she said.

"Then why —" Dovella started, but Pandil held up a hand.

"I know Plais is wrong, and if I could change his mind I would. Yet, this may be to the good."

"How can that be?"

"I think Elder Master Faris will be a more congenial teacher, but there is more than that." She studied Dovella for a moment. "I'm going to tell you something that not even your parents know. Not that I don't trust them," she added quickly. "Only that it's safer for everyone." She stopped as if waiting for Dovella to agree to carry the secret.

"All right," Dovella agreed. "If you think it's best."

"Your mother was in a coma after the attack and she ..." Dovella started to interrupt, but Pandil rushed on, "She's recovering well. Truly she is, Dovella. Now this coma — it wasn't only because of her injuries. Her mind was being held captive by a sorcerer." Here Pandil paused and gazed at Dovella again, no doubt remembering how Dovella had once laughed at the idea of sorcery. "It was Jael who worked to free her."

"Jael!" Dovella sat heavily on the side of the bed and stared. "But how? Surely he isn't a ... sorcerer." She could hardly bring herself to say the word.

It looked as if Pandil were smothering a smile, but she only said, "No, but Jael has Plains blood. In his village the wise men of power are called *shagines*. It is ... a kind of sorcerous power, yes, but there are many constraints on its use. Not that a *shagine* couldn't misuse his power, but that is true of any kind of power, sorcerous or not. Anyway, Jael is learning. It was a very brave thing he did trying to save Avella, for his training is not complete and he could have done great harm to himself. As it was, in the process of freeing her, he exposed himself to the sorcerer's mind, and that may have put him and his teachers in danger."

Dovella stared at Pandil. It was almost too much to take in: her mother held in a coma by a sorcerer, Jael with sorcerous power, Jael and his people in danger. "And now Havkad has escaped," she said, her voice filled with dread.

Pandil nodded and studied Dovella for another moment. "But Jael doesn't think it was *Havkad* who captured Avella's mind, even though he was the one who attacked me; Jael believes there is another sorcerer, one much more powerful. That is why I have kept Jael's role quiet, for although I think Avella is quite free of the sorcerer's hold, we can't know whether he might be able to lay claim to her mind again. And I would never ask Safir to keep a secret from her." Again she subjected Dovella to a searching gaze. "And I do not ask that of *you* lightly."

"I know," Dovella said, "and I understand your reasoning. But why tell me at all?"

"Because I am hoping that you might learn something of this mind healing while you are there. I'm not sure if it can be taught to one not having Plains blood, but I'm hoping that it can. I fear that we may face more such attacks in future, and it would be well if we had healers here in the Village who could do what Jael did, although ... well, he did say that the sorcerer just let Avella go. Still, he had almost freed her when that happened." Pandil studied Dovella with a worried frown. "We'll need you, Dovella, need your training if you can master this. And it may be soon. That's why I'm pushing for you to leave at once."

"So who do I ask? Jael?"

"It is a delicate matter, not something you just ask for. You can only be patient. Get to know them. Let them get to know you. When they are sure of you, I'm sure they will offer to teach you."

"Do I tell them how I heal?" Pandil was one of the few people who knew that Dovella was a somapath; others just thought that she was skilled with herbs. After years of Safir's cautioning silence, Dovella had feared her gift, thinking it might in some way be shameful. She now knew that was not the case, but she also knew that others might not feel the same. And yet, if what she did *was* magic ... maybe she'd been right all along. And here was Pandil wanting her to delve even deeper into this dark knowledge.

"I don't think you need tell them, not at first, anyway," Pandil said, "though the elder *shagines* may well sense it. No, just show that you are an eager learner, and if they offer to teach you more, think well before you refuse."

Dovella nodded. "I learned a lot on my journey, Pandil," she said. "However uncomfortable I may still be with the idea of sorcery, I know now there are many kinds of power of which I've never even had a glimpse." Saying so didn't make her any more comfortable with the idea of using such power, but she trusted that Pandil would not encourage her to gain knowledge that was evil.

Pandil touched her cheek, much as Avella had done earlier. "It grieves me that you have had to learn things so harshly," she said. "Still, it's better to know than to live in ignorance. And the Village needs you and what you can learn about this mind healing as much as it needed what you accomplished with the machine."

Although Dovella hated to leave home again, she accepted the urgency of Master Pandil's request. She would study with Elder Master Faris. She would learn whatever the *shagines* could teach her. And once she returned and Master Faris convinced the Guild that she should be accepted by the Guild despite missing the Rites, she would begin her work here in the Village as a healer.

She smiled grimly. And there would be nothing *Master* Plais could do about it!

Two

I N THE LIGHT OF THE EARLY MORNING SUN, DOVELLA EYED
the tall man who was to be her guide. In Outlander
fashion, he wore his shoulder-length hair tied back with red
thong but was dressed, as she was, in tan tarvelcloth breeches
and tunic.

Dovella sighed when she saw the horses. She wasn't a
very experienced rider, and though she'd come to feel fairly
comfortable with riding on her recent trip, she didn't look
forward to the sore leg muscles she knew would follow. She
hoped at least they wouldn't have to do hard riding.

"Greetings, Dovella," he said with a smile. "I've been
looking forward to meeting you. I'm eager to hear about your
journey."

"Greetings, Drase," she replied, feeling a bit uncomfortable.
It embarrassed her to have people make a fuss over what she
had done. "Maybe we can exchange tales. I've only heard a
little of what went on in the Village while I was away."

"That we can," he said. "All set?"

She nodded that she was ready, and mounted her grey
mare. Once they were well away from the Village, Drase
turned toward the thick of the forest. Tall, with dark hair and
eyes, the guide reminded Dovella of her father. Clearly, Drase
was of old Village blood, but because he didn't reside in the

Village, he was called an Outlander — as if he were somehow not as good as a Villager. Dovella felt her colour rise when she thought of that. We should be ashamed, she thought.

There was little in the way of a path, so they rode single file for a long while. As they rode through splotches of sunlight and shadow, birds chattered from the trees that towered above them. Alongside the path grew scarlet and blue ladyflowers, their centres like small replicas of golden Hari, one of the three moons of Edlena. Many flowers were scraggly and wilted because of the long drought, but the ladyflowers still flourished and their fragrance filled the air. Although Dovella had often accompanied her father when he went into the woods in search of herbs, it had been her journey through Hill Country that had brought her to a better appreciation of the forest and all it contained. Caught up now in the beauty of her surroundings, she forgot her guide.

Then the trail widened and he waited for her to catch up with him. After agreeing to ride a couple more hours before halting for a rest, they rode side by side, their companionable silence occasionally broken as Drase told her what had been happening in the Village and the Outlands during her absence. From time to time, Dovella caught a glimpse of burned-out cabins; sometimes an entire settle of five or six lay in ruins. Drase rode on stiffly without a word, but finally, at one of the cabins, he pulled his mount to a halt. Grim-faced he studied the blackened heaps of wood.

Dovella caught her breath. "I know this place," she exclaimed. "Once, when I was out with my father, we stopped here." She fell silent. There had been a tow-haired boy of about ten and two younger girls, one fair and one with dusky skin. While Safir had talked with their parents, Dovella had sat with the girls, who were making a garland of blue ladyflowers. In trying to get the yellow centres to line up, the girls had crushed the delicate petals. They took it to their mother and the older fair-haired girl had stood with hands clasped behind her back, one bare foot rubbing across the arch of the other, watching anxiously; the younger one had danced around, clearly harbouring no doubt as to what reception their gift would receive. Carefully, the mother put the garland around her neck, smiling as if she had received a necklace of rare jewels.

What had become of them? Dovella wondered, blinking her eyes against tears.

Drase gave himself a little shake and kneed his horse forward. "So many," he said, "and we could do nothing for them."

"Raiders —"

He snorted. "Raiders? Then why did they never attack farms owned by followers of the New School? No, this was New School work. In fact, most of the Raiders are in New School pay. They are determined to gain power by whatever means possible, and anyone they can't convince to follow them, they terrorize or murder."

His lips firmly pressed together, Drase pulled ahead, but after a short spell, he dropped back and said, "I don't know how much you need to keep secret about your journey to repair the machine, but I'd be happy to hear whatever you can tell me."

Dovella paused. "Pandil didn't want anyone to know about it while I was away," she said, "but now that it's done I don't think it matters." She told of her journey deep into Hill Country and of how the people there, led by their leader, had accompanied her to the source. They had fought off Havkad's men and helped Dovella repair the machine that had been sabotaged on his orders. "It's thanks to Zagoad that I made the trip safely." She felt a tinge of satisfaction that she could make that admission so easily.

"I dare say he deserves full credit for what he did," Drase said. "Nonetheless, it was a big undertaking. And the last part of the journey, facing the Hill Folk ... *that* you had to do on your own. For Outlanders such as myself or for a Forester like Zagoad, it wouldn't be hard as we have known Hill Folk all our lives, but I know that Villagers are taught to believe that they are savages. It must have been difficult for you to see past your differences."

Dovella nodded, not wanting even to think about how afraid she had been. "But they treated me gently even before they learned about my mission — more gently, I'm sure, than one of them would have been treated in the Village. It shames me that I used to think they were dangerous enemies."

"It's the schoolmasters who keep the hatred burning."

"The New Schoolers do too," Dovella said. "It's not just the Village they want to control. If they got in power, they'd start another war with the Hill Folk as well. That's why Havkad had the machine sabotaged: he was hoping to make people believe that the loss of power was a sign that the gods were displeased with our leaders. Then, when he gained control of Council, he'd have the water restored to make it look like he was right."

"And when that plan failed, he tried to kill Pandil with sorcery."

Dovella shivered. She had to admit that some kind of mysterious power actually existed, but the thought of magic being real still made her very uncomfortable.

"We can all be thankful that you succeeded," he said. "It's too bad you had to give up your chance to go through the Rites in order to make the trip — I hope the Village appreciates what you've done." He gave a little snort. "Though I doubt that they do. Plais is only one example of that ingratitude."

They had been riding for quite some time; the sun was now high in the sky. Just as they were about to stop for food, two men rode toward them from a fork in the road. As the men drew near, one pulled his horse to a halt. "A healer," he cried out. "We were just riding to find someone."

Dovella's hand flew up to her medallion. She'd not thought to conceal it, but that was as well, she thought, for the men would have had a long ride to the Village to find help. Still, she glanced over at her guide. She didn't want to offer help without his approval. "I see no reason not to help," Drase said. "It will delay us, and we may have to sleep outside tonight, but we've both done that before."

"Oh, no need," the man said. "If it delays you too long, we can offer lodging."

They turned their horses and accompanied Dovella and Drase down the other fork of the road. As they neared a shabby hut, a group of five or six more men strode out. They were unkempt and Dovella didn't like the looks of glee on their faces. One of them Dovella recognized as Brakase, the son of Barte, who was one of the most vocal Outlander supporters of the New School. Two of them wore their long, tawny hair loose and were dressed in rough tarvelcloth. Clearly not Outlanders, but they didn't look like Foresters either.

Before she could voice her reservations, one of the men grabbed the reins of her horse while another pulled her down. She kicked and fought, but there were three of them and soon her arms were firmly pinned behind her. The others went to assist those manhandling Drase, who had two of the attackers sprawled on the ground screaming in pain. By the time Drase had been downed by the reinforcements, they too were nursing bruised jaws and slashed arms.

"How can you treat a healer so?" Drase yelled.

"We're not going to hurt her," Brakase said. "There was no need for you to attack us."

"It was you who attacked *us,*" Dovella snapped.

"Only because you resisted."

"I came willingly when I thought you needed help," she said. "But you seem determined to keep us by force."

"And we will if that is necessary," one of the tawny-haired men snapped.

"You can't force her to help you though," Drase said.

Dovella turned sharply, then dropped her eyes. He would know, of course, that she could never deny healing, not even to an enemy, but their captors didn't need to know that.

Drase's words didn't fool them though, for the leader just laughed. "By the time we need her skills, we'll have ways of ensuring her co-operation. Anyway, no one wearing that medallion can refuse to help."

He was right, of course, so despite the circumstances, Dovella offered healing to the men injured in the fight. They were unwilling to trust her, though, regardless of what their leader had said.

The camp was comprised of two small huts built in the ruins of burned-out cabins, and a stable in between the two, kept none too clean she reckoned, given the stench that came from it. Weeds abounded in the yard and vines crept up the side of the cabins. One of these had bars across the small windows, and it was there they were herded, the door locked behind them. The floor and walls were bare, and there was nothing in the room but a rough-hewn table and two chairs. Dovella and Drase stood a moment, studying their spartan surroundings, but when they heard the sound of horses leaving, Drase went to look out of the window.

"Four of them," he said. "The two injured in our scuffle won't do any more fighting for a while, so that just leaves two. If we can get out of here, we can surely manage them between us." He prowled around the room, pushing at the door and prying at the bars. "No way out. Still," he said, "someone has to come in eventually. Maybe we can overpower them."

When the door opened later, there were two men; one stayed at the door while the other brought in a wide-mouthed jug of water and two plates of food. "Don't waste that water," Brakase warned. "We're running low and there won't be any more until late tomorrow."

He smirked as he put the plates on the table, then turned and left, locking the door behind him. Dovella shivered. She looked at the small serving of stew on the plate. It smelled good but she was feeling too angry and jittery to eat. Drase picked up a spoon and took a bite.

"Tasty enough," he said, and took another, larger bite. "You should eat something." But then, when she picked up the dish, he flung out an arm to knock it out of her hand.

"Don't —" His face was red. Sweat had broken out on his forehead.

"What is it?" Dovella reached out to steady him. Her voice shaky, she asked, "Is it poison?"

He shook his head and, hand to his mouth, stumbled to

the corner of the room and vomited. "Not poison, but a drug of some kind. To disable —"

She didn't understand how he could have detected this, but something about the way Pandil had spoken of him had told her that Drase was something more than a simple Outlander guide. Did he have some kind of *magic*? Dovella grimaced even at the thought of the word. She could *not* overcome her distaste for the idea. How was she supposed to toss aside a distrust that she had been taught all her life?

Dovella went to her guide and felt his head. With her healing sight she could see the drug already coursing through his body. It was like nothing she had ever seen before.

*

Maleem stood at the kitchen table cutting up great hunks of vesson to be prepared for the noon meal to feed the workers from Barte's fields. Barte's wife stood across from her chopping a large turnip. With her wheat-coloured hair and hazel eyes, Tavile was likely descended from Plains people — Maleem's people — but the woman's blood had been tainted with that of Villagers and Hill Folk. Foresters they were called: *mongrels* was what they were, all of them. But the woman was a fervent follower of the New School, thus useful to the Plains People.

Nothing of Tavile showed in her son, Brakase, who had the same old-blood Villager colouring as his father. But where was Brakase? Maleem hadn't seen him for several days. Giving her head a little shake, she turned her attention back to the meat, for Tavile had been glancing at her with a frown. No doubt she wondered why Maleem was having such a hard time cutting the meat.

"Are you afraid of the knife?" Tavile asked at last. "I'll do that if you are." "No," Maleem answered. "I'm just not used to this kind of knife."

Among the Plains People, women were not permitted to use anything other than a small knife suitable for peeling and cutting vegetables. Men would prepare the meat and even large vegetables, slicing everything into portions small enough to be finished with the woman's knife. It felt strange working with such a large blade. And with bare hands at that. Only a loose woman would let anyone see her bare hands.

But Maleem could not speak of this. It would not be good for Barte to know of the traditions and faith of her people, not yet. Later, once their sorcerer had control of the Village, everyone would learn to prostrate themselves before the Goddess Machia, whom they had long ago abandoned. But for now Maleem's people needed Barte and others like him. Barte was one of the richest Outlanders, owner of many farms. Barte had visited the camp where her people lived, had been flattered and praised for his help. He would be persuaded to make a place for more of her people to work these farms, and eventually the Plains People would take them for their own. Maleem smiled. Barte didn't know about *that* part of the plan.

She glanced around the kitchen, which was as richly furnished as the rest of the house. It would be good to own a house such as this, and perhaps she would, if she and Brakase came to an understanding.

"I noticed many burned-out steadings as we were coming here," Maleem said.

"Yes, but none of ours have been burned." Tavile smiled.

"That is what comes from following the true path of the New School. We've had the protection of the gods."

More likely, the protection of the Goddess and her servants, Maleem thought, for Machia would look kindly on those who came to the aid of Her people. She would protect them from Raiders while leaving other non-believers to their ravages.

Maleem turned her attention more carefully to her work. She had put on one of her best green tunics, hoping to see Brakase, and she didn't want to get blood on it. She knew that Brakase was attracted to her. With her wheat-coloured hair, she probably didn't look that much different from the Forester women he knew, but her way of dressing and speaking had set her apart, and he seemed not to be bothered by the small mole on her left cheekbone. To her people, it was a lack of perfection on her otherwise flawless olive skin. She'd always been ashamed of it before, but only a few nights ago, Brakase had touched it, called it a mark of beauty.

She had just finished cutting up the last chunk of meat when Barte came in. He was a big man. Just as Brakase would look when he reached Barte's age — brawny without being fat, black hair and dark eyes that could burn through you ... or caress you. Again, she asked herself why Brakase was not with his father, but dared not voice the question.

Barte gazed at his wife, and though he didn't speak, Tavile appeared to understand, for she shook her head. He tightened his lips and let out a sound that seemed to be part worry and part exasperation. Perhaps he too was wondering where Brakase was.

Glancing through the window, Maleem saw Lofel walking toward the barn. Of her people, only she and Lofel had been brought by their leader into Barte's home. She was sure that Fvlad had chosen Lofel for his strength, but she wasn't sure why he had honoured *her* so. Perhaps because Fvlad knew that he could trust her, knew that she was a true believer. He was asking her to taint herself by using a knife and baring her hands before these mongrels, and though she would have to go through a great purification when she returned to live among her own people, she was willing to defile herself in doing the work of the Goddess, and for the good of the Plains People. Unlike some, she could remain silent when these people raved about their false gods. Despite the fervency of her faith, she knew when to keep still.

Perhaps, too, Fvlad wanted her to get close to the young Outlander. Brakase's father had a great deal of influence among the Outlander followers of the New School. Eventually, Fvlad would have to reveal their true purpose. It would be well at that time to have some of the leading New School people closely allied with them. If she gained Brakase's love, she would be able to persuade him to follow Fvlad, to worship the true Goddess, Machia, and defeat those who denied Her.

While Tavile made ready the table, Maleem went to call in the children from their play. These were the younger children of the field workers. She would see to it that they washed their faces and hands, put on clean aprons, and went in orderly fashion to their tables. Most of her time here was spent with the children, and she enjoyed that much more than the kitchen work. She had always been good with the little ones. That was a big part of her work with her own people, but it was difficult with these mongrels. It was hard to conceal her feelings about the degradation. Fleetingly she thought of Brakase. If she were to wed him, their children would be mongrels ... but if she could convert him to the true faith and bring up their children in the true faith, perhaps everyone would overlook this.

After the food was ready, Maleem prepared a bowl of the savoury stew to take to Lofel. He preferred to eat outside near the stable where he worked. He said it was to keep an eye on people who came and went in order to report to Fvlad, who was staying in another Outlander house nearby, but Maleem didn't think this was the reason. Lofel had once shown that he was interested in Maleem and it was true she had given him reason to think she might feel something for him, but once she had met Brakase, she had discouraged Lofel's attention. He knew the reason and resented it. He didn't want to be around Brakase — *that* was why he chose to eat outside.

Lofel took the bowl without looking at her. His hands, large but surprisingly graceful, gripped the bowl as if he would crush it. Then he looked at her, his grey eyes hard as the stone water trough behind him.

"Haven't seen your new man around lately. Are you sure he isn't betraying us?"

"He wouldn't!"

"And you know this? How?" He reached out one hand and grabbed her wrist. "What is between you? It is one thing to debase yourself by baring your hands before these dogs, but that at least is for the good of our people. There is no call for you to flaunt yourself."

She twisted her arm out of his grasp and rubbed it. "There is nothing between us," she said, as stung by that truth as she was by his accusation. "I'm doing the work I was asked to do."

"You are doing more than that."

"Indeed she is," said a mild voice.

She and Lofel swung around. A tall, thin man with skin almost as white as his hair, their leader Fvlad looked from one to the other. His approach had been so quiet Maleem had not even sensed it.

Dressed in the tan tarvelcloth favoured by Foresters and Outlanders, Fvlad looked even paler than usual. Despite his pallor, he was an attractive man. He stood tall and proud and his dark eyes seemed to glow when he smiled, as he did now.

But when he was angry ... Maleem didn't like to think about that. She remembered once when a woman had challenged him — Fvlad had sent a ball of fire that consumed her. His eyes had shone then too, but with an icy fire rather than the warmth Maleem saw now. The woman had deserved to die, of course, for her defiance, but Fvlad had insisted that it wasn't he who had killed the woman but Machia Herself. "I am but Her servant," he'd insisted. All the Plains People were Her servants, but not all of them had Fvlad's power. He was special.

Fvlad touched Maleem's shoulder, pulling her away from the memory. "But," he went on to Lofel, "she is doing nothing that does not aid our people and further our aim."

Maleem glanced at Lofel and smirked.

"Nonetheless," Fvlad said, turning his smile on Maleem alone, "I will be asking you to return to our people."

Maleem gaped. "But I thought I was helping."

"You are, child. I'm not sending you as punishment. But I am returning and I need you there."

Maleem swallowed hard. Although it made her proud that

he wanted her with him, she had thought she was helping her people by staying here, thought she had been honoured by Fvlad's trust. Had she been so wrong? She dared not ask, for he was her leader, the true prophet of Machia. Obedience to the Goddess meant obedience to Fvlad.

She bowed her head. "I'll pack my things," she said, choking back tears.

Three

Dovella knelt by Drase, who was still heaving, though his stomach must surely have been empty by now. This drug that he'd been given was completely foreign to her, yet she decided to try to leach it from him in the same way that she would draw out any other affliction. Since he'd only ingested a small amount, it didn't appear to have spread throughout his system, but even if she could draw it out, she was reluctant to try to absorb and transmute it. She knew too little about the actions of drugs. That was something else she needed to learn. Thankfully, she could see how it travelled through his body.

She fetched the jug of water. The mouth was just wide enough for her to slip in one hand. "I think I can take the drug out of your system," she said, "and transfer it to the water."

He rocked back on his heels and looked up at her for a moment, his dark eyes assessing her. "You *think* you can?"

Dovella felt her cheeks redden. "I've never tried anything like this before," she said, "but I have to do something."

"And if you can't?"

She hesitated for a moment, then knelt beside him. "Then we will both be affected. But I don't think I can escape without you, for I don't know this part of the country and wouldn't know where to go for help. And even if I could disable both of them, you are so big, I'm not sure I could get you away while you are in this condition."

He nodded, but she could see that he agreed with great reluctance.

She placed her hand on his forehead, which was coated with fine beads of perspiration, and, tracing the course of the drug in his body, she drew it out into her hands. This was a filthy kind of energy, different from that associated with disease or injuries; but it was still energy, and Dovella was used to dealing with such. She focused until she was sure that none of the poison remained in his system, and then dipped her hands, one after the other, into the jug and let the drug drain into the water. She sat back and turned her sight inward. She was clear of the noxious energy.

Depleted, Dovella sagged against the chair. The procedure was unlike anything she'd ever tried before. She drew in a deep breath, replenishing her strength.

At the sound of steps approaching the door, Drase dropped to the floor and motioned for Dovella to follow his example. The door opened and the men entered the room.

"They're out," one of the men said with a laugh.

"Don't know why it was necessary," said the other. Dovella recognized the voice as that of Brakase. "We could have handled them without drugs."

"We didn't do such a great job of handling the Out-lander."

"We managed."

"After two of us were nearly killed."

"I still think we should make her heal them, she's responsible for their injuries," said Brakase.

Dovella bristled at the accusation. It was just like a New Schooler to blame others when it was his own actions that brought harm.

"She'd only make it worse. Why would she help willingly?"

"She's a healer, she'd have to."

"If you have so much love for Villagers why are you fighting against them?"

"I don't love them," Brakase said hotly. "But Village healers are honourable."

Unlike you New Schoolers, Dovella thought. Hard as it was to listen to him, she made herself lie still. She had to wait for Drase to signal his readiness. It would take the two of them to defeat both men, especially as she had no weapon. And she needed time to gather strength after the effort of healing Drase. In the meantime, maybe they'd hear something useful.

"Well, I don't want to count on it, not till we have a means of making her help. Anyway," the stranger added in a laughing voice, "Rhahol fancies himself as a sorcerer."

"Was this sorcery?"

Dovella thought she heard a note of distaste in Brakase's voice. Strange that he should feel so when his own leader, Havkad, was a sorcerer.

"Of course. Some kind of spell he put in the food."

So that's why emptying his stomach didn't rid Drase of the drug, Dovella thought. Well, whatever it was, it was now in the water.

The men walked closer, and as one of them bent over Drase, the guide made his move, grabbing the man's shoulders and dragging him down. Dovella immediately threw out one foot and kicked Brakase's leg out from under him. Surprised by the attack, it took him some seconds to realize what had happened. By that time she was on her feet and ready to fight, even though she had still not fully recovered her strength.

Brakase was a good fighter, she had to give him that, but she'd been trained by Pandil. If only I had my stave, Dovella thought, this would be over already. Dovella grabbed the chair, rammed it into Brakase's stomach. He wobbled a bit then twisted the chair out of her hands and flung it to the floor. Still, when he came toward her, his knife drawn, she was ready. Remembering the moves Pandil had taught her, she managed to knock him down. Drase also put his man out of action. Seeing both men disabled, Dovella gladly sank to the floor for rest.

Drase came and knelt beside her. "Are you all right?"

"Just tired from the healing."

He glanced at the men. "We need to tie them."

"I'll go look for rope." She pulled herself up and hurried out to the stable. It stank so badly she could hardly stand to enter to search, but finally she found several coils of rope as well as the weapons that had been taken from her and Drase. She grabbed the weapons and rope and rushed back into the cabin.

Quickly they worked together. When the men were secured, she and Drase headed for the door, but then she stopped and motioned for Drase to wait. She went back for the jug of water and the two plates of food. She grinned at him as she took them to the cistern and dumped the contents in with the other water. "Some of their own medicine. Let's see how it agrees with them. Whatever sorcery is still in it may slow them up a little unless it's too diluted."

"Even a little will help." Drase gave an approving smile.

Their horses were in the stable, still saddled, together with four others. "They must have been planning to take us somewhere else," Dovella said.

Drase nodded and grabbed the reins of the other horses. He mounted his own. "Just in case the men are able to get free, I'd rather they not have mounts at hand," he said as he led the horses away. After they had gone some way into the forest, Drase stopped near a small stream and loosely tethered the four horses they had taken from the camp. "We'll leave them where there is grazing and water. I've a good mind to take them with us, but even from such men as those, I'd rather not thieve. After a bit, they'll work themselves free and return to camp."

"Those men with Brakase," Dovella said. "I don't think they were all Foresters."

"They weren't. It looks like some Plains People are here."

"Plains People?" Could the sorcerer be one of them? Dovella wondered. Pandil had spoken of sorcery as being a practice of the Plains People. "But what are they doing here? I thought they had left this part of the country ages ago."

"It looks like some of them are back," Drase said, "and to no good purpose. Sorry, but we should avoid the roads. I'd just as soon not meet up with anyone else. And you might want to tuck away your medallion. If they are only interested in healers, another party might ignore us."

Dovella stuffed the medallion inside her shirt, where she also wore the Kavella medal that had been given to her by the Kaftil, the leader of the Hill Folk. They belong together, she thought, for she had received both from her friends in Hill Country.

Soon they were racing through the woods, the shod hooves of the horses kicking up dust. Dovella had to duck to keep from being thrashed by low branches. Suddenly, Drase held up a hand in warning and pulled his mount to a halt. At first, Dovella heard nothing but a few birds, but then came the faint thud of horses' hooves on the road nearby. She felt her throat tighten. The pounding came nearer, nearer — and then it passed by. She swallowed hard and fixed her eyes on Drase. His head was still tilted a little, then he nodded, flicked his reins lightly, and they were on the move again.

As they rode, Dovella considered Drase's fighting techniques back at the cabin. Some of his moves she recognized as ones she had learned from Pandil, but others were new to her. Only they were slightly familiar all the same, she realized, for she had seen both Pandil and her father use them in the recent riot. Had her father ever studied with Drase? Even now, long after it was over, she felt the same wonder at how Safir had fought. Wonder at his skill, yet sadness that he should have had the need.

When the path widened enough that they could ride side by side, she asked Drase about Safir's fighting.

"Many Villagers have trained with me," he replied. "Your father often travels alone, searching for herbs, and even though he is a healer, not everyone in the Outlands will respect that enough to leave him in peace. But fighting aches his heart."

Dovella was grateful for his understanding. She herself didn't have as peaceful a nature as her father, yet it had torn at her spirit as well when she'd had to bring harm to those she had been born to heal. Nonetheless, without the training she'd received from Pandil, Dovella knew she would have had little chance in that scrap. She'd been well trained, this she knew;

but she could fight nothing like her father and Pandil.

Could she ask Drase for additional training? Pandil had said she should not ask Jael's *shagines* for teaching, only be prepared to consider it should they offer. Did the same apply to asking Drase? Perhaps he sensed the question, for he replied, "One thing at a time. Right now, what you have to learn from Elder Master Faris is much more important. Fighters we need, yes, but healers we will need even more, especially those who can heal the mind."

Since their escape, Dovella and Drase had ridden hard. As the sun disappeared behind the trees, they came upon a small camp. Several young men were seated around the fire and one of them jumped to his feet as she and Drase approached. Dovella was inclined to hold back, but Drase lifted a hand in greeting and the figure came running toward them.

A stocky young man in Forester dress grinned as he called out, "Welcome, Drase. What brings you this way?" He glanced at Dovella but made no greeting.

The camp was surrounded on three sides by a thick stand of high trees. The fourth side looked to be a wall of solid stone except for the opening to a cave. That must be where they sheltered, Dovella thought.

Drase dismounted and gripped the young man's arm in greeting. By now the others had also risen and come over to make Drase welcome.

"I've brought someone from the Village seeking Elder Master Faris who is guesting with you," Drase said.

Dovella was a bit surprised at his not giving more information. Surely here there was no need for secrecy. But, of course, whether there was need for secrecy or not, it was for her to reveal her business, not for him to do so. Before she could say anything though, these thoughts were driven from her mind by the man's response.

"I don't think there is anyone guesting here by that name."

"But he left the Village to come here," Dovella burst out. "He was invited by Jael."

The man glanced over at his companions, all of whom shook their heads. "It's possible that he came while someone else was on guard, but I think we would have heard. Still, it's best to ask in the settle." The young man's eyes moved from Dovella to Drase. "You know we have to cover her eyes?"

Dovella stiffened, but when Drase smiled and nodded, she relaxed. If Drase saw no reason for concern, she would not worry. She thought about a long dark road through the mountain she'd had to travel in Hill Country. Surely this could not be worse.

"I've guested here many times," Drase explained, "but you are new. Until you are given guest rights by the *shagines*, the guards can't let you see how we go in."

Her eyes bound, Dovella stepped carefully beside the man who held her arm. There was no sense of coercion. He only guided her so that she would not stumble. She had thought they would be led in the direction of the cave entrance, but could sense that they were walking away from it, back along the side of the stone wall. They turned then, and she felt a coolness and a sense of enclosure. A tunnel through the stone, perhaps? Only she'd seen no sign of an entrance other than the cave. It must have been disguised. Underneath her feet she felt the softness of a forest floor. After another twenty steps or so, they stopped and the cloth was taken from her eyes. She glanced around, but there was no sign of a cave or tunnel entrance, only the stone wall.

Coming toward her was an old man, moving swiftly for someone of such advanced age. Behind him came several other people, including Jael. Dovella felt her pulse quicken and swallowed hard. His eyes widened a bit when he saw her, then relaxed into a smiling welcome.

Dovella was glad to see Jael, glad to see he had not been injured in the Village unrest, but she kept her feelings in check. She thought she felt a spark of pleasure coming from him, but she couldn't be sure. She smiled shyly in return.

"Is there an Elder Master Faris here?" asked one of the men who'd brought them into the village.

The old man looked at Jael. "He was to follow you, was he not?"

"Yes, Master Tostare, I expect him to arrive some time around now."

Drase reached hurriedly for his horse. "He should have been here long since unless he was captured as we were."

"What?" There was much consternation on the faces of the men surrounding them. "What happened?"

"Let Dovella tell you," Drase said as he mounted up. "I must go look for the Elder Master."

"You'll not go alone," Tostare said. "Bide a few moments while we prepare to go with you."

Tostare nodded at Jael who glanced at Dovella again. "I will see you later," Jael said with a worried frown, then turned and raced away toward the stables nearby.

"We were captured by a small group of men, not all from around here judging by their appearance," Drase said. "Some looked to be Plains folk. They saw Dovella's medallion and said they wanted healers. They must have injured men somewhere, or be planning some fighting. We saw no trace of the Elder Master with them, but perhaps there is another such band."

"What will they do to him?" Tostare asked.

"I don't think the Master is in danger if they mean to make use of him. But we must find him." Drase turned to Dovella. "I know you'd like to come with us ..."

She smiled. "But you'll be riding fast and hard and it would be difficult for me to keep up. I understand."

Jael and several other men returned, mounted and armed. Drase nodded. "We'll be back soon," he said.

Dovella recognized one of the men as Maidel, who was Pandil's senior Security associate. He gave a nod in her direction but remained silent.

"Had we known exactly when he was coming we would have already been searching," Tostare said, touching Dovella gently on the shoulder. "But now, be assured, we will find him and bring him here safely."

Dovella watched in amazement as one by one the men disappeared into the hillside wall.

*

Before returning to work after her nooning meal, Security Master Pandil wandered through the Village trying to assess the mood of her people. The long drought continued unrelieved but the machine was working properly, and now both water and power had been fully restored in the Village. They had that at least to be thankful for. As she walked along the pebbled path leading to Security Hall, Pandil caught sight of a thread caught on a bush outside the entrance — a small red thread. What does my redbird have to sing to me today? she wondered. A smile flitted across her lips.

Pandil didn't quite know why she thought of her informant in those terms. Possibly because he almost always left a strand of red, signalling her to go to the park as soon as she saw the thread. Occasionally it was white. That meant they should meet in the evening, he'd told her. Black would mean deadly danger. So far, thanks be to Kavella, there had been none of that.

She made her way down to the park, stopping on the way to buy a couple of sausage rolls. Anyone who might be watching would assume that Master Pandil simply wanted a relaxing supper on her own in the quietness of the park; it would have been a welcome rest, indeed, to sit and enjoy the shady nook surrounded by the scent of zalebush, bakul and wild roses. She only wished that were the reason for her seeking this bench. She had scarcely finished the last bite of spicy sausage and wiped her mouth and fingers on the fine handkerchief that was one of her few vanities, when she heard the faint sound of boots on hard earth.

How her informant knew when she had arrived, Pandil couldn't understand, but he always turned up shortly after she did. She could, of course, have arranged for one of her people to watch so as to discover who he was, or even turned to look at him herself, but she never had. Once, he had asked her why she hadn't done so.

"I gave my promise the first time we talked. Isn't that reason enough?"

He'd chuckled. "Master Pandil's honour. Ordinarily, yes. Everyone knows how you value your word. But I'm sure that if you felt it would best serve the Village, you'd break it soon enough, for it is also known that you hold nothing higher than Village security. So again I ask, why do you think it would be in the interest of the Village for me to remain anonymous?"

She had brushed aside his words, not wanting to think too deeply about his question. Just how far would she go to ensure the security of the Village? It was a question she'd hoped she would never have to answer, but she'd had to do so recently when she'd been forced to truth-read one of Havkad's henchmen.

"All right," she'd told her informant then, "as you muffle your voice, I assume you are someone I come into contact with, if not frequently, at least often enough. And probably in the presence of others. Although I am able to dissemble better than most people, there is always the chance that — through a slight difference in my behaviour toward you or through a glance we might exchange — I would betray that something lies between us. That would not be in the best interest of the Village."

"The very reason I come in secrecy," he'd replied, and she'd heard something like satisfaction in his voice.

Today though, he made no general conversation, as he sometimes did, but went straight to their business. "You are putting a lot of effort into trying to trace Havkad, and I understand that, but you need to know that he is not the real threat."

"His sorcery —"

"He is only a dabbler and, as you must realize, not a very talented one at that. Anyone could see he had no control over the dark spell he attempted to cast on you. No, he isn't a danger ... but there *is* a strong sorcerer behind him."

She nodded grimly. Jael had said the same thing. She had known he must be right, but here was concrete confirmation.

"Perhaps," she said, keeping her voice even, "but Havkad seemed to have some power."

"Oh, no doubt the sorcerer taught him enough to satisfy him temporarily, but not enough to give him any mastery. There is still the deeper question, however: why is the sorcerer helping Havkad? The name he uses, in case you haven't already discovered it, is Fvlad."

"No," she said. "I ... had reason to think that perhaps there was someone else besides Havkad, but I had not heard a name." She ran her tongue across dry lips.

Her informant snorted. "Nor had I until recently, and I have to wonder why it was kept from me." He paused for a moment. "Well, never mind that now. For the moment, Fvlad is living in the outlands with a man named Bissel, Master Bokise's uncle."

Pandil certainly knew Bissel, but that he was Master Bokise's uncle was news to her.

"Bissel claims that Fvlad is a cousin whose settle was burned," her redbird continued. "Nonsense, of course. And there are more of his people around, though just how many and where they are camped I haven't yet discovered."

Not prepared to tell him just how little she did know, Pandil replied, "It's all useful information."

"Humph." She could imagine his smile, if only she could picture the face behind it. Something tugged at the edge of her consciousness. She had ways of following a half-formed picture like that, but she did not attempt to do so, for the same reasons she'd made no other efforts to discover his identity.

"Then another question," he went on. "Given the New School position on purity of blood, why do you suppose they enjoy the support of so many Forester people in high positions? And what about New School women who hold positions of authority? Why would they support leaders who hold to a philosophy that calls for removing women from power? Are they just fools? Deluded? Or is there some deeper purpose?"

"I have asked myself the same questions," she said.

"Then I suggest you continue following those questions," the informant said. "Foresters have Plains blood — some more than others. And some of them may well have a great deal. And perhaps that has some bearing on why the sorcerer is prepared to help. As you know, Plains sorcerers never did anything from the goodness of their hearts."

"Some were good people."

"Yes, all right, I'll grant you that: some were. But believe me, this one is not. I do not yet know his purpose, but I greatly fear that New Schoolers are being used by, rather than using, this man. In either case, it does not bode well for the Village, I agree, but if Fvlad gains control of the Village, I suspect that what the New Schoolers have promised will look good in comparison with what he will surely bring."

"But why does he want control of the Village?"

"I wish I knew, Master Pandil. I only wish I knew."

Pandil heard footsteps move away, and after a short space of time, she rose and left the park. She wished the Master Archivist were here for her to discuss this with, but as soon as he'd heard Dovella speak of the archives in Hill Country, he'd arranged to journey there to see if he could study them.

But maybe Avella would have some ideas.

When Avella opened her door a few minutes later, Pandil felt again the flare of anger that came each time she saw her friend's wan face covered with a patchwork of fading bruises. Avella had still not fully recovered from the beating she'd been given, but today she greeted Pandil with a smile and it seemed that her cheeks held a touch of natural colour.

"Come in." Her blue eyes gleamed in welcome. "I was just making tea. You'll join me?"

"With pleasure."

A few minutes later Avella handed Pandil a cup and sat down across from her.

"I've just had confirmation of what Jael suspected," Pandil said. "There is another very powerful sorcerer behind Havkad."

Although Pandil had never told her friend of Jael's role in freeing her from the coma, Avella had been present at the Council meeting when Havkad attacked Pandil with sorcery and was defeated through Jael's efforts.

Avella leaned back heavily. "This is ill news indeed." She listened closely as Pandil related what she had learned.

"Well, that explains why Councillor Bokise supported Havkad in Council disputes despite New School teachings about women in positions of power," Avella said. "I always found it strange that she would side with him. And if there is a Plains sorcerer behind the New School attempt to take over the Village, it bodes ill for all of us."

"But what do they want with the Village?" Pandil asked.

"A place to live that they don't have to make the effort to develop, I suppose," Avella said. "With so much of our knowledge lost, even we would be hard-pressed to make anything similar to what we have here. They were never able to do so."

"I'm sure of that," Pandil replied, "but why now? Why them? Why go about it in such a way? None of that makes sense."

"What better way than to have someone else do the work for them?" Avella asked. "And they will reap the benefits."

After leaving Avella, Pandil made her way to New Town for the early evening patrol. No one from Security liked working that detail, for this part of the Village was dirty and depressing, the people either unable or unwilling to care for their homes. Feral cats scrounged in the garbage-strewn streets and carousing residents were usually looking for trouble. Like it or not, however, Pandil was careful to take her share of the burden. Perhaps people were saving themselves for the upcoming Festival time, she thought, for the streets were unusually quiet.

It was nearing twilight when she headed back to Security Hall. Returning through the park, she paused for a moment to enjoy again the mingled fragrances that surrounded her. It was in that moment of inattention that three men material-ized menacingly in front of her. Senses sharpened, she whirled just as a fourth assailant came from the rear, and caught him with boot and fist. He crumpled but, just as Pandil swung back around, two men grabbed her arms and the third advanced, long knife in hand. He raised his arm to strike, then his eyes widened. His mouth opened in a scream of pain as he fell to his knees and sprawled forward.

The two men holding her loosened their grip a little, giving Pandil the opportunity to break free. As they gaped at the sight of the dagger protruding from her assailant's back, Pandil grabbed them by the necks and slammed their heads together. Stunned, they wobbled and fell. Quickly, Pandil dragged each of them to opposite sides of a tree, laying them on their backs. She stretched their arms over their heads around the tree and, pulling out her leather thongs, bound one man's wrists to those of the other. As the first man she had downed was rousing, she towed him to another tree and bound his wrists together surrounding the trunk.

Panting, she leaned over and took a couple of deep breaths, then straightened and peered into the shadows. Someone was obviously looking out for her. Not one of her people — they would have helped her secure the men. Why the secrecy? Could it be her redbird? Or perhaps someone from the New School who didn't hold with the fanatics? Or maybe an Outlander, one of Drase's friends, left to guard her back?

Pandil looked around, listened. Whoever had thrown the blade must be far away by now. She knelt by the man with the knife in his back and felt for a pulse. Faint, but there. As her hand brushed across the shoulder of his tunic, she paused and looked closer. The material was of tarvelcloth, but it seemed rougher somehow than that used by most Villagers, and he wore a woven sash around his waist that was unlike any she'd seen. A thought flashed across her mind, but she rejected it: surely this couldn't be a man of the Plains People. Yet no Outlander would wear his hair loose. Perhaps it was true: a man of the Plains People had come into the Village and attacked her.

She rose and gave her shoulders a shake. The only thing she could do now was fetch a couple of her apprentices to help her get these men to Security Hall and find a healer.

Pandil gazed at the knife — she'd need to examine it in better light, but the handle seemed to be carved with a pattern of leaves and fruit, much like the pattern on the Kavella medal that she wore concealed beneath her shirt.

She didn't like leaving these foulheads here unattended, but she had to go for assistance. Pandil reached for the knife, then drew back her hand. She'd leave it in place, for removing it might worsen the bleeding; later, she'd take it to the knife maker to see what he could tell her.

As she ran from the park, she saw a Villager and called out to him, asking him to hurry to Security Hall and bring a couple of her apprentices and a healer. She watched for a moment as he raced off, then hastened back to the prisoners, but as she approached, she stopped short and stared at the dark patch on the sprawled man's shirt. The knife was gone.

four

A s Dovella watched Jael and the other men ride away, she fought back tears. The elderly *shagine*, Tostare, had disappeared as well, no doubt to see about things that needed to be done, leaving her standing there alone. She looked around wondering where she should go. With relief, she saw a woman approaching.

"I'm Calisa," the woman said. Tall and slender, she had green eyes and light greying hair. Unlike Village women, who for the most part wore trews and tunics in sombre hues, Calisa had on a bright green blouse and what at first glance looked like a skirt, but was actually wide-legged trews. Calisa was very attractive despite the deep scar that split her cheek.

Touching Dovella's arm with a calloused hand, she said, "Let's take your horse to the stable. Then you can come home with me."

As they were making their way to the stable, a short, slender woman came out. She was dressed in similar trews but with narrower legs and a sleeveless tunic made of tarvel-cloth that had been dyed a deep blue. Under the tunic, she wore a blouse of bright blue with tiny white flowers embroidered on the long, full sleeves. Her light brown hair had been cut short and curled softly about her face.

"That's our horse master, Lata," Calisa whispered. "She's Jael's mother."

The woman was short and slender, but when they approached and Dovella saw Lata's high cheekbones and met her measuring grey-green eyes, she thought she might well have been looking at Jael's face.

Calisa introduced them and Lata smiled warmly. "Welcome to our village."

"Thank you," Dovella said. She turned and lifted down her pack, and had begun to take off the saddle when Lata stayed her hand. "I didn't hear what brought you here," she said, "but I can guess from the speed with which our men left that there has been trouble, and you've tasted some of it. I'll see to your mount. You go on with Calisa and refresh yourself."

Dovella looked at Calisa, who gave a little nod.

"My thanks," Dovella said, but Lata had already started leading the horse away.

"Come," Calisa said.

As they walked along the paths made of hard-packed dirt, Dovella looked around. The houses were small, some made of logs, others of dressed boards brightly painted, and decorated with painted flowers.

Dovella followed Calisa to a small blue cottage where an elderly man sat on the porch in a red wicker rocking chair. "This is my father, Vrillian," Calisa said.

Vrillian was slighter of build than Tostare, yet there was something in his wiriness that suggested strength. Tostare had greeted Dovella kindly enough, but there was real warmth in Vrillian's grey eyes. "Welcome," he said, holding out both hands to take hers. "Welcome to our village and to our home."

"Thank you." At the touch of his hands, Dovella felt the

tension drain from her shoulders. Something about the man exuded peace.

While Calisa busied herself with preparing the meal, Dovella sat on the porch and talked with Vrillian, who was full of questions. "But I'll save most of them," he said, "for others will want to hear your story as well. Tell me only what befell you on the way, for I think others have already heard that tale."

And so Dovella related all that had happened to her and Drase since leaving the Village that morning. As he listened Vrillian pursed his lips and shook his head. "It grieves me that anyone of Plains blood could bring such evil. I suppose it should be no surprise, given the history of our people, but it still saddens me."

He ran slender fingers through his thatch of silver hair. "It troubles me even more," he went on, "that we are ill-prepared to fight them. Besides Tostare and myself, there are only three other *shagines*, and none of us young. We have eight younger ones training, but too little time to prepare them as thoroughly as we need to. We have had to expend far too much energy in fighting the drought."

"Can you fight a drought?" The dry weather had lasted two years, which was part of the reason Dovella's recent journey to restore water to the Village had been critical.

"If it is caused by sorcery — as this one has been — you can. But, just as it takes great power to cause such a disturbance in the weather, it takes great power to fight it. We have been only partially successful as we have not been able to devote the energy needed. It's made worse by the fact that the sorcerer keeps moving around so we can't direct our energies against him as well." He looked around at the yellowed grass.

"We've managed to bring enough rain to keep our crops from withering completely, though we've had to transport water from the lake also. But here ... we've had to leave things to die."

Using sorcery to fight sorcery. Dovella shivered.

Calisa called them to come in and wash up for the meal, sparing Dovella further discussion of that topic. Just inside the front door she found a small bathing room with running water and a small stove, which would, no doubt, be welcome when the weather was cold. She adjusted the taps to get a stream of warm water, then doused her face and washed her hands. After drying on a fluffy towel, she went to join Calisa.

While they were waiting for Vrillian, Calisa showed Dovella to an alcove concealed by a woven blue curtain. Her pack had been stowed beneath a bed. "You'll sleep here," Calisa said. "I have the other alcove and Father sleeps in an adjoining room. I hope ..."

"It's fine. I'll be comfortable here," Dovella said, running her fingers over the soft blanket. And she would.

Although the cottage was small and had little in the way of furnishings, the walls were covered with tapestries much like the ones hanging in her bedroom at home, and the table was covered with a woven cloth of gold and orange. The compact kitchen was tidy and the shelves appeared to be well stocked.

Near the front door stood a table covered with a blue cloth like the one that concealed the sleeping alcove. The table held a white pottery vase with a pattern of dark blue flowers twining around it.

"How beautiful!" Dovella exclaimed.

Calisa touched the vase gently. "Yes, it is. Our Master Potter made it for us. He is Jael's father. And Jael's younger brother wove this cloth." She smiled. "He didn't want to give it to me for it was an early piece and not perfect, but that makes it all the more precious to me."

By this time Vrillian had joined them and he put an arm around Calisa. "My daughter is our Master Weaver," he said, "and every piece her students make is precious to her."

"Everything anyone makes is precious," Calisa said. "We also have a small harp that Jael made. He is a talented musician and was a promising instrument maker before he turned aside to become a *shagine*. We need more *shagines*, of course, but he's a great loss to our musicians."

"But a greater gain to us as a *shagine*." Vrillian patted his daughter's arm and turned to Dovella. "We all missed Jael when he was away in the Village but the experience was good for him. Only, it pains Calisa that he has trained as a warrior."

"Well, doesn't it pain you?" Calisa's voice sounded ragged and full of unshed tears.

"It pains me that we *need* to train anyone as a warrior. But given that we do — and will — need warriors, I'm glad that Jael has received such good training."

Calisa took his hand. "I know, Father. I know the need. But it pains me all the same." She smiled at Dovella. "Come. You must be hungry."

The meal was a simple stew of vesson and root vegetables with a thin flat bread, and though Dovella had thought she was too nervous to eat, the aroma made her mouth water. Soon she had cleaned her bowl.

"Do you know where Elder Master Faris will be staying?"

Dovella had to believe he would be found and brought here safely.

Perhaps Calisa read her worry for she smiled. "Don't worry, they'll find him. And yes, he will be staying in a small house just down the way. It's really only a single room, but it does well enough for one person, and we thought he'd need more work space than we could give him here with us."

After they finished the meal, Dovella helped Calisa clear away the dishes. The woman was friendly enough but clearly not one given to talking while she worked. When everything was tidy, she said, "We'll gather at the meeting fire and discuss what is happening."

They wandered through the village, past an altar that made Dovella shiver. She remembered the broken shrines, vandalized in ages past by her own people, that she'd seen during her previous travels and felt the same flare of shame. Even so, the altar made her uncomfortable.

As they walked, she noticed that although there were lamps along the streets, none of them were lit. A few people carried lanterns, but mostly they made their way by the light of the moons.

"Has your village lost its power?" she asked.

"Not exactly," Calisa said. "But with the drought, we agreed that the water we'd use for power could be put to better use in the fields. Also, Father and Tostare drew on the water to help make the rain they've been able to bring our way."

Others joined them as they walked and Calisa introduced Dovella. The villagers greeted her with friendly words and no one questioned her presence, but she sensed the curiosity in their glances and heard them whisper among themselves when she and Calisa moved on.

The meeting place was at the edge of the village in a small depression that allowed those sitting on the tiered sides of the bowl-shaped area to see and hear the leaders, who were seated around a fire that had been laid in the base of the area. Calisa led Dovella down to join Vrillian who was already seated by the fire. Dovella didn't know what kind of wood was burning, but it gave off a fragrance that reminded her of collitflower tea.

When everyone was settled, Vrillian rose to speak. Despite his apparent frailty, his voice was steady. Quickly he told what he knew, then invited Dovella to share her story with the entire gathering. There was silence while she spoke, but when she sat down a man called out, "But how did they know to capture you?"

Dovella drew out the medallion which she had earlier concealed. "I'm a healer," she said, "and they have need of healers. Though I don't understand why they would not have healers of their own."

"They are surely renegades," another said. "No decent healer would go with them."

"But why did you come here?" This from a young woman with honey-coloured hair and dark eyes. She was slender and beautiful, but her face held the frozen expression of a statue. She too wore a divided skirt, much like Calisa's, but her blue blouse was cut low in front. And though she smiled, there was a harshness to her voice that made the others look at her with a frown.

"That is hardly a gracious welcome, Mandira," Calisa said.

Dovella silently agreed, but answered the question as if she had not taken offence. "I had thought to find Elder Master

Faris here. Although I wear the medallion, I still need training. Master Plais refused to teach me because I missed the Rites." Each time she told the tale of Master Plais's rejection, Dovella felt her anger burn ever brighter. "But while I was on my journey," she went on, "I spent some time with the Khanti-Lafta and she awarded me the medallion."

There were excited whispers when Dovella mentioned the name of the Great Healer of the Hill Folk.

Mandira frowned but said nothing more. Still, Dovella could feel herself caught in the young woman's hostile gaze.

Calisa rose. "I'm sure you must be tired after what you've gone through this day," she said. "Come, I'll take you home." Something about the way she said "home" felt comforting to Dovella, but she saw the blood rise to Mandira's face. Dovella wondered why the girl should resent her, for clearly it was resentment that had made her speak so.

Dovella stood up and bowed to Vrillian before following Calisa back to the cottage. She was tired and it was kind of Calisa to recognize this, but Dovella was sure that it was not only out of kindness that Calisa took her home. Surely the people had decisions to make and it would not be appropriate for Dovella to be there for their deliberations.

When they entered Vrillian's house, a yellow kitten came running toward them, meowing loudly. "There you are," Calisa said, laughing. "You've been hiding." She scooped up the kitten and stroked it on the nose, then turned to her guest. Dovella had seen feral cats back in the Village, mostly scavenging in the streets of New Town, but she'd never held one, never even seen one close. For a moment she faltered, but then she stretched out a trembling hand to pat it gently. She smiled in surprise. She'd had no idea a cat could feel so soft.

Calisa must have noticed her hesitation for she said, "I'll put it out tonight, otherwise it will be up in the bed with you."

Dovella felt a wave of relief, followed swiftly by a feeling of reluctance to have the kitten ejected. "No," she said. "Don't. I'm not ... I've never been around cats, but I think ... I'd like it to stay." She had no idea where this feeling came from, but she was sure she would like the kitten's company.

After she pulled the curtain closed on her alcove, however, Dovella found it difficult to sleep, for she couldn't stop worrying about Elder Master Faris. Nor about how she would react when she was finally able to talk to Jael. Then she felt a slight jolt as something landed on top of her. Feeling the warmth of the kitten as it curled up in the curve of her stomach and listening to its contented rumble, she fell into a deep sleep.

*

Jael and his companions rode frantically, their horses kicking up plumes of dust that coated the boots of their riders. Though none of them voiced any fears, Jael sensed that they felt as pressed as he did to find Elder Master Faris.

The news they'd gleaned from the Guild Master of the Guides had only served to feed Jael's fears. Guild Master Hidele had not wanted to give them any information at first. "You know the Forester Guild protects the privacy of its clients. You would not want us to publish your business to anyone who asked."

"You are supposed to protect your clients as well," Drase had snapped. The big Outlander's face was tight. "Elder Master

Faris was to have been taken to Jael's village but he has not arrived. And just today there was an attempt to capture a young healer in my care."

"No!" Hidele looked from one to the other. He must have read them as speaking true for he said, "Young Landar is a good guide. If they have not arrived, something must have happened to him as well."

"Then we'd best seek him out." Drase said.

"I can take you to his home," Hidele said, "but you'll not find him there. Not if the Elder Master did not reach Jael's village. Some harm must have befallen them both."

"Let's find out," Jael said, more concerned with rescuing Faris than with whether or not Landar was a traitor.

At their insistence, Hidele rode with them immediately, though he'd fussed the entire time that the journey was in vain, that they would do better to trace the road Landar would have taken.

Drase, Maidel and eight others from Jael's village pounded along the road. Would there be enough of them? Jael wondered, not knowing what to expect at Landar's cabin.

As he rode, his thoughts turned to his own village. Tostare and Vrillian, the two senior *shagines,* were getting old. He needed desperately to complete his studies while they were still able to teach. What would happen to his folk if the Plains People came wanting to take over while there were still too few *shagines* to fight the mind attacks that would surely follow? What would happen to Villagers and Outlanders who had no idea of how to ward themselves against such attack? He shuddered as he remembered the eyes that had sought to probe him when he was freeing Avella from the sorcerous snare that had held her in a coma.

His thoughts also kept turning to Dovella. He'd left the Village before the young healer had returned from her journey, so he knew very little of what had happened to her while she was away. On his last night in the Village, Pandil had finally revealed that Dovella had made the trip to the Hill Country, hoping to repair the workings of the machine. The restoration of power, which had come just in time to ward off the New School attempt to oust Master Pandil, had proved that Dovella's journey must have been successful, but more than this he didn't know.

The brief moment of time that he had seen her back in his settle, she had seemed well, but there had been a wariness in her eyes that told him her adventures had not left her unscathed in spirit. Sensing this left him unaccountably sad.

The forest became thicker as they neared Landar's home, but with the brightness of the three moons, all nearing to full, it was easy to find their way. The house itself was little more than a hut, but there was a neat vegetable garden, a coop for fowl and a small stable. A horse grazed just beyond the garden.

"That's Landar's mare," Hidele whispered. "Perhaps the Elder Master was unable to complete the journey in one day." For the first time, Jael heard doubt in the man's voice and feared the worst. When they drew up in front of the small cabin, a young man came out carrying a lantern. He stopped short. It looked as if he would run back in, but before he could turn, Hidele's voice sliced the air. "Landar! Give account of yourself."

Of medium height and a wiry build, the young man trod slowly forward. His neatly groomed blond hair gleamed in the light cast by the lantern. As he drew near, Jael saw that his face was haggard and his hand trembled, sending the light from the lantern in jagged patterns across the dirt.

"Where is Elder Master Faris?"

"He's safe! No one is going to harm him."

"That was not my question." The Guild Master's voice thundered and Landar shrank back.

"Our brothers need him," Landar said. "Will need him even more in days to come." When the others continued to stare silently at him, Landar went on, stumbling over his words. "The Plains People have come back. They are our people! What loyalty do we owe Villagers and Outlander mongrels?"

"You are a fool!" Hidele shouted. "But even if I could agree with such nonsense, you have given an oath to your Guild and your Guildbrothers. Your actions smear them as well as yourself." He gave a snort. "Besides, you are a mongrel yourself, if truth be told."

"I'm still of Plains blood, and my duty to my people comes first."

"Your 'people' are your Guildbrothers and other Foresters. We have no duty to any renegade Plains People who may have returned."

Jael glanced over at Hidele. Clearly the Guild Master knew something about the return of the Plains People even if he was not in sympathy with them.

"Their sorcerer is powerful!"

"No doubt he is. That is no reason to follow his wickedness. Now tell me where you took Master Faris."

Landar looked as if he would refuse until he saw Drase dismount. Before Drase had let go the reins of his horse, the young man was shaking. "To Bissel's house," he cried out.

"I took him to Bissel. But he's safe. I promise you he is safe. They only want him to help them when the battle comes."

Hidele dismounted and he and Drase bound Landar's hands and put out the lantern while Jael went to saddle Landar's horse.

"What will you do with Landar?" The Guild Master's voice was unsteady.

After exchanging a glance with Jael, Drase said, "We'll leave him in the hands of the Guild. If you'll take charge of him, we'll go on to Bissel's. Do you want one of us to go with you?"

"I can manage Landar," Hidele said. "You'd best all go to Bissel's house since you don't know what you will find there."

Jael watched Drase search Hidele's face. What Drase saw clearly convinced him that the Guild Master took this breach of duty seriously, for the big Outlander nodded and remounted. Leaving Landar in Hidele's care, Jael and his companions continued toward Bissel's farm.

The sun had not quite risen when Jael pulled to a halt beside Drase and Maidel. They studied Bissel's farm from a distance.

"Bissel's farming operation has expanded a great deal." Maidel's voice held a note of puzzlement.

Jael glanced over at him. Pandil's senior apprentice was a handsome man who looked younger than his years and that often led people to underestimate him. They always regretted it. Jael smiled at the thought.

"We knew he had a lot of extra workers but had assumed he was taking in others whose farms had been burned," Drase said. "Now I wonder if instead he is using Plains People who have been brought in by the sorcerer."

"He certainly hasn't been affected by the drought as much as others have." Maidel gestured toward the fields, green with young vegetables.

"The drought was a sorcerer's work," Jael said. "Clearly, he spared Bissel."

Maidel shifted uneasily. "That means Bissel is in league with the sorcerer. But why?"

"Bissel is of Plains blood. Maybe he feels as Landar does," Jael said.

"Likely so, but knowing Bissel, I expect he has been promised a great deal. I'm sure that was why he was such a strong supporter of Havkad." Drase shook his head. "And the riot that freed Havkad from prison was surely the work of Bissel's people."

"Havkad escaped?" Maidel exclaimed.

Jael turned sharply in his saddle. "What happened?"

Briefly, Drase related what had taken place. "While Pandil and her people were putting down the riot, others went in and freed Havkad."

"He should have been better guarded!" Maidel burst out.

"I agree," Drase said, "but the healers were convinced that, with his injuries, he couldn't be a danger."

"That may well be, but he still commands a lot of loyalty," Maidel said, "and if he is free, we have no way of bargaining with them." He pounded a fist on his thigh. "I knew I shouldn't have left the Village."

"One more person, even of your strength, wouldn't have made a difference," Jael said. "You would have been fighting alongside Pandil, and Havkad still left in Healer's Hall with too light a guard."

"Jael has the right of it," Drase said. "Pandil sent you to study with the *shagines* and me for a good reason." The big Outlander reached over to clap Maidel on the shoulder. "She'll have great need of the skills you can develop. I fear that the threat posed by Havkad is nothing compared to what the Plains People plan."

"But what *do* they plan?" Maidel grimaced and raked his fingers through his dark hair.

"I wish I knew," Drase replied. "But the least of it will be to reclaim lands surrendered when their ancestors left. What more ... I don't even like to think of it."

"I knew you were coming out to Jael's village to help with our training," Maidel said, "but why did you have Dovella with you? I would have thought after her journey, her parents would have wanted to keep her close."

Jael fingered the sleeve of his tunic, listening for the answer.

Drase frowned. "No doubt they did, but Plais refused to acknowledge her right to wear the medallion."

"What medallion?" Jael asked. "I saw nothing."

"After we escaped, I counselled her to hide it. It seems she was given the Medallion of the Healer by the Khanti-Lafta when she was in Hill Country, and Plais was furious. Since she didn't go through the Rites in the Village, he refused to accept it."

"But the only reason she missed the Rites was that she was journeying to save the Village!" Jael protested, outraged on her behalf.

"That wouldn't matter to Plais," Maidel said. "He's far too rigid to make an exception."

"Especially for a woman," Drase said.

"But why?" Jael looked from Maidel to Drase. "He gets along well enough with Avella and Pandil."

"He gets along with women anywhere except as healers," Drase said. "It's a long story, and I only know a few rumours of it, but it has something to do with a woman healer he worked with years ago. Whatever the truth, he has always searched for some way to exclude Dovella, and when she missed the Rites, he had all the excuse he needed."

"So she's come to work with Elder Master Faris then." Jael gave a careless nod, hoping that would disguise his true feelings. "Well, she couldn't do better." He'd had a few dealings with the Elder Master, and in the short time he'd been around the old healer, Jael had become very fond of him. He was glad Dovella would be working with someone who would help rather than hinder her learning. More than glad that she would be guesting in his settle.

As the sky brightened, they drew closer, concealing themselves in the forest bordering Bissel's land. In the yard surrounding the farm house were three men.

"The two tall ones are Havkad's men, fierce fighters both, but we can take them," Drase said. "I'm not sure who the other man is."

"That's Bissel's son, Govan," Maidel told them. "He likes to think he's a fighter, but he avoids a fair fight."

Drase again looked at Jael, deferring to him as leader of the men from his village. "How do you want to do this?"

"You know them," Jael replied. "It's best if you decide how to approach them."

Drase nodded. "You and I will go up with four of your men. Maidel can stay here with the rest to see if anyone tries to leave by another door, and then join us if it turns out there are more men inside the house."

Jael glanced around, gave slight nods in the direction of four of his men and, without further words, they set off. As they drew their mounts to a halt near the cabin, the young man Govan rushed toward them, tucking in his shirt.

"My father isn't here." Govan stopped and stared at them defiantly, hands on his hips.

"We haven't come to see your father," Drase said, "We've come for Elder Master Faris."

"I don't know anyone of that name," Govan replied, but he wouldn't meet Drase's eyes.

"Now, that's a lie," Jael said. "You've spent enough time in the Village to know the Elder Master."

Govan's eyes flicked toward the house and quickly away. For a moment, it looked as if Havkad's men would intervene, but then one of them sidled in the direction of the stable. Drase lifted a hand, motioning Maidel and Jael's remaining men to ride forward. "Let's go to the house," he said.

The other New Schooler reached for his knife, but before the man had a chance to draw his blade one of Jael's men pinned his arms behind him. Meanwhile, Jael, Drase and their men raced for the house. Flinging the door open, they found the old healer lying on a cot in the front room, guarded only by a boy.

Jael let out a long sigh of relief. His old friend looked tired but none the worse for his captivity. Still, Jael asked, "Are you all right?"

Faris sat up and smiled. "Better now," he said, "but I've been done no harm except to my pride. I trusted young Landar, and it always hurts to know your trust has been misplaced."

Govan rushed in behind them. "You've no right to take him away," he shouted. "We need healers. A lot of our people were injured by your Village security people."

"Many Villagers were hurt too," Drase said. "If your people were hurt, it was at their own asking. They were the ones to start the riot."

"Havkad was being unfairly held. Falsely accused."

"That's rot and you know it," Jael snapped.

Govan glared at him. "You are the one who turned the spell on him, aren't you? You should be ashamed. You carry Plains blood."

"Which Havkad does not," Jael said. "In any case, it was his own lack of discipline that caused the spell to recoil."

The young boy, who did not look more than twelve, cowered in a corner as the men argued. Sitting with his back against the wall, his legs drawn up against his chest, he glanced from one to the other.

"Come," Faris said, his voice gentle, "no one is going to hurt you." He turned to Drase, "He has taken care of me. I don't think he's part of what's going on here, but his father is dependent on Bissel, so the boy had little choice."

"There's always a choice," Drase said. "Maybe not a good one, and the price may be high, but he's going to have to decide for himself regardless of what his father does. He's old enough." Drase motioned the boy forward. "Come along, lad, I'm not going to hurt you, but you have to go into the Village with us and account for your actions."

They tied his arms in front of him, but loosely enough not to hurt, then led Govan and him outside where they found four other men tightly bound.

"They were in the stable," one of Jael's men said. "I'm afraid the other one got away. These men fought so he could escape."

"That must have been Ancel," Drase said. "He's one of Havkad's top renegades."

"What now?" Maidel asked.

"You and I will take these *skrev* to Pandil." Drase looked at Jael. "I expect Ancel has gone to get help. Can you spare some of your men?"

"I can spare six of them," Jael said.

"But you have Elder Master Faris to get safely to your village." Drase turned to Faris. "Assuming you still want to go."

"Oh, yes," the healer said. "I most certainly still want to go. I see now more than ever that we will need whatever I may be able to learn from my fellow healers in Jael's village."

"Then —"

"I and my remaining men will be enough," Jael said. "They won't be able to follow us." Jael was confident he knew the forest better than most; besides, with his training, if need be he would be able to hide all of them from prying eyes.

Drase looked over at Faris, then grinned. "Yes, that should do well."

Jael and his two men helped Faris collect his things and mount the gentle horse he'd been given by the Forester's Guild for his journey. That it had been left at Bissel's farm told them there had been a plan to take Faris somewhere else.

As they rode away, Faris asked, "How did you know I'd been taken?"

"Dovella came looking for you."

"Dovella?" Faris frowned, then shook his head and smiled.

"I have a feeling there is a great deal I need to know, but perhaps it's as well that we get underway and I can ask questions later. Tell me only this: is she all right?"

"Yes, but Master Healer Plais has refused to let her train further."

Faris sighed heavily. "Poor Plais. He is a gifted healer, but he can be such an ass. Well, never mind. Take me to your village, young Jael, and I'll ask my questions there."

*

When Dovella arose the next morning and discovered that Jael and his companions had not yet arrived home, her fears returned.

No doubt Vrillian noticed her restlessness, for after they had eaten a breakfast of porridge and berries, he invited her to walk with him into the forest. Before her journey to Hill Country, Dovella's only experiences in the forest had been the outings she'd made with her father in search of herbs, but her recent trip had entailed so many dangers she had not been able to absorb the peace a forest walk could give. Thanking Vrillian, she went to fetch her herb pouch, for she was sure she would be introduced to herbs that were unfamiliar to her. She took up the Medallion of the Healer and started to put it on, but then with a sigh, she laid it aside. Although she had every right to wear it, she was not in the Village now. Besides, she was here to learn. She tucked it into her pack, strapped on her pouch, and went to meet the *shagine*.

As they walked, she could see that the drought had caused less damage than it had nearer the Village; still, the grass was not as lush as it should have been, nor the flowers as plentiful. But there was a yellow zalebush perfuming the air.

Vrillian spoke little, only pointing out certain plants he thought would be of interest and watching without comment as Dovella pinched off a few leaves here and there, smiling when he saw her making the small motion with her hand that she had been taught was the proper technique for the taking of herbs.

The settle was nestled in a valley with steep hills rising on all sides. "It's very beautiful," Dovella said. In the distance she could see the fields and a large corral which seemed to hold very few animals. Closer by were the sheds of the tradesmen: weavers, potters, boot- and saddle-makers and such.

"It is beautiful," he said. "And safe. There are only three entrances to the settle and they are all disguised. There are also alarms that will let us know if anyone should somehow breach our shields."

When they had walked a little while, Vrillian motioned to a small glade. "We can rest there."

At the edge of the glade was a small shrine that Dovella recognized as being similar to those she had seen in broken heaps near Hill Country. Here, the figure was of a beautiful woman seated on a stool, the base of which was carved with vines and fruit. About her feet a child played with a forest cat and a bear cub. In her lap was a small bowl. A shrine to the Goddess Kavella.

Although Vrillian's eyes wandered briefly to the shrine, he said nothing. Dovella reached up to touch the medallion of Kavella hidden under her tunic. She wore it to honour the Hill Folk and the work they had done together, but it made her a little uncomfortable, for she worshiped the unnamed gods, the true gods. Still, despite the discomfort, and even though she would never wear it openly, she did not want to put aside the Kavella medal because of the friendship it represented.

As they sat quietly, a deer passed close by. It paused briefly and looked at them with moist brown eyes. After a moment, it scampered away. A bird with bright blue and red feathers darted from tree to tree while another, hidden in the foliage, sang.

Vrillian cocked his head to listen. A smile touched his lips as if the bird had given him welcome news. A snake slithered in their direction, then stopped and tasted the air with its tongue.

Dovella felt herself stiffen, but after a moment the snake veered away.

"It almost looked as if you are talking to it," she said.

"Not talking, exactly, but communicating all the same." Vrillian smiled. "Snakes do not attack because they are evil. They attack for food or because they feel threatened. Because a small snake like that cannot eat a person, it attacks to protect itself. There is a way to send a message that says 'no danger here, run along.'"

"But how do you do that?

Vrillian laughed. "That is not so easy to say. It can be taught if you are willing to learn, but it will take a little time."

Dovella hesitated for a moment. Pandil had advised her to accept what learning she was offered and Dovella was prepared to do so, even if she was a bit uneasy about it. "I'm willing."

"First you must know something about the creature with which you want to communicate. That snake, now, it paralyzes its prey."

Dovella wrinkled her nose in distaste.

Vrillian studied her for a moment. "How is that different from killing with an arrow or a stone from a sling?"

She reflected for a moment. "It isn't really, I suppose. Just ... I'm more used to the idea of shooting a bow or a sling."

"The snake can hardly do that."

Dovella laughed. "No, I don't suppose it can."

"So, by knowing something of different creatures, why they attack and how they attack, you can picture in your mind a block to that attack, surrounded by peaceful actions on your part. This tells the creature that you understand its need and fear, but offer no threat. Once you've studied enough to understand what picture you need to send, it's only a matter of making the picture in your mind and sending it. That part can be learned fairly quickly. It's knowing which messages to send that takes time to learn."

"Could you also send messages asking for help?"

"You can send almost any kind of message if you can picture it in your mind."

Was this magic? she wondered. All her life she'd been taught by the schoolmasters that magic was mere superstition, and that anyone who sought to learn such a thing was evil. The Hill Folk had spoken quite openly of magic. One had even thought that Dovella was using some kind of magical ritual when she repaired the machine; yet, it had been only a matter of knowing what oiling technique was needed and then following that pattern. Not magic at all.

"You see," Vrillian went on, "we are all one — people, creatures, plants, we are meant to work together. But we must have knowledge. For instance, some people have a horror of poisonous plants, yet these plants have their uses. They harm no one by just being, and are often beautiful to look at. Only if they are used wrongly do they cause harm. Kavella put everything here for a purpose. It is up to us to discover that purpose."

Dovella looked away. Even after her time with the Hill Folk she felt uncomfortable with the mention of their Goddess. Although they had made no attempt to convince her that Kavella was the true deity and should be honoured over the unnamed gods, she still felt a small tingle of revulsion run up her spine. She glanced over at the shrine. It hadn't been right for her forefathers to destroy the shrines in Hill Country, she thought; yet, how were people to be taught the ways of the true gods?

five

MALEEM TIED THE WOVEN WHITE SASH ABOUT HER WAIST
and glanced toward the corner of the room that had been
given to her family. A small chest held all of her belongings,
including the red sash she would wear when she married.
That was one of the first things a young Plains woman wove.
Sometimes she wondered if she'd ever get to wear it. She could
have married already, of course — Lofel would have taken her
gladly — but she'd sworn not to wed until she could do so
in the Village, after the Plains People had taken it for their
own.

Most girls her age already wore the red, and some even
wore a second sash, to show they had borne a child. Her
mother wore five — her red sash and four more for the
children she'd brought the people. By rights, she should only
wear three sashes, Maleem thought; Gzofie shouldn't lay
claim to the two children who had not come to share the
destiny of their people.

Walking outside, Maleem looked around with a grimace.
True, this camp was better than the others they'd lived in
during their long journey, but after the comfort of Barte's
steading, she found it hard to come back to this shamble of
lean-to shelters, crudely patched houses, tents and hastily
erected huts, all set amidst the burned-out ruins of a small

settlement. Even the ground was mostly bare, the few patches of grass seared by fire and drought.

Everyone, except the obstinate prisoners, took their meals together in the largest of the buildings, which had a makeshift kitchen at one end. The wood-burning stove was good enough but, because of the drought, water was scarce. Cutting the chunks of vesson with her small knife, Maleem remembered the feel of the big knife she'd used in Tavile's kitchen, remembered how it had felt against her bare palm. It was an abomination, she knew, still ...

She understood why she needed to keep her hands covered. When a woman married, it pleased her husband to know that his wife's hands had not touched another man, had not even been seen by another. Too, covers kept the hands smooth and soft. And in pleasing her husband when they came together, a woman would help raise more energy for the good of her people.

This Maleem accepted, but she couldn't see why it was so wrong for women to use a large knife; she'd handled it as well as any of the men she'd seen cutting meat. That thought she quickly thrust away before she examined it too carefully: it was part of their faith and not to be questioned, no matter how unreasonable it might seem.

As she and her mother worked, Maleem listened to her father crow about how they would not only reclaim the land that had once been occupied by Plains People, but would take over the Village as well. Flinging his arms wide, he shouted, "We'll have it all!"

Rhahol was tall but he'd put on too much weight, so he was no longer the fine figure who'd once enchanted Maleem. And he boasted too much. Yet, something about his smile made women follow him with their eyes whenever he walked by.

"It won't be that easy," Gzofie broke in.

"Doing the will of Machia is not meant to be easy," Rhahol said, "but we will do it. By whatever means necessary."

"I still don't see why we have to fight them," Gzofie said. "We've been welcomed by many Outlanders and Foresters — given a chance to work. Why can't we just find land and work with them for a better life? We could live with them in peace."

Gzofie was almost as tall as her husband and she carried herself proudly. Too proudly, perhaps, for she was quick to challenge Rhahol. And although her mother never challenged Fvlad, Maleem could see that she sometimes looked at him askance.

"Woman, what are you saying? There can be no peace with those who do not follow Machia." Rhahol eyed Gzofie for a moment. "You are not falling away from the faith?"

"Of course not. But I've seen nothing that says we have to make war on them."

"Fvlad says we do. Are you such a prophet that you can question his word?"

Gzofie glared at him, but she said nothing more. Maleem let out her breath. She hated it when her parents argued. She knew that Rhahol was right, that her mother was too weak in her faith, but Maleem loved Gzofie. When they left their home to follow Fvlad, they had left behind Maleem's older sister and brother. She missed them, especially her brother Pharvin, who had refused to follow Fvlad. She couldn't admit this, though; she couldn't even mention his name, for her father had disowned him, saying Pharvin was not a faithful follower of Machia. And truly Pharvin was wrong not to support Fvlad's plans. Maleem knew that she should cut her brother out of her heart, just as her father had, but so far she had been unable to do so. Ever since she could remember, he'd been the love of her young life. He'd made a pet of his baby sister, protected her against harm.

As she was growing up, her sister was kind enough, but she had had little time for Maleem. And her other brother, Ramis ... Well, the less said about Ramis the better. Not that he'd ever been unkind to her, but he'd been too caught up in learning sorcery to have time or patience for anyone. And now, with his twisted arm, he seemed crippled in mind as well. She was one of the few people who knew that he'd received his injury in a magic fight in which his opponent had died.

At nineteen, Ramis was only two years older than Maleem, but he acted as if he were one of the elders. Although he was a true supporter of Fvlad, she was suspicious of his desire for power. Would he use it for Fvlad, or for himself?

She gave a low snort. Ramis believed that Fvlad was unaware of the cause of his twisted arm, but Maleem knew better. Not that she had been the one to tell him. She had felt torn between loyalty to her brother and duty to their leader, but Fvlad had told her that he knew the truth of it, releasing her from her guilt. "Be patient with Ramis," he'd advised. "He is a good support for me despite his arrogance."

So, feeling isolated as she did now, she wanted — needed — her mother's companionship and love. It was hard to cling to Gzofie though, she was so weak in faith. Some day Maleem would have to choose; she knew this. She knew too how she would choose, but her stomach clenched at the thought of renouncing her mother, just as it clenched each time she thought of her beloved brother, Pharvin.

Looking down at the small knife clasped in her leather-covered palm, she remembered how Lofel had accused her of flaunting herself in front of Brakase. But she'd paid for those uncovered hands, paid for using a man's knife. Even though it had been for the good of her people that she had soiled herself, she'd still had to undergo the purification ritual.

For two long nights she had sat in front of Machia's altar, her face, hands and feet smeared with dirt. She had gone without food and had felt the scourge on her naked back. True, her flesh had not been torn, but the humiliation had cut deeply. The priest, Bratan, had proclaimed her guilt in a loud voice, though she'd felt that he had some sympathy for her since she had been following Fvlad's orders. Bratan, it seemed, was uneasy about many things, but he was young still, not yet thirty summers old. He'd been a good hunter, or so she had been told, before Machia had called him to be Her priest.

And when the second night of Maleem's humiliation had passed, everyone gathered again and Bratan proclaimed her clean. She'd been taken to bathe and put on clean clothes, and there had been a celebration of her purification.

Food was scarce, of course, but Gzofie had taken enough flour to make a small sweet cake layered with honey, and there was dancing afterward even though they had no musicians. One of the prisoners had a harp, but even if they could have persuaded her to play, Maleem would not have wanted it. Instead, the small children sang and their beautiful voices had been music enough.

Now, as they sat with their vesson stew, Rhahol said, "I

don't know why Fvlad continues to bother with Havkad. He has failed us at every turn."

"He has," Ramis replied, "yet we could not leave him in the hands of the Villagers. In his state, he might have said something of Fvlad."

Maleem eyed her brother. He was fairer than most Plains People and his tall, slender form would no doubt be attractive were it not for the withered arm and his dour expression.

"What is to be done with him?" Maleem asked.

Rhahol shrugged. "He'll be kept safe until Fvlad decides whether we have further use for him. It seems he still has supporters in the Village, and we have need of them yet a while."

After dinner, Maleem went to another building where all the younger children were kept. They jumped up and clapped when she walked in, a few running up to hug her. This was the best time of day for her, for she loved telling them stories as much as they enjoyed listening. "We missed you," they had sung out when she returned from Barte's. "Don't go away again."

Tonight, as was appropriate when it neared the time of the three moons, she would tell them about Machia and how Her people needed to serve Her so that She would not be defeated by Her sister Kavella and the unnamed gods. Always they sought to take what was Hers, and only the faithfulness of Her people defended Her.

Maleem stroked the hair of one of the little girls who had snuggled in close to her. What would it be like to have such a child? she wondered. She pushed aside all thoughts of Brakase. However much he sent her pulse racing, she would never wed an unbeliever. But, if he could be brought to the true faith ... Maleem sighed. She had followed this train of thought many times, but always arrived at the same inevitable fact: their children would still be mongrels.

When she'd finished her storytelling, Maleem went to perform her least favourite task, taking food to the prisoners: a half-Giant girl and a young woman with fiery hair, and skin as pale as clouds. Maleem wasn't sure where Fvlad had captured them, or why, but the fiery-haired woman had been held prisoner for three seasons. Other prisoners had become passive enough to send to the fields, some even taken as field wives. Gzofie had argued against this, but Rhahol pointed out that Fvlad had said it was permitted as long as the man's first wife agreed.

"And if she doesn't agree, what then?" Gzofie asked. "Her man will just put her aside if the new woman pleases him more."

"Then it is up to the wife to see that the new woman doesn't please him more," Rhahol replied. "And that will be for the good of Machia."

The two that remained as prisoners were treated well enough, but kept in a kind of cage. Fvlad had said that the women could be useful in rites; if not, eventually they could be made to work the fields. The fiery-haired woman muttered curses when anyone came near, invoking the names of gods Maleem had never heard of; but the other girl only glowered, a silent hatred burning in her dark eyes.

"They'll come to our way of thinking," Fvlad had said. "If not, well, there are ways to handle that too."

Rhahol had argued that these two should be broken and sent to the fields at once, for it was too much trouble to look after them. Not that he had anything to do with their care.

Maleem shivered when she thought of how her father dared question Fvlad. One part of her was proud that he was so bold, but another part felt anger that he would dare challenge their leader.

"Why does Fvlad let him argue with his decisions?" she'd asked Ramis one day.

Her brother had laughed. "By letting one person put forth questions that no doubt many are asking, Fvlad disarms those who might oppose him. He makes it look like he doesn't object to questions."

"Why should any oppose him? He is the spokesman for Machia."

Ramis had shaken his head and looked at her, smirking.

When Maleem reached the cage, she unlocked the door, shoved the pot of stew onto the floor, relocked the door and raced away. She didn't want to hear the woman's curses or receive the venomous glare of the half-Giant girl.

From the prisoners' cage, she went to evening worship. The altar was a broad stump, waist high, the top covered with a fine black cloth. After Bratan had lit candles, he poured a small measure of vesson blood onto the earth, then turned to bless those who had gathered. Maleem was glad to see that everyone was there — everyone but Ramis. When the service was over and only Bratan remained, she approached. She wanted to ask the priest about the sacrifices, for seeing the sacrificial knife had made her think back to the knife she'd handled at Barte's house.

"Our old priest did not always offer blood," she said.

"Many of the older ones do not," he said. "According to them, that was not part of the original idea of sacrifice.

Rather, it was a part of one's baser self that one gave up. But we learned that Machia demands more of us."

"Blood?"

"Blood has power."

"Does human blood have more power?"

He hesitated, then nodded. "The Great Sacrifice uses human blood, but we do not perform it except for the greatest need. And then, only a small amount of blood given willingly. We do not sacrifice life."

"But why not, if that is what Machia wants? If there is very great need, would not a life bring greater blessings from Her?"

"I do not know, Maleem, but we must be sure that a sacrifice is what Machia wants and not what *we* want to give Her out of our own fear of Her displeasure. And that sacrifice must be given willingly. We are to give that which is ours to give, not that which belongs to another."

"Surely the Holy Books tell us."

"The Holy Books were inspired by Machia, but they were still written by people, and not everyone hears Machia's voice in the same way. Besides, words can be read with different meanings." He turned back to the altar then, but she still heard the quiet words he uttered: "Just like prophecies."

She knew there was a prophecy that said the Giants' shield would fall one day, and Fvlad believed he was the one chosen to bring this about. Maleem turned away, wondering if Bratan was as true in faith as he should be. She wondered too whether she should report his words to Fvlad.

Six

PANDIL HAD JUST RETURNED TO HER OFFICE IN SECURITY
Hall when one of her apprentices came running to tell
her that Maidel, accompanied by several Foresters and an
Outlander, had ridden in with prisoners.

She rushed from her desk and met them just as Maidel
and the others were herding the prisoners through the door.
The dungeon cells would soon run short of space. Most of
her prisoners were only misguided, having been persuaded by
Havkad and his New Schoolers that rioting would be pleasing
to the unnamed gods, but she couldn't free them until they
had been tried. And there were many more convicted prisoners
than usual since the unrest had begun. Most Villagers were so
incensed that those chosen as jurors were likely to be harsher
in their judgements than she would have been.

Once the new prisoners had been locked up in the crowded
cells, Pandil returned to her office with Drase and Maidel,
and asked her senior apprentice for his report. Maidel's tale of
what had happened was quickly told. She dropped into the
chair at her desk and ran a palm over her black hair. What
more devilment was in store? She needed Maidel here, especially with Jael being away, but she also needed the training
Maidel had gone to gain from Drase and the *shagines* in Jael's
village. She weighed the two needs: much as she regretted it,

she had to send him back to complete his training.

"What about Landar?" she asked.

"We left him to the tender care of the Guild Master." Drase perched one hip on Pandil's desk.

"I could almost feel sorry for him," she said. "The Guild will punish him severely."

"I can't say that I have much sympathy," the big Outlander replied. "He knew the code and swore to it willingly. He also broke it willingly."

"But they'll mark him. He'll get no work as a guide for years." She knew Landar was in the wrong, but she believed that he, like many others, was misguided rather than malevolent.

Drase shrugged. "Then he'll have to labour, just as others who were never given his chances."

"He may yet redeem himself," Maidel said.

Pandil smiled. Already, Maidel's short sojourn in Jael's village had coloured his attitudes. "Or he may go for an outlaw," she said. She didn't like to puncture his optimism, but it was a possibility they had to consider.

"That's his choice," Drase said heavily, "just as it was his choice to betray a trust. And, if he's caught as an outlaw, he'll pay the price." He ran calloused fingers over his chin and met Pandil's eyes. "I hate it as much as you do, but unfortunately we don't have the luxury of being too forgiving. That's something else they have robbed us of."

She'd never heard so much bitterness in his voice.

"Who is behind capturing healers?" she asked.

Drase shrugged. "I expect it was Bissel. I don't think Havkad is up to such decisions even though two of his men were there — Ancel and Keelow. Unfortunately, Ancel escaped."

"I doubt you'll get anything out of Keelow," Maidel said. "Or Bissel's son either."

"No, but the boy guarding Faris may know something," Drase said.

"I'll talk to him, then," Pandil said. "You two need to head back to Jael's village to get on with your duties. I'd also like you to keep an eye on things from there."

"I should stay here," Maidel protested. When she shook her head, he rushed on, "Do you really think the New Schoolers are going to settle down now that they've freed Havkad?"

"No, but I've arranged for help from some of the Villagers."

"It's too dangerous," Maidel said.

"And likely to get more dangerous," Pandil said. "I'll have need of what you can learn from Drase and the *shagines*. It is best that you travel back with Drase."

Pandil had scarcely finished questioning the boy, and finding that he knew very little, when an apprentice came in to tell her that Councillor Bokise was there to see her.

The Master of Agriculture was one of the most adamant New School followers on Council now that Havkad was gone. Pandil had often wondered why Bokise, who was both a woman and of mixed blood, would support Havkad. But if there *was* some kind of plot by a group of Plains People, that could explain her stance, for Bokise clearly carried Plains blood. Yet, if the New Schoolers were in league with the Plains People, why would those followers who were most definitely of old Village blood support them so fervently? Follow the questions, her redbird had said — and she had. Over and over. She still had no answers.

Pandil sighed. "Show her in," she said to the apprentice.

A beautiful woman with amber-coloured hair and green eyes swooped through the door. "Why do you hold my cousin and his men prisoner?" Bokise demanded.

"He abducted Elder Master Faris," Pandil snapped back.

Bokise waved a hand as if flicking away the answer. "That had nothing to do with Govan, nothing to do with my uncle Bissel."

"He was held at Bissel's farm. Govan was guarding him, fought to keep him."

"My uncle has been away from the farm on business and Govan is easily led, his trust easily abused, as it clearly was in this case. Ancel is the one responsible, yet your men let him escape."

This was not the story Pandil had been told by the boy, but she had no intention of betraying what she had learned from him. She had even put the boy back in a cell so that no one would suspect that he had told her anything.

"How would you know what happened at your uncle's farm?" Pandil asked, "unless you've been talking with Ancel? In which case you should have turned him in. I might have been a little more willing to believe you then."

"Be careful that you do not overreach yourself, Pandil."

"And you be careful lest your sorcerer prove not to be so tame as you New Schoolers think."

Bokise took a step back. Clearly she was surprised that Pandil should know about a sorcerer. Still her little smile showed that Pandil's suggestion that the sorcerer might betray the New School did not worry her. Whatever his purpose, Bokise was in on it — and it was not for the benefit of the New School.

*

Dovella and Vrillian walked on slowly and again the *shagine* pointed out different plants. Some were known to her from her work with her father but many were new. Vrillian explained their properties, promising there would be time for more leisurely learning later. "I expect your Elder Master Faris will also want to explore the plants," he said. "We'll be coming here often."

They went to an oak tree and he told her to put her palm upon its trunk. "Close your eyes now, and feel the energy coursing through the tree."

When she laid her hands on the surface, Dovella stiffened in surprise. It was almost like touching a person. Her sight showed her the sap running through the tree, the strength of the roots reaching deep into the ground. She tried to close her healing sight and just feel. Her fingers tingled with energy.

"All life has such energy," he said. "With time you will be able to distinguish different life forms by their energy just as you now recognize them by sight."

Could that be possible? she wondered, still too astonished by what she had felt to offer comment. Would she one day handle these energies as easily as she now worked with the healing energies that were so natural to her?

In silence, they continued. Every once in a while Vrillian would stop and place his hand on a tree or perhaps gently cup a flower in his fingers. Dovella followed suit and tried to feel the differences in the energy from each plant.

When the sun was high in the sky, Vrillian said, "We

should think about food." Here and there, he stopped to dig up a root, pick some greens and take a few leaves of various herbs. Always, he bowed his head and Dovella almost felt as if he were talking to the plant. He gathered some mushrooms and picked a few berries, which he put in the pouch that hung from his shoulder. Then they went back to the glade.

Vrillian took the things he had gathered and laid them out on the ground in front of the shrine. He then lit a small fire, sprinkled some of the herbs over it and turned inward in meditation. Though she felt uneasy at being so near to someone honouring the Goddess, Dovella stood silently and watched. When Vrillian had finished his devotions, he gathered up the things he had picked for their meal and brought them back to the centre of the glade where Dovella waited. From another small pack that he had brought with them, he took out a small pot. "If you don't mind going down to the stream," he said, "I'll ask you to rinse the root and bring back some water." He handed her a water skin.

She raced down to a narrow stream that flowed swiftly over glinting pebbles of many colours. A light breeze ruffled the leaves of the trees, painting a wavering pattern of sunlight and shade on the ripples of water. Kneeling on a white rock that jutted out over the stream, Dovella leaned forward and splashed cool water on her face, then dipped the water skin down into the clear stream to fill it. Afterward, she brushed off the loose dirt from the root vegetable and then, according to custom, poured some water over it from the skin. When most of the dirt was removed, she held the root down in the stream and scrubbed it until it gleamed.

She took everything back to Vrillian, who had built a larger fire in the centre of the glade. He cut up the root and greens and put them to cook. "Now," he said, "while we are waiting, let's talk more about making pictures in your mind."

He spoke in a low voice, encouraging her to relax. Since this was something she did spontaneously when she touched someone with healing, it was easy, but to make her mind a blank page was difficult. Trying to envision something was harder still. After a short space of time, Vrillian had led her to picture a tree, to imagine herself approaching that tree and touching it, to experience again the energy she had felt earlier when she had touched a living tree.

"Making such images is important in setting shields on your mind also," he said. "Once you have opened your mind, you will find that the thoughts and emotions of others can be overwhelming, so you must learn to shut them out, in part to protect yourself, but also because it is wrong to spy on the thoughts and emotions of others. You should practise building a wall around your thoughts. When we come out here again, I will test you on that. If you are willing, of course."

Dovella didn't think she would ever be able to access the minds of others, nor did she want to, but she was equally loath to have anyone in her mind, so she determined to work hard at building her shield. "I would like to learn," she said.

By the time their meal was ready, Dovella was surprised to find that she was ravenous. It seemed somehow that the food tasted richer than that she was used to. When she said as much to Vrillian, he smiled. "In part it is because we are in the fresh air, but mostly, I think, it is because you are eating with attention."

After they had eaten, Vrillian put out their fire and restored the sod he had displaced to make the firepit, while Dovella returned to the stream to rinse the pot. When they'd tidied everything, Vrillian also put out the small fire in front of the shrine, then gathered his pouches. They turned their steps toward the village.

"Once the Elder Master is here, we'll set up a plan for exchanging knowledge. From what young Jael tells me, we *shagines* also have much to learn." Vrillian seemed to have no doubt that the Elder Master would be rescued, and his certainty reassured Dovella.

As they neared the village, Vrillian pointed out an herb with blue flowers. He stopped and made a sign with his hands before pinching off a few leaves. It was similar to the kind of sign she had been taught to make when she prepared her healing herbs. When she'd asked why, Safir had replied that it was tradition and that, though they no longer knew the reason, the healing herbs were too important to risk making changes in the way they were gathered.

Wondering if Vrillian would give the same answer, she asked shyly, "May I ask why you made that sign? It's only that we do too, but I've never known why, except that it's our tradition."

"It is, in part, to give thanks for the gift, but it is also a way to focus the mind." He placed the herbs in his pouch and turned to her. "The herbs are important, of course, but true healing comes from your link with the energy that surrounds you. You have to create a connection between yourself and that energy."

Dovella grimaced. She was uneasy with the idea of linking herself to something beyond her own skill. "Are you talking about ... magic?"

Vrillian laughed, his eyes merry. "It's just a word, Dovella.

Call it something else if that will make you more comfortable. It is a natural use of power. Call it focusing the mind, call it a gift."

Like her healing power, she thought. She didn't like to call *that* magic. And if it *was* magic, did that mean it was evil? Was that why Safir had cautioned her to keep quiet about how she healed? Despite everything she had learned in recent days, Dovella found it hard to dismiss this worry from her mind.

When they reached the village, Jael and Elder Master Faris were seated by the fire in the meeting place. Dovella raced forward to greet the old healer. Kneeling in front of him, she grasped his hand. "Did they hurt you?" she asked softly.

"They treated me well enough," he said, patting her hand, "save in the taking of me at all. Now, come and sit beside me. My tale is soon told, so I'll get it out of the way first."

A few other foresters had gathered and listened quietly as Faris recounted being taken to Bissel's farm by Landar. "I think they were planning to move me somewhere else later. They had people injured in the riot that freed Havkad, but of more importance, I think, they were expecting additional injuries in whatever wickedness they have planned and they wanted to be sure to have a healer to help. Doubtless, they were delighted to have captured Dovella as well."

"Did you get any feel for what they plan?" Tostare asked.

Faris shook his head. "I caught only a glimpse of their leader. Name of Fvlad." The old healer paused and it seemed to Dovella that there was a tremor in his voice when he went on. "The man radiated such ... rank evil, it was almost painful to be near him. Thankfully, he left shortly after I arrived. I didn't see Bissel at all."

"Likely he was in the Village," Jael said. "He was probably the one who arranged Havkad's escape."

"In any case, I was kept confined but comfortable — and then Jael and his friends came to free me." Faris smiled at Jael. "I was most grateful to see you. Now, that's my tale done," he said, facing Dovella. "And Jael tells me it was thanks to you that they discovered I had been taken. I understand you have come to continue your studies with me?"

"If you'll let me," she said, suddenly afraid that Pandil might have assumed too much in sending her here to ask for his help.

"I'd be delighted," he said with a gentle smile that seemed to say he understood her anxiety. "But now," he went on, "I'd like you to tell me about your journey to the source."

As she told of her previous journey, Dovella was aware of Jael sitting across from her. Though he had not yet spoken to her, she could feel that his grey-green eyes often lingered on her face. She was also aware that she was not the only one who had noticed this. Mandira, too, often turned toward her, but the look in the young woman's eyes spoke of a rising jealousy that would cause trouble.

Seven

EARLY THE NEXT MORNING, DOVELLA AND ELDER MASTER Faris followed Vrillian out to the forest. All was quiet except for the occasional call of a bird and the sighing of the leaves. Zalebush perfumed the air and as they walked a light breeze ruffled Vrillian's silvery hair. Blue ladyflowers swayed beside the path. Dovella stopped and lifted her face to the sun, trying to feel something of the energy Vrillian had talked about. She wasn't sure if she sensed it or not, but the warmth and breeze felt good.

As they walked along, the *shagine* stopped from time to time to point out herbs that he thought would be of interest to Dovella and Master Faris. Some had fared more poorly than others in the drought and looked limp and withered. These he touched tenderly. "We could not bring enough rain to save all." His voice was heavy with sadness.

Vrillian and Master Faris had taken a liking to each other at once and chatted easily, but always included Dovella in their discussions as an equal.

Although Dovella had known Master Faris since she was a child, this was the first time she'd had close dealing with him. She trusted him and had come to trust Vrillian, but she was not yet ready to reveal her way of healing. In any case, she had to concentrate on learning more about herbs and using her new way of seeing if she wanted Faris to vouch for her before the Healer's Guild.

She had put aside the Healer's Medallion for the time being, but she still wore the Kavella medal, though she kept it concealed under her tunic. Somehow, feeling the medal rest against her chest comforted her even as it increased her confusion, for she held no belief in Kavella.

Vrillian stopped suddenly and pointed to a yellow flower almost concealed below the large leaf of another plant. "Giants' Ease," he said. "It is rare and we don't really know what it does, but it was important to the Giants and so we preserve it."

"I met a Giant in Hill Country," Dovella said. "I had always thought they were only part of the legends of Edlena. He wasn't as huge as I would have imagined, but he was much taller than anyone else."

Vrillian's grey eyes, usually filled with calm, took on an angry cast. "The Giants truly are little more than legends now and it is a great pity. They were good to all our people when we came to Edlena. We repaid them poorly for their generosity."

"What happened?" Dovella asked.

Vrillian motioned to the small glade where they had rested before, and when they had made themselves comfortable, he began his story.

"When our people landed here, the Giants helped them settle, provided food and shelter, taught them how to use the ... gifts they received."

Magic, thought Dovella, thankful that he hadn't used the word. She *knew* that it existed, no matter what the schoolmasters said, *knew* it didn't have to be used for evil, but her former beliefs were too deeply engrained. No matter how she reasoned with herself, she just couldn't throw off the distaste.

"Each group employed this new power in its own way," Vrillian went on. "The Technols, forefathers of you Villager people, used it to strengthen their own knowledge and skill with building. The Hill Folk increased their ability to work with plants and animals. The Fisher Folk excelled in navigation, music and poetry. They went their own way early, however, so we know little of what they accomplished. The Plains People were the explorers, the map-makers and the philosophers. Although they settled in small steadings as they moved about on their explorations, they became hunters out of necessity."

Here, Vrillian paused as if he found it difficult to continue. Dovella waited quietly although she was eager for him to go on. She'd heard so much about the Plains People and yet, on consideration, not much of what she'd heard was specific — only that they worked evil with their magic. She glanced over at Elder Master Faris, who was sitting with bowed head as if he understood how difficult it was for Vrillian to speak of what his people had done. And yet, that had been long ago — and not the doing of those of his people who had stayed behind. Why should he bear the guilt of what others had done long ago just because they were of the same blood?

"They found that they could call to the minds of animals," Vrillian continued, his voice sounding weary, "so they decided to try the same on people and found that they could do that too. But they wanted more, for they did not think they had prospered from their gifts as much as the other settlers." He looked up. "Greed can so easily lead to evildoing, and with our people, it did: manipulating minds, causing pain, using secret information. Naturally, the Giants did not like how the Plains People used their new powers, and held back from teaching more."

Again he looked away, fingering the grass around him. He obviously found the story painful and Dovella was grateful that he was willing to share it with Master Faris and her.

"This made the Plains People angry," Vrillian went on at last, "and they worked to stir up resentment in the Technols and the Hill Folk. The Hill Folk stayed apart, refusing to take part in the attacks, but they didn't fight against their brother settlers, either."

"But if the Giants were so powerful, couldn't they have defeated everyone?" Dovella asked.

"At their full strength, yes, but they had been weakened by disease brought by the settlers and it took time for them to learn how to heal themselves. Also, because they are not a warlike people, they had no knowledge of fighting. It went against their teachings to kill wantonly, as doing such a thing would have damaged their *seraise*, so they put up a shield and cut themselves off instead. It was a great loss to us."

"What is *seraise*?" Dovella asked.

"Ah!" Vrillian placed his hand across his mouth for a moment then gave a shrug. "It's hard to explain. It's like ... the essence of a people, what makes them whole. What makes them one. Their living spirit, perhaps. A person also has *seraise*, of course. Integrity. Character. Essence." He smiled and shook his head "It's hard to find any other name for it than *seraise*. Without it, a person — a people — cannot thrive, but will wither inside."

Was this what was happening at home because of all

the dissension? Dovella wondered. Had Village *seraise* been damaged beyond all repair?

"But when our people had been given so much, why did they join the fight?" Dovella looked to Elder Master Faris for an answer.

"I don't know, Dovella." He too seemed to find this a difficult story to tell. "Some of our ancestors blamed the Giants for the shaking of the earth that made them move from their original settlement, but they received land enough from the Hill Folk, who had already claimed land further away. And with the enhancement of their technology, they could build quickly and well. Even after all these years, their works still stand. But ... well, in part it was because some of them resented the honour paid Kavella, preferring to worship the unnamed gods. And as for the Plains People — they turned from both Kavella and the unnamed gods to worship Machia alone."

"Machia? I've not heard this name before," Dovella said. "She must be an evil goddess for the Plains People to behave as they do."

Vrillian shook his head vigorously. "No, no. Not evil at all. We Foresters too honour Machia in her season. She takes that which makes us less than we can be and returns it to us for our growth. She also metes out judgement. I fear the Plains People will learn to their sorrow that She does not tolerate those who defile Her name."

"Judgement?"

"Yes. The Giants had a complex religion. They honoured all the Mighty Ones: Kavella, Machia and the unnamed gods. Each had a time for that honour to be shown and all had special times of celebration. Because the great moon

Lucella — which means 'face of the Goddess' — is thought to reflect the time of Kavella, She is honoured on a more regular basis. Machia is Kavella's sister, and Her time comes when the great moon is dark. At this time, the Giants would come to sacrifice before Machia. But what they sacrificed was a part of themselves that was ... not evil, exactly, but something not worthy. A resentment, a lie, a hurt they had done to someone else, any wrong not settled by the Council, anything that would damage their *seraise* or the *seraise* of their people — these ill feelings and deeds were brought to Machia and confessed. In this way, anything that would take away from the peace of the community was sacrificed to Machia. She transformed these negative energies and returned them as blessings to the people."

Dovella felt as if her heart had stopped when she realized what he was saying. Taking something that was harmful to the body and transforming it to health — this was what *she* did when she healed. Surely, her gift was not something that came from Machia!

Vrillian must not have noticed her distraction, for he had continued with his tale. "Nothing would be left to fester because the Giants settled their differences each time bright Lucella's face was hidden and, because they trusted that Machia would judge them, they were honest in bringing differences before Her. This is why the Giants were such a peaceful people, unused to war. And that was, in part, their undoing."

Vrillian was silent for a moment then heaved a great sigh. "But the Plains People turned that sacrifice into something else, perverting the honour due Her. This is what caused my own ancestors to split from the Plains People. We are of the same blood but our people disagreed and would no longer claim kinship with them, so we and others like us broke away to form new settlements in the forests. And though we have many of the same powers, we use them differently. That's why we call our gifted ones '*shagines.*' It means 'blessed power.' We strive to use our powers for good — to help and defend rather than to control and hurt. That is what separates us from the sorcerers of the Plains People."

"So it was greed for power that made the Plains People evil."

Master Faris leaned forward and touched her arm. "Not all of them, Dovella. Among all people there are those who do evil, even among our folk. Witness the evil done by New Schoolers, and the old Schoolmen before them. The difference is that we try to fight it, as I'm sure many of the Plains tribes do."

"But these people who have come among us now, it appears that they celebrate this foul use of the power." Vrillian's face became grim. "They will face the judgement of Machia, but in the meantime ... we must defend ourselves."

After returning to the steading, Dovella went with Master Faris to review her knowledge of the herbs and techniques, or rituals as Vrillian called them. Master Faris seemed comfortable in the little house he'd been given. There was a cot, a table and chair and, beneath one window, a chest for clothing and other possessions, which was covered by a green tapestry. On a shelf in one corner he'd lined up small containers of oils and dried herbs, which he asked her to identify for him. As they worked, Faris studied her. After a while, he said, "Your sight has been opened."

She nodded. "The Khanti-Lafta did that when I told her that I feared Master Plais would refuse to teach me."

"Well, she hasn't left much for me to do," Faris said, "especially as your father has trained you so well. But we need to work on strengthening your sight and making sure that you understand what you can now see. With a little practice, you'll be able to send your mind through all the body's pathways. Given your knowledge of the body and its various illnesses, the herbs and the techniques for healing, I see no reason why you shouldn't be accepted by the Guild."

"Master Plais won't like it."

Master Faris paused for a moment, looking down at his wrinkled hands, then brought them together and interlinked his fingers. "No, he won't, but it's time he got over his prejudice."

Dovella looked up at him with interest. Maybe he knew the true reason Plais had taken this stance against her. "Why does he think women can't be healers?"

Elder Master Faris threw back his head and laughed. "Bless you, child, he knows well that women can be healers, and good ones. No, it is a matter of hurt ... and guilt, though, in truth, there is no cause for that. You see, when he was a young apprentice our Guild's Master Healer was a woman, greatly gifted but not overly patient. Much like Plais himself, in fact."

The old healer glanced away and his smile faded. "In any case, Plais and another apprentice, a young woman of whom he had grown very fond, were working on a child who had been badly injured. One of the first things we learn is that healing is not always possible and, when this is the case, we must pull back, no matter how loath we are to give up, for otherwise we drain our own lives to no avail."

Dovella nodded her understanding. Once she had been in a similar situation and had been reluctant to pull away. Had Safir not been with her and disconnected the link himself, Dovella would have been drained of her life energy and died.

Perhaps Faris had heard the story, for he reached over to give her hand an encouraging pat before he continued his story. "But when Plais pulled away, the young woman helping him ... she didn't pull back. She died."

Dovella leaned forward. She'd never felt any liking for Master Plais, but the story touched her. "It must have hurt him dreadfully, I can see that. But why did that make him turn against women healers?"

"It is part of our nature that we must hold someone responsible when anything happens that we find hurtful." Faris clasped his hands together, gave a little shrug. "Plais could not blame his young friend for not following her training. He could not blame himself ... at least, not openly, though I think that in his heart he did and perhaps still does. So he laid the burden on the Master Healer, saying she had not emphasized strongly enough the need to pull back. From there he jumped to the idea that women have too little discipline to be healers, though by that he means they have too much compassion. If he ever absolved the Master Healer, he would have to blame himself, or the young woman. This he cannot do. But however much he may oppose you, Dovella, he knows well that you are a good healer."

But he'll never admit it, Dovella thought. She almost told Faris then about her way of healing, only she wasn't sure how he would feel about it. Vrillian would surely accept it, but would Faris? Or would he think it was magic and therefore evil? Just as she had once feared it might be — still feared, in some measure, despite all she had learned.

When Dovella returned to Vrillian's house, she found the yellow kitten sleeping on her bed. She was reluctant to wake it, so she sat on the floor and watched the rise and fall of its tiny belly, listened to the rhythm of its breath. Just so it would be, she reflected, to be in rhythm with all the energies of the earth if she could only learn how. If only she could let go and just be ... as the kitten did.

That evening, after Drase and Maidel had returned from delivering their prisoners to Pandil, everyone gathered around the fire and the talk centred on what had happened in the Village while Dovella had been away on her journey. She listened eagerly, for having been back in the Village such a short space of time, she'd heard little about what had occurred other than what Drase had related.

"And do we know anything more of this sorcerer?" Maidel asked. "We had been so sure it was Havkad, yet Pandil has had word that it was not."

"I always believed there was someone else behind him," Jael said. He told them then, just as Pandil had told Dovella before she left the Village, about how he had tried to pull Dovella's mother out of the coma that had resulted from the vicious attack on her. Dovella leaned forward to listen more closely.

"I looked into his eyes," Jael said, giving a shudder, "and they were not Havkad's eyes."

"When we delivered the prisoners to the Village," Drase put in, "the young boy who'd been looking after Master Faris whispered something about a sorcerer named Fvlad. He told us that there had been Plains People at Barte's farm as well but that they had gone away though he didn't know where nor why."

"Fvlad!" said Elder Master Faris. "Yes, I saw him when I was held at Bissel's farm." He turned to Jael. "Perhaps that's who was behind Avella's coma. I wonder what his purpose is."

"Well, whatever these Plains People want, you can be sure it's not for the good of the Village, nor of our people," Tostare said. "We need to find out what they are planning and stop them."

"If we can," Maidel said.

"Yes," Tostare agreed, "if we can."

"We must," Drase said. "Whatever the cost. We must stop them. Or we'll be slaves."

"Or dead," Maidel added.

Vrillian gazed up at the sky and lifted his hand. "The three moons," he said. "They are now joined in fullness. Let us put aside our worries for a time."

A wave of longing swept over Dovella. In the Village, there would be a rowdy celebration. Villagers and Outlanders would throng the streets, buying the savoury meat pies and spicy fruit pies and sharing the Edlenal bread, loaves made of braided strands and filled and decorated with small candied figures of animals and plants. There would be harps and pipes — instruments not heard often in the Village for they were not a musical people and few Villagers played with skill — and there would be dancing.

Two years ago Dovella had been encouraged to join the harpists though she had worried her playing wouldn't be good enough. She felt a jolt of sadness that she would not be playing this year.

Here, the celebration that followed was not so boisterous. First, the villagers gathered at the shrine of Kavella where Vrillian sang a song of praise and danced, his movements sure and fluid as those of a child. Afterward there was feasting, with both sweet and savoury pies, though these were different from the ones she would have eaten in the Village. Dovella was happy to find that they also served the Edlenal bread and that it was the same. Then came the musicians with pipes and harps and there was dancing, yes, but not performed with the same abandon as in the Village.

She edged closer to the harpists and listened as Jael played. She remembered how sad Calisa had sounded about him putting aside his music to study with the *shagines* and, later, to apprentice with Pandil. She could understand that sadness now, for he played with skill and passion, weaving a web of peace with his music. Was this magic also?

After a few minutes, one of the girls offered her harp. Dovella was reluctant, but the girl motioned her to come on over, grinning as Dovella shyly took the instrument. Feeling her cheeks burn, Dovella joined in the playing and found that the others nodded their approval. Jael looked over at her and smiled, his eyes warm. Vrillian came closer and listened, but though he smiled too, *his* eyes were uneasy.

Later, after they had put aside the harps, Jael came and took her hand and led her toward his parents. "You haven't met my family," he said.

"I met your mother when I first got here," she said. "At the stable."

When Jael introduced Dovella, his father took her by the

hand. "Welcome," Jolan said.

"Thank you." She felt a bit nervous, but after a moment, she said, "I saw the vase you made for Calisa and Vrillian. It is very beautiful."

"My father does beautiful work," Jael said.

"As did you with your music," Lata said.

"As he still makes beautiful music," Jolan said. "It's just music of a different kind."

Jael then introduced his brother, who appeared to be shy, but the boy smiled and murmured a welcome. Lata, however, seemed strangely cool. Not that she was rude, but her eyes were troubled.

After they had exchanged greetings, Jael took Dovella's hand again and led her into the circle of dancers. It felt right, having his hand at her waist.

"I'm glad your journey was successful and that you returned home safely," he said. He held her gaze. "I'm even more glad to have you guesting in our settle."

"I am too," she said.

Jael drew her closer. "Dovella, I've thought about you so often. I don't know if you ... have someone close."

"No," she said quickly, hardly able to speak. She moistened her lips and tried to quiet her breathing, then added, "No one."

"I'm glad. Maybe we ... can get to know each other better now that you are here. I'd like that."

"I'd like it too," she said, feeling that her feet were suddenly lighter.

He grinned and twirled her around, his eyes laughing.

When the dance ended, Dovella saw Mandira staring at them, her eyes filled with pain and anger.

*

In the camp of the Plains People, Maleem and Gzofie prepared the evening meal while Ramis talked about the Village and all it had to offer. "It has everything we need. There may even be information about the prophecy in their archives."

"They have no knowledge that is not false except maybe their technology." Maleem could not keep the disdain from her voice though she knew that Gzofie didn't approve of the way she despised the Villagers.

"Perhaps that is so," Gzofie grumbled, "but I think it is more important to get in touch with them and co-operate to find out what they know. I have always thought we could live in harmony. There's no need to conquer. Afterward, we might make peaceful contact with the Giants and gain more power that way."

"Why should we want peace with them?" Maleem asked, her voice rising. "The Giants betrayed us. The Villagers and Hill Folk betrayed us. The time for peace is past. Now we will take what we want."

"Our people betrayed themselves," Gzofie said, "wanting more, always more."

Not wanting to listen to such treacherous talk, Maleem went to the door. Across the way she saw Fvlad speaking with the Village traitor. The tall man had the colouring of the Hill Folk, but she knew that he was descended from the old Plains People. *Mongrel.* Still, his loyalty was to his Plains blood, as indeed it should be. Master Trader Rancer sat on the Village Council, but it was he who had invited her people here. Rancer had met Fvlad on one of his trading trips and told the sorcerer of the New Schoolers, how they had plunged the Village into disarray, leaving it ripe for conquest. Maleem had heard Fvlad talk of this with her father, but few others knew of Rancer's role in this; and of the mongrels, only Rancer, Bissel, and Bissel's niece knew what Fvlad had planned. The few others who knew anything about Fvlad believed that he was helping the New Schoolers gain power in the Village out of friendship, asking nothing in return except a little land. Fools!

Maleem prepared plates of sliced vesson and root vegetables and took them over to the table where Fvlad and Rancer were talking, hoping to hear more of what was planned.

They took the plates and Rancer muttered thanks, but they scarcely noticed her. Fvlad said nothing when she stayed to listen.

"I'm disappointed in the failure of Havkad," Rancer said.

Maleem bristled. It sounded as if he were chiding Fvlad, as if Havkad's failure were the sorcerer's fault rather than a weakness of the New School leader himself.

"He was a defective vessel," Fvlad said, his voice even. "You said we could depend on him."

Maleem smiled. Fvlad was laying the blame back on Rancer, where it belonged, for he was the one who'd said Havkad could be made to do their bidding.

"Havkad still has supporters in the Village." Rancer took a bite of vesson and chewed slowly, as if Fvlad's words didn't bother him.

Fvlad flicked a hand. "There are others with support. Bokise is powerful."

Rancer nodded. "But she hasn't the support Havkad has. And she's a woman. Of course, there is Councillor Granzie, Bokise has him under her thumb."

"As long as she keeps him there." Fvlad gave a little shrug. "Still, our plan would have worked except for that boy who turned Havkad's spell against him." Fvlad frowned. "I think he may be the same one who interfered when I was holding the Engineering Master in a coma."

Although Fvlad spoke calmly now, Maleem remembered what a rage he had been in when that had happened. Even she had trod with care when she'd had to serve him. He'd spent days weaving spells to try to capture the person who had defied him. Finally, he had given up, but, though he had held it in check, his black mood had not lifted.

Rancer stared at the plate then shoved it onto the table. "Our plan still might have worked except for that wretched girl who went to the source and got the water going again."

"What do you know of her?" Fvlad asked. He spoke as if it were of little matter, but Maleem knew him well enough to recognize a tone in his voice that spoke of more than passing interest.

"She's an apprentice to her mother, the Master Engineer. She's also something of a healer, I gather, probably from working with her father." He slammed his fist on the old table. "I still don't know how she managed to get the machine going again. Havkad had men at the source, but the only one who returned was ripped open by Pandil."

"She tortured him?" Fvlad gaped. "I thought ..."

Rancer gave a little snort. "Pandil holds herself above torture. She truth-read his mind though."

"She has magic?" Now Fvlad was openly intrigued. Maleem took a step closer. Could it be possible that Villagers knew aught of Plains magic?

"Nah, she just learned somehow to dip into minds. It's nothing to be concerned about."

"I wasn't concerned," Fvlad said, his voice cold. "But

you spoke of healers. Your people had two and lost both of them."

"That isn't the fault of my people." Rancer reddened and his voice grew agitated. "In the one case, we were given some kind of spell that didn't work. In fact, it backfired on my people. So maybe you need to talk to whoever made the spell."

That accusation stung, for Maleem knew it was her father who had made the spell, but she kept her peace as she knew Fvlad would be angry if she spoke.

"As to the other one, my people were outnumbered," Rancer continued.

"Then you'd best see to getting greater numbers," Fvlad said, his voice like ice. "I didn't come this far to be defeated. Now leave me."

Rancer, obviously realizing he'd overstepped himself, jumped up, bowed apologetically and hurried off.

Maleem and Fvlad watched Rancer as he strode away and Fvlad let out a little laugh. "Fool!" he said, echoing her earlier thought.

He looked up at Maleem and laughed again, his dark eyes full of malicious glee. "Those mongrels think I'm doing this for them, but they will soon find that they are only doing my bidding. When they have conquered the Village for us, I'll send for the people we left behind. Weak vessels, yes, but when they arrive, they will recognize their folly in not following me. And I will forgive them, for they are of our blood."

Maleem peered at him anxiously. Although he hid it from others, she could tell he was tired. He'd used so much energy making and maintaining the drought. He needed more, much more, and she didn't know how to help him. Like all Plains women, she could draw energy and direct it but she couldn't shape it for much except shielding. And she'd already given him as much as she could without draining her life force. There were the prisoners, of course. Perhaps it would be possible to use them. She must give that some thought.

Fvlad pushed back his stool, rose with a little grunt and glanced up at the sky. Maleem followed his gaze. The three moons were full. This was a time for celebration for others, a time for praising Kavella. But for Machia's people, it was a time of mourning.

Eight

As Pandil left Security Hall to meet Avella and Safir for Festival, she spotted another red thread and made a detour to the park where she took a seat with her back to the entrance, waiting for her redbird. Although eager to meet her friends for the festivities, she was happy to have a few minutes to relax in the last of the afternoon sunlight. She just hoped that the news she was about to hear wouldn't mean more trouble. Hearing footsteps, she sat up straighter.

"Have you learned more of the sorcerer?" she asked when the footsteps stopped.

"I think he may have had something to do with the drought. He seems to be very powerful. Apart from that, I've learned little. Information is being kept from me and I have to wonder why."

"Could they have learned that you are speaking to me?"

A low chuckle followed. "No, I think rather it is because they have something planned that they know I would not go along with — which convinces me that the New Schoolers are being used and that all the riots and destruction of Outlander farms have been, in truth, for the good of the Plains People."

So, Pandil thought, if they knew he would not agree with their goals, he must be a true New School follower; but she wouldn't try to pierce the secrecy with which he surrounded himself. Whoever the man was, his information was good. That was all that mattered.

"What of Bokise and her uncle?" she asked. "Are they shut out as well?"

A little silence, then, "I think not."

"Which supports my evidence that Govan and Bissel are not as innocent as she claims."

"And they are planning something. I don't know yet what it is, but be on your guard."

"I'm always on guard," Pandil said.

A low laugh, then silence. Well, her redbird was an odd one, but he'd brought her good intelligence over the last few moons. She was happy to take what she could get, she thought, as the scuffle of boots faded into the distance.

There was nothing more to do right then and she was looking forward to spending some time with Avella and Safir enjoying Festival, though as always she'd have to be alert for trouble. But both Villagers and Outlanders were eager to celebrate, and with the restoration of water and power, everyone was now more content. The foulheads would be foolish to start trouble this night. And yet, perhaps that was what they wanted her to think. Be on guard, her redbird had said. Well, she would.

Pandil felt a lump rise in her throat as she walked through the Village she loved so much, greeting people — some known to her, some not. But they were all her people and she'd protect them or die trying.

She found her friends waiting outside Healer's Hall, and together they made their way to a booth that sold meat pies. They breathed the rich aroma in deeply as they waited for the hot pies to be wrapped. Moving aside to make way for others to reach the stall, they bit into the flaky pastries. They laughed as the rich gravy dribbled down their chins, then found a spot where they could talk without too much noise from the revellers.

"Have you heard anything more of Dovella?" Avella asked Pandil. "We don't know what is happening or what dangers she may be facing."

"And you miss her," Pandil said with a smile.

"Well ... that too," Avella agreed and joined Pandil's laughter. Avella had become well known for worrying about her daughter when she was last away.

"And she always loved Festival so much," Safir said. "It's a shame she has to miss it."

"Well, as to that," Avella said with a sly smile, "I've no doubt she's found some compensation."

Pandil and Safir stopped in mid-bite and looked at her.

"Well, they *do* celebrate Festival in Jael's settle, don't they?"

"Well, yes, but —"

"And Jael will be there." When they continued to gaze at her with puzzled faces, Avella broke out laughing. "Well, I'm her mother, of course, so perhaps I saw things you missed. It seemed to me that her eyes roved in his direction quite often, though she was careful not to be obvious."

Well! Pandil didn't quite know what to make of this information, but after a moment she said, "Neither of them could do better than to walk with the other, but if what you say is true, working together on Dovella's studies may be more difficult for both of them."

"She's a sensible girl," Safir said. "And from what little I've heard of Jael, he's a sensible young man. They won't do anything foolish."

"No," Avella said, "they won't. And although that's for the best, I find it very sad that they can't be more carefree."

Have I made a mistake? Pandil asked herself. And yet, what alternative would have been better? She shrugged away the worry, telling herself she'd think about it later. This was a time for celebration.

Near the musicians, Avella's young apprentice, Carpace, leaned against a tree, listening with her eyes closed. She looked lonely and Pandil felt a wave of sympathy. Here was another whose life had been irrevocably changed in the struggle between the New Schoolers and the Villagers. Carpace was a sincere New Schooler who had been pitted against her family when her brother and father took part in a riot, led by New School foulheads, in which she had been badly beaten. Because Carpace had fought against them, she was as if dead to them now. Perhaps the young woman felt Pandil's gaze, for she opened her eyes and looked around. When she caught Pandil's eyes, she gave a little nod.

Councillors Granzie and Bokise passed nearby, arm in arm. Granzie was dressed in silk robes of gold and blue. They were among the most outspoken New School supporters, though Granzie, like Carpace, was one who spoke against violence. Pandil wondered if Granzie knew about the sorcerer and that Bokise's uncle was likely in league with Fvlad. And, if Granzie did know, how did he feel about it? As if he could read her thoughts, Granzie smiled and gave a little bow, but Bokise haughtily turned her head away.

Avella and Safir had moved closer to the stage where the Doll Masters were performing, and the laughter of her friends drew Pandil over. Soon she too was caught up in the antics of the dancing dolls, her worries forgotten for the moment.

*

The morning after Festival, Dovella rose early and went out to the little glade where she had worked with Vrillian the day before. She stopped to inhale the fragrance of the zalebush, then seated herself before a large tree where she reached out to feel the energy the *shagine* had talked about. Once she felt connected, Dovella settled into the exercises Vrillian had set for her. She was so caught up in her assignment that she forgot all about time and was surprised when she opened her eyes and saw her teacher standing a few feet away. She blushed, wondering how long he had been watching her.

Vrillian smiled. "You seem to be meditating very well."

"I think I can shield my mind against thoughts and emotions others might broadcast unawares, but I'm not sure I can shield myself against anyone who might try to invade my thoughts."

Vrillian smiled. "I suspect you can do a lot more than you think," he said. "It's a matter of practice and confidence. We'll work on that later. But if I'm not mistaken, Master Faris is expecting you."

Dovella glanced at the sky then stumbled to her feet. How had so much time passed? Although she was feeling a bit stiff from sitting at meditation for so long, she hurried with Vrillian back into the village, then made her way down to the one-room house where Elder Master Faris was waiting.

As she told Faris about her morning and her misgivings about delving deeper into the study of magic, the old healer said, "I know that you are uneasy about this, Dovella, but these skills are to the good. I'm trying to master them myself."

"But we've always been taught that things of magic are evil."

"Our ancestors have a lot to answer for," Faris said. "Throughout history, there have been others who, like the New Schoolers now, tried to force everyone to believe as they did, and frightened many into joining them whether they shared their beliefs or not. You must remember hearing mention of the Schoolmen in your history classes. They were in large part responsible for the Village warring with the Hill Folk, and it was people like them who joined the Plains People in their persecution of the Giants. But the Schoolmen didn't get rid of magic — they just took it for themselves, keeping secret what they did."

"But ... why?"

"To have power over others. They knew that the rituals were important in keeping up the technology and medicine of the Village, so they taught those rituals and called them 'traditional techniques.' But it's all the same. The problem is that, because the Schoolmen hid the true meaning behind them, these techniques have become empty rituals and are not as effective as they would be if we truly understood what we were doing and the reasons for doing it."

Dovella thought about the little hand movements that were part of the Engineering techniques for maintaining the machine, thought about the signs she made when gathering herbs, how she'd been taught to prepare those herbs in a precise way.

"Magic is neither good nor evil, Dovella. It just *is*. What matters is how it is used. So don't worry about what to call the things you are learning from Vrillian. Just learn them well, and be sure to use them for good." He studied her for a moment. "But I sense there is something more."

She looked away, not sure how to express her uneasiness. Last night at Festival, she had stood as far away as possible when Vrillian was performing his song at the shrine of Kavella, but she had seen Faris standing much closer. He didn't join in, exactly, but neither did he distance himself from the idolatry.

"It's ... last night, when Vrillian was singing ..."

"You are troubled that I did not stand apart." Faris's voice was quiet.

She nodded, still unable to look at him. The Elder Master took her chin gently but firmly and turned her face toward him. "I try to show respect and honour for the beliefs of others even if I do not hold those beliefs myself, for how can I be sure that the face the Mighty One shows me is the same that others see?"

"But surely the unnamed gods are the only true gods."

He was silent for a moment, his gaze resting behind her though there was nothing there.

"Tell me, Dovella, do you know your father well?"

Dovella frowned. What did her father have to do with this? She shrugged. "I think so, yes, as much as a daughter can know her father."

"Exactly: as much as a daughter *can* know her father. And does your mother know him well?"

"Of course."

"And Master Plais? And Pandil? And I? And the other healers Safir works with? And those he has tended as a healer?"

"Well, yes ... but not in the same way, of course."

Faris's eyes lit up. "*Of course!* For each person who knows Safir knows him in a different way. Yet, he is who he is. And he is more than all of what people know about him. Would this not be even more true of the Mighty One? How can anyone claim to know the whole of It and the truth of It?" His smile faded. "We are like the blind arguing about who can best describe the sunset."

It made a kind of sense, and yet it left her uneasy. "But ... does that mean it doesn't matter who we serve?"

"Oh, it matters a great deal." As he reached out to take her hand, he looked her firmly in the eyes. "Dovella, you can only truly honour the face that you are able to see, only serve the voice you can hear, but you can still understand that others might see a different face, hear a different voice and respect that. So it is that I can respect even the vision New Schoolers share of the unnamed gods and their desire to return to the ways of the Founders. But — and this is what is important — I cannot, *will not*, respect their attempt to force that vision on others."

"Are we wrong in sharing what we believe?"

"In sharing, no. But a forced worship is no true worship and I cannot believe the unnamed gods would be pleased by the praise of those who come to their altars by force. Nor would Kavella or Machia. The Mighty Ones have no need of slaves. I think the gods must weep at what we do in their names." Faris smiled wistfully and stood up. "I stood with Vrillian because of the respect I hold for him and for his beliefs. I assure you that took nothing from my loyalty to the unnamed gods."

"Thank you, Master Faris. I ... will think about all you have said."

After her talk with Faris, Dovella had taken a walk out to the glade and spent some time pondering what he had said. Returning now to Vrillian's house, she felt much better. Thinking over her talk with Faris had cleared a lot of questions in her mind. As she neared the house, she noted that a small group of young men had gathered around Jael. One of them she knew was Mandira's brother, Kriat; another one was also studying with Vrillian, though she didn't know his name. The others she didn't know but had seen with Jael before. They seemed to be arguing, while he just shook his head, making no answer. He glanced over at her, then looked quickly away. Now what was all that about?

She shrugged away the concern and walked on. Just as she reached the house, Jael's mother approached. Lata paused for just a moment as if she would speak, but then only nodded and smiled. Yet it was an uneasy smile and, again, Dovella wondered why.

Vrillian was waiting in the small closed-in porch at the back of his house that he used for study and teaching. The room contained a stack of dusky green mats and a small brazier at one side; the walls were covered with softly coloured tapestries. He placed two of the mats on the floor on opposite sides of the brazier and motioned for her to sit.

They began by reviewing what he'd taught her about shielding her mind, then he started teaching her how to protect herself against mind attacks.

"Neither the New Schoolers in the Village, nor these Plains People who are threatening us, are going to give up their drive for power, Dovella. In the days to come, you might well come under attack, just as your mother did. It would take long training for you to defend yourself as Jael defended her, but if you can learn to shield your mind, it will at least make it more difficult for those who would attack you."

Dovella shivered at the thought of ever having to fight off an attack by someone with power, but she nodded and concentrated on what Vrillian was teaching her. He seemed to be pleased with her progress, even if slightly puzzled and ... worried.

She thought about how he had reacted when she'd finally come to trust him and Faris enough to tell them about how she healed. "I take the illness or hurt into myself and transform it to healing," she had told them. "I don't know how I do it, I just ... do it."

They'd both looked at her as if stunned, and she had cried out, "Is it wrong?"

Faris had recovered first. "Oh, child, no. No! It is just ... something so wondrous, I don't know what to say. It is truly a great Gift."

"Indeed it is," Vrillian had agreed. And yet, for all that, it had seemed to Dovella that he was uneasy, as if her telling him had reminded him of something that made him afraid.

It was that same look he gave her now.

Over the next few sessions, Vrillian arranged for her to work with Jael on reaching into the mind and shielding against intrusions. She trusted Jael, but found it uncomfortable working with him, for what if he read in her mind how she felt about him? Even though he'd said he wanted to get to know her better, they'd had little opportunity to be together except when working; until they could have more time together alone, her feelings *must* be shielded.

This shielding practice was one in which Jael was truly skilled, for he was able to open a part of his mind, the part showing how to shield, without letting her see any other thoughts. Would she ever be able to do that?

As she walked through Jael's mind, Dovella was astounded at how orderly everything seemed to be. And, with her newly awakened healing channels, it seemed to her that, unless shielded, the mind was as perceptible to her as the body.

When she opened her eyes, Vrillian said, "This kind of mind walking is what you'll need to do when you attempt to heal a mind."

It was the first time he'd made any mention of her healing gift.

"But how will I know what is wrong?" she asked.

"Sometimes you won't, but you will see when everything looks twisted. Now that you've seen a healthy mind, you know what it should look like." He turned to Jael. "What was Avella's mind like when she was in the coma?"

Jael reddened. "She has a wonderful mind, but it seemed as if something was shrouded. Caught and tangled, yet the tangling was not from within." He lowered his eyes and shuddered. "I can still remember the sorcerer's eyes searching for me as I pulled her from the coma. I've never seen such malevolence. It was ... confusing, and I wasn't really sure ..."

"One can't always be sure," Vrillian said. Turning back to Dovella, he added, "But with experience and with your gifts, you'll always know what to do."

Jael was always friendly when he and Dovella worked together. His eyes seemed to say one thing, but his manner always held her at a distance. After what he'd said at Festival, she found this new formality confusing. Was it because they were working together and he needed to keep some separation, or was it because of Mandira? Yet the times Dovella saw Mandira approach him, Jael seemed to be equally as distant with her. And, of late, Mandira had stopped glaring at Dovella. It was all very puzzling.

That night when the kitten nestled against her chest, Dovella found herself drifting into the mind of the tiny creature. Seeing the tidy channels of its mind, a memory came unbidden of a deranged beast that she had encountered on her journey to Hill Country. How could anyone warp the mind of an innocent being as that poor creature's had been? She realized now it must have been the work of that Plains sorcerer. If he had done nothing else, for that alone he deserved to be destroyed.

Had Dovella ever doubted the need to learn what Vrillian could teach her, had she ever feared that knowledge, she now swept both doubt and fear aside and embraced completely the desire to master those skills. Call them gifts, call them ... magic. She would learn.

Nine

THE NEXT AFTERNOON, DOVELLA WENT ONCE AGAIN OUT into the forest on her own. She'd practised the technique of communicating with animals, but always Vrillian had been with her and she had to ask herself whether he had been helping her. She would go alone, she decided, to see if she had equal success.

Dovella found the small glade where she often worked, and made herself comfortable. The scarlet ladyflowers at the edge of the glade nodded gently in the breeze and the sun felt warm on her face. She couldn't remember when she'd last felt so content. She closed her eyes and focused on setting the shields, but had scarcely got them in place when she felt the presence of something near her. When she opened her eyes, she saw a tawny forest cat. Dovella drew in a sharp breath and tried to quell the rising panic.

She had seen these beautiful creatures at a distance before, but Vrillian had said they were not dangerous for they avoided people. This one, however, was only a few feet away and as it stalked toward her, it did not appear to be friendly.

Frantically she tried to make an image in her mind. But what would you say to such an animal? Certainly, it was nothing like the kitten that snuggled against her at night. And yet, it was not a thing of evil and she didn't want to hurt it, even supposing she could. She couldn't think how to picture: *"I am not a threat; go away."* Clearly, she was not a danger to the cat, but it was a danger to her. She sent out a silent cry of anguish, then gathered her courage to try again.

It lay almost flat on its belly now, eyeing her, and she could see a quiver in its haunches as if it were preparing to spring.

Perhaps she needed to make it see her as a danger, someone to be avoided. In her mind she built a wall between her and it and showed the wall embedded with spears. Then she tried to picture a rabbit in the bushes nearby. *"Go: there is your prey."*

The cat stopped for a moment as if startled, but then continued to come toward her, slinking low, eyes appraising. Dovella looked more closely. With the knowledge she had gained from Vrillian and her newly opened sight combined in a way she didn't yet understand, Dovella could now see waves of sticky, foul energy radiating from the cat. She was used to dealing with the tangled energies of the sick and wounded, but this was something tainted, like the sorcerous energy in the food she and Drase had been given. She didn't want to take in this energy any more than she had that. Now thoroughly frightened, Dovella pushed with her mind, deflecting the wave of energy back toward the animal. The cat jumped back with a yowl and glared at her for a moment, then steadied itself and resumed its measured movement in her direction. Encouraged by that bit of success, Dovella drew a deep breath and prepared to repel the next wave of corrupted energy that she could see gathering around the cat.

*

The sun warming his back, Jael sat cross-legged on the ground near the high pass that led from his village and focused on the shield that concealed the entrance. His task today was to reinforce that illusion and check the warning signals that would alert his people if anyone managed to bypass the shield. It was not a difficult task, but it demanded concentration and he was finding it difficult to focus. His mind was awhirl with thoughts of Dovella, worry about what the Plains People were up to and the work he yet had to do in order to become a *shagine*.

He needed to free his mind of these distractions. He drew the small coiled shell that he wore concealed in the neck of his tunic and blew on it softly, remembering the sound of gentle wind. Letting his thoughts float with the breeze he'd called up in his mind, he felt the stiffness in his shoulders dissipate and when he was sufficiently relaxed, he turned his attention once more to weaving the illusion.

He recognized the weaving that had been done by Tostare and Vrillian, though he could not say which was which, for all their work was neat and closely knit. The other work he could not place, but some of it made him shake his head in disgust. Any trained illusion-worker would have been able to break through it. Whether it was bad work by one of his fellow students or work set by the *shagines* to test him, Jael couldn't know, but he set to weaving it aright.

Finally satisfied that his work had been well done, Jael fingered the shell. Tostare had given it to him when he'd passed his first stage of training. He returned it to its resting place and glanced down at the valley where the gardens flourished. It had been hard work pulling in enough rain to keep them from dying, but Vrillian and Tostare had managed. The number of herd animals had diminished considerably however, for the farmers hadn't been able to grow enough fodder to maintain them all. He felt a stab of guilt that he'd not been here to help. His work in the Village had been worth doing, but it had left the *shagines* without the aid he could have given.

While he was away, Jael had missed this valley, missed his family and friends. Yet, he'd been happy in the Village, working with Pandil. Happy to see Dovella at Council meetings or on Village streets even if he'd seldom spoken to her. Now she was here and, much as that pleased him, it made him uneasy.

When he'd first seen her walk through the gate, he'd felt as if his chest wasn't large enough to contain the pounding of his heart. Not being able to tell her how he felt was unsettling, but he knew it wouldn't be right to do so, not for either of them. She was just starting her training with Vrillian and emotional distractions would impede her learning. As for himself, knowing for sure how she felt about him, whether she cared for him or not, would only make working with her more difficult. He could not teach her properly how to walk minds unless he was able to keep the doors to his feelings well closed — and that was hard enough even now.

Thinking of their work together brought a smile to his lips. Helping her learn was like ... strolling through a garden in spring. Her mind was ordered but not rigid, and she picked up the techniques so quickly. In turn, when she walked though his mind, it was with easy steps.

Not like working with Kriat. That thought pained him. He, Kriat and Mandira had been like brothers and sister from the time they were babies. When had Mandira begun to look at him as something other than a brother, and how had he failed to notice? He loved her still, as he always had: like a sister. But her attitude toward Dovella when she first arrived both hurt and angered him. It had been uncomfortable for everyone in the village. Mandira seemed to be less hostile of late, so perhaps she was no longer jealous, but her earlier behaviour had not only caused tensions in his own house — his mother and Mandira's mother had been friends since childhood — it had also made working with Kriat difficult. Whenever they mind walked together it felt like Kriat was stomping through his thoughts, not exactly trying to pry but making no effort not to.

And that was why Jael was still sitting here instead of heading back to the village, where he was scheduled to meet Kriat at Vrillian's house.

Jael heaved himself to his feet and headed back, greeting friends as he hastened on his way. As he passed near the pottery shed, he paused. Perhaps he'd stop in to speak with his father. Then Jael shook his head ruefully. Stopping would only be an excuse to delay the work ahead.

He wished he had time, for he'd like to ask his father's advice about easing tensions with his mother. Jael understood Lata's unhappiness. No doubt she and Mandira's mother had hoped that Mandira and Jael would someday wed. Now, Lata was caught between her dearest friend and her son; more to the point, caught between her own wishes and Jael's. Her unhappiness was affecting the entire family, even Jael's younger brother, whose weaving had lately been filled with knots. As for the village ... the *seraise* of his people was deeply wounded by the dissension.

Yes, he would dearly love to stop and talk with his father, but it would have to wait.

As Jael neared the edge of the settle, he spotted Vrillian and Kriat heading toward him briskly. Had they given up on him and decided to come to get him? He loped toward them with long easy strides, calling out, "I'm sorry I'm late."

"It's Dovella," Vrillian said. "I sense distress emanating from the forest. She may be in trouble."

Jael spun around but before he could take off, Vrillian grabbed his arm. "Trouble," he said, "but not danger. Not yet."

"Then I need to get to her," Jael said. He could scarcely speak for the tightness in his throat.

"But *she* needs the chance to prove her skills," Vrillian said. "We'll be there in time to help if she is unable to protect herself, but we must give her the chance."

It was hard for Jael to restrain himself but he knew the *shagine* was right. It would be demeaning to rush in without first giving Dovella the opportunity to use what she had learned.

They walked quickly and stopped at the edge of the glade. Jael stared. A tawny forest cat faced Dovella, snarling its defiance yet clearly stymied. Dovella had control of the animal, but it was straining to break those bonds.

The rustling of the bushes as they moved into the glade must have distracted Dovella, for her eyes flickered in their direction, but then she focused on the cat again, made some kind of motion and it jumped back, yelping in anger and pain.

That moment when Dovella seemed to waver must have disturbed Vrillian as much as it did Jael, for the *shagine* ran into the glade, Jael and Kriat, at his heels. As they came into view, the cat growled, looked from one to the other, then sprang away. Kneeling by Dovella, Vrillian asked, "What happened?"

"I thought they stayed away from people." Dovella hugged her arms tightly, but Jael could see that she was trembling.

"And so they do," Vrillian said. "I've never seen such a thing."

"It stank of mind control," Jael said, fighting to harness his anger. "The kind the rogue Plains People would use."

"But who would do such a thing?" Kriat asked.

Something in his voice made Jael whip around and stare at him. Kriat looked away.

"Who indeed?" Vrillian asked, his voice heavy. "Either the rogues have found their way through our shields or, far worse, we have someone in the village infected with the old filth."

"No!" cried Kriat.

Vrillian looked sharply at Kriat, then turned back and touched Dovella's cheek. "Yet, you held it at bay."

"If I had been stronger I could have fought it better," Dovella said. Jael could see that she was fighting tears but she kept her voice steady. "I didn't want to hurt it, but ..."

"You did better than I could have ever hoped," Vrillian said.

"Thanks to your teaching." She took Vrillian's hand. "I can see now how much you have taught me, but I've so much more to learn. I could have done better if only ..."

"You will learn," Vrillian said. "It takes time. But it troubles me deeply that there was such a need, and in our settle." He helped Dovella to her feet and they made their way back to the village.

Leaving Dovella in Calisa's care, Jael and Vrillian went into the *shagine*'s workroom. "How could Mandira have done that?" Jael burst out.

Vrillian jerked his head around. "Why are you so sure she's the one responsible?"

"I don't know. Just ... I sensed it. And who else has such anger toward Dovella?"

The *shagine* was silent for a moment. "I don't know either," he said, his voice heavy, "but where would she have learned such a thing? Certainly not from anyone here."

"No," Jael agreed. "Not from anyone here."

The two men gazed at each other and finally Jael said, "But lately, she is often out hunting. Is she perhaps meeting someone when she leaves the village?"

Vrillian stared at him blankly. "We must take good care of Dovella," he said. "Not just because she is our guest, not just because we care for her. She has all the Edlenal gifts, I believe, and that could put her in great danger."

"Why?"

"There is a prophecy. I'm not sure exactly what it says, I'm not sure anyone knows, but it's something about the many-gifted ones gathering and bringing down the Giants' shield. That has long been the goal of the Plains People and I can't believe it has changed. They would give much for one such as Dovella."

*

Maleem watched Fvlad as he prepared for the evening worship. His white hair blew in the warm breeze and he smiled down at his small granddaughter. Yet, for all the love he showed the child and her mother, Maleem felt sure he must be longing for the daughter he had left behind, the daughter who refused to follow him. Or had he been able to cut her out of his heart as Maleem had not been able to deny her brother, Pharvin?

Fvlad had taken on a great burden, leading his people here. But, Maleem thought, we followed willingly, unlike the weak ones who stayed behind. Fvlad understood the will of Machia as those who opposed him did not.

"We have a great destiny," he had told his followers when they set out. "We will take the Village for our home and from that base we will defeat the Giants to become the masters of Edlena's magic. Then we will be able to spread Machia's rule everywhere."

But to do all this, he had to use great sorcery and the weak ones did not approve. Approve! As if they had the right to judge Machia's sorcerer. But to do the work set before him, he needed power and ... something else. Maleem didn't know what it was, but she knew he believed that the fiery-haired prisoner might be part of it and that he hoped to find someone else in the Village who would further his plan.

Fvlad patted the little girl on the head and turned away to talk to Lofel, who had recently returned from Barte's farm. Maleem sighed as she thought of the days she had spent there. It had been almost like home. Again she thought of her brother Pharvin and how much she missed him. She shook her head as if to dislodge the thought. She had done right to follow Fvlad. The Plains People deserved to have the Village. They would fight — *she* would fight — for what was rightfully theirs.

Now Lofel approached smirking. "Your friend Brakase is not much good to our cause despite your flaunting yourself in front of him."

She shrugged as if she were unconcerned, but wondered

what had happened. She was glad when Rhahol joined in to complete the story. "Yes, he complained that it was the bespelled drug that was to blame for their losing the healer, but I know there was no fault in what I made. It is the guards who should be blamed and Brakase was one of them."

Maleem shrugged again. It pained her to think that Brakase was not strong in their cause. She had felt drawn to him, but if he was not true to them, if he hindered their just mission, she would kill him herself. She would kill anyone who stood in Fvlad's way.

Rhahol crossed his arms over his broad chest and smirked. "Fvlad has not said so, but he too thinks it was a flaw in my spell, and frowns on me. But he will soon smile instead, for I will bring him a greater prize than he has hoped for. Before long, we will gain entry to a Forester settle, but before that, I will bring him a new prisoner, one that will please him greatly."

Ten

SEVERAL TIMES, DOVELLA HAD SEEN MANDIRA COME IN
from the forest bearing a string of rabbits or ducks. Clearly,
the young woman was a good hunter, but, though she was
generous in sharing her catch, she seemed to prefer hunting
on her own. Of late, when the villagers met by the central
fire in the evenings, she smiled at Dovella and occasionally
engaged her in conversation about herbs. It appeared that
she had put aside her animosity; and though Dovella still
felt uneasy, she told herself that she should give Mandira a
chance to be her friend. Being a very accurate shot with her
sling, Dovella had thought several times that she might ask
Mandira if she could go hunting with her. So when the young
woman approached late one evening with a shy smile Dovella
welcomed her.

"I wish I knew more about herbs," Mandira said. "When
I'm out hunting, I often come on some that I don't recognize.
I'd like to bring some back for Vrillian and Tostare but I'm
afraid I won't harvest them properly. Would ... would you be
willing to help me?"

"Of course," Dovella agreed.

"There's a field with some kind of small gold flowers. They
seem to be quite fragile, and they close at daybreak. The leaves
look like hearts."

Dovella's interest quickened. It sounded like a variety of toutile, the plant used for making the healing oils. The Village's supply had been exhausted because of the blight on the toutile plants in the Outlands, and although the Hill Folk had very kindly replenished it, Dovella was eager to make some oil for herself. If this were a different variety of the same plant, and one that bloomed at night, it would be interesting to see what manner of healing properties it had. This would be a way of showing Faris how much she had learned from her father. It would also be a test for herself, confirming whether she could sense the healing energy of an unknown plant, as Vrillian was able to do.

"If you like, the next time I go out early, I'll come by for you," Mandira promised.

"Yes, please," Dovella said.

Grateful as she was that Mandira was trying to be friendly, Dovella was even more pleased at the opportunity to work with a new herb. Perhaps she should ask Vrillian about it, but she decided to wait. She wanted the opportunity to discover something on her own.

Early the next morning, well before sunrise, Mandira shook her awake. "I'm going out now," she whispered. "If you could show me how to harvest the herbs I told you about, it would make a wonderful surprise for Vrillian and Tostare."

Dovella swung her feet to the floor and dressed, making as little noise as possible. "Should I tell someone where I'm going?"

"It's early to awaken anyone," Mandira said. "I told my brother I was going to take you with me."

Quietly they made their way through the village and

entered the forest. The first part of their trek was familiar to Dovella from her walks with Vrillian, but soon they reached a deeper part of the woods, one unknown to her. Here, the trees grew taller and closer together and the underbrush was thicker. In the near darkness, Dovella had to go carefully to avoid getting snagged on twigs.

Then they passed through a stretch of hazy air and Dovella assumed that they must be leaving the valley, but through a different pass from the one where she had entered the settle.

There was a tinge of pink in the sky ahead, and she turned to Mandira. "Will we be too late to gather the blooms before they close?"

"I don't think so," Mandira said, "but we need to go more quickly if we are to be in time." She hastened her pace.

Dovella glanced up at the sky. If the flowers closed at daybreak it was already too late. Hearing a noise behind her, Dovella turned. A tall man stood grinning at her. A Plains man, she realized instantly. This was trouble.

She called out, but before Mandira could raise her bow, the man had grabbed Dovella and pulled her up against his chest. She struggled to get free, but felt that something held her besides his strong arms. Some ... magic?

"Help me!" she cried out.

Mandira stared at them for a moment then set off running back toward her village.

"Get help," Dovella called, struggling against the man's grip.

He laughed. "Oh, I'm sure she'll get help." He twisted her arm and then, without touching her further, stunned her in some manner. She couldn't move, but didn't lose consciousness.

She cursed at her slowness. Perhaps she could have protected herself with a shield if she'd thought of it. Dovella felt herself being tossed across the back of a horse, then the man mounted behind her.

After a short ride, they arrived at a camp set amidst the burned-out ruins of a farm. They had come upon it so suddenly that Dovella felt sure it must have been hidden in some manner, just as the entrance to Jael's village had been concealed by sorcery. It wasn't a farm Dovella had ever visited before, but it was very like other destroyed farms she'd seen: destroyed by Raiders everyone in the Village had said, but Drase had said the destruction was New Schooler work.

A tall man with white hair stood, arms crossed, watching with a frown as Dovella's captor pulled his horse to a halt.

"I thought you didn't like keeping prisoners, Rhahol," the man said.

"Only useless prisoners, Fvlad."

Dovella tensed herself warily. This must be the sorcerer they had talked about in Jael's settle — the sorcerer who had held her mother in a coma.

Dovella's captor gripped her arm. "But this one will be very useful. She's the healer girl Rancer's men let go. The one who fixed the Village machine."

Fvlad raised his eyebrows at Rhahol, then turned his dark eyes on Dovella.

How did they know what she had done, Dovella wondered, and what did Master Trader Rancer have to do with anything? He was a Village councillor. But even as she wondered, she knew the answer: clearly, Rancer had betrayed the Village. Just as clearly, Mandira had betrayed Dovella to these people.

"And what did you have to give for her?"

Fvlad's voice was soft but Rahol must have sensed some threat, for his shoulders slumped. "Only a bit of training." Then he straightened and his voice took on a hint of bravado. "Met a Forester girl out hunting who wasn't too happy. Seems she was studying with a *shagine* but he wouldn't teach her some of the things she wanted to know. She was glad to offer me this one in exchange. I haven't convinced her to lead us to her settle yet, but she does tell me what's going on."

Rhahol dismounted and pulled Dovella down to stand beside him.

"Did she tell you this one has a mind shield?" Fvlad asked.

Rhahol jerked around to gaze at Dovella. She felt a kind of tug and focused on keeping her shields tight. Rhahol shrugged. "I'm sure we can break through," he said carelessly.

Fvlad's lips curled into a twisted smile and his eyes were like those of a woodcat studying its prey. "Are you? Well, then, perhaps I'll leave it up to you to do so." A young woman had come up beside him and he nodded to her. "Maleem, put her with the others for the time being."

The young woman, who looked about Dovella's age, came forward to take hold of her arm and none too gently. When Dovella jerked it away and turned on the girl, the man they called Rhahol stepped forward and grabbed her other arm. "Best behave yourself, girl. It will go easier for you if you do."

Half pushing, half dragging her, Rhahol and Maleem took Dovella to a building at the edge of the camp, a makeshift cage that nonetheless seemed to hold the prisoners securely. It was closed in on all sides except for the front, which had metal bars. The top also looked to be made of some kind of metal.

As they shoved her into the cage, a girl who appeared to be of Giant blood hurried forward and kept Dovella from falling. "Are you hurt?"

Dovella shook her head. No, she wasn't hurt, but she felt bile rise in her throat. How could she have been so naive? She had *known* that Mandira couldn't be trusted, but she'd felt guilty about not responding to the seemingly friendly overtures. Now, here she was with important information about two traitors and no way to get the information to those who needed it.

Dovella looked around the cage. Crouched at the back was a fiery-haired young woman who gazed at Dovella without speaking. The Giant girl, who'd rushed forward to keep Dovella from stumbling, said, "I'm Vebelle." Although the girl was clearly much younger than Dovella, she was as tall. Vebelle had the same silver hair of the Giant that Dovella had met in Hill Country, but her skin was not as fair as his and her eyes were dark.

"I'm Dovella."

"I'm Narina." The fiery-haired woman had joined them so silently that Dovella hadn't noticed her movement. The young woman was unlike anyone Dovella had ever seen.

"Where do you come from?" Dovella asked. She knew it was rude to stare but she couldn't help herself.

"My people are seafarers, and I'm ..." She raised her head as if in defiance. "I'm training as a bard. I was abandoned by ... one I should never have trusted."

Dovella was too astounded to speak. Another legend, the Fisher Folk. And here was one of them.

"We must collect stories," Narina went on, "and I wanted to find what stories were told by the inland people. I was angry and foolish. I thought that if I had some stories no one else knew, it would make a difference. *Wanted* to think that. So I wandered away from the little town where I'd been stranded. By chance I came on a place where these Plains People were camped. At first they seemed friendly, but when I tried to leave, they put me in this cage. I've been in here for three seasons."

"And I have been here for two," Vebelle said.

"What magic caught you?" Dovella asked. "I thought the Giants had stronger magic than anyone else."

"I wasn't caught by magic, though I might have been. I have little training," Vebelle said. "I am only half Giant, and I was brought up by my mother, who was of Plains blood."

So that explained why she was not behind the safety of the Giants' shield.

"When Mother died, I no longer felt welcome in my village." Vebelle gave a little shrug. "Well, I never felt welcome, but as long as my mother lived, I was treated ... not kindly, but at least ignored. But then ... well, I decided to run away, see if I could find some way to contact my Giant relatives. I ran into Fvlad." She spat out the name as if it tasted foul. "He spoke kindly and assured me he would help me. Well, he helped me into this cage."

"How about you?" Narina asked.

Dovella told them how she'd been betrayed. "Is there no escape?" she asked.

"I tried once," Vebelle said, "and they set the dogs on me. I could have hurt them, I suppose, but then —"

"She stayed for my sake," Narina said. "They told her I

would pay if she escaped and she was too kind to leave me to them."

"But if we all escaped —" Dovella began.

"How?" Narina asked. "If I'd had any magic, I would have tried already."

"I have some, but it isn't just the strength of the magic that matters," Vebelle said. "It's also the kind of magic. And how it's used. I've been keeping them out of our minds, keeping them from finding out what we know. Shielding takes a lot of energy. And I haven't had the training to do much more."

Narina looked at her sharply. "I didn't know," she said. "Thank you."

I haven't enough training either, Dovella thought, wishing she'd had more time to learn from Vrillian. She had been taught to shield her mind, but was she strong enough to stand against one such as Fvlad?

Narina excused herself and retired to the back of the cage where she had a harp. She seemed to lose herself to her surroundings as she played.

"I think that's all that keeps her sane." Vebelle smiled. "Sometimes I think it's all that keeps *me* sane as well."

"It's very beautiful," Dovella said. She sat back and listened, felt the tightness in her throat disappear.

For Dovella, the next few days followed the same pattern. Twice each day the prisoners were taken out of the cage and herded to the edge of the camp to relieve themselves and wash. Then, there was a period for exercise. They could sit if they liked, but after being crowded together in the cage they were all eager for a bit of movement. At first, Dovella did exercises on her own, but then Vebelle and Narina beckoned to her.

Although they had developed a pattern of working together, they invited Dovella to join with them. The ways in which each of them had been trained for fighting differed greatly, but soon they found a combined pattern that worked for all three. If only we had weapons, Dovella thought, perhaps we'd have a chance.

"Why do they let us train?" Dovella asked later. "It keeps us strong."

"They need us to be strong enough to walk if they have to move," Narina said. "They don't want to spare a cart or horse to carry us, but neither do they want us to slow them down. Besides, they don't believe we could ever be a threat. I think it amuses them."

Whatever the reason, Dovella was glad. If she could keep fit, there was some hope of escape. Not while they were exercising though, for even if their jailers didn't think their drills were worth studying, they kept the area closely guarded. There were only a few guards, but they were accompanied by half a dozen large, rangy dogs.

After their exercise period they were taken back to the cage where they were fed, and though the food was not of the best, there was enough of it to keep them from going hungry. From the time they left the cage till the time they returned, Narina loudly cursed every Plains person who came near them, calling on gods Dovella had never heard named before. When they reached the cage, Narina let out a little laugh. "Too bad I don't have the power to make my curses real." Then she retreated to the back of the cage and played her harp. The plaintive sound swept through Dovella, filling her with a powerful urge to weep.

As there was little to occupy them otherwise, Dovella used

her time to practise the mind exercises she'd been taught by Vrillian. Vebelle and Narina watched and when Dovella was done, they asked if she could teach them.

"I'm just a student myself," she told them, "but I'll tell you what I know."

Soon all three were working on the drills Dovella had been taught. When they weren't practising, the prisoners talked of their homes and lives.

"Most of our people live on their boats," Narina said, "but we still have to come into port from time to time to get supplies."

"But ... are there villages there?" Dovella had always believed that no one lived beyond the Hill Country. Her history books had dealt only with the Village itself except for the bits that accused the Hill Folk of all manner of evil.

"Of course. That's where the traders and craftsmen live and work."

"But who are they?" Dovella asked.

"A mix. Some of Fisher blood, folk who married inlanders. Some of the old Technols, some Hill Folk."

"Can't be," Dovella said. "The Technols are the ones who built the Village. The Founders."

"You must mean the ones who left after the earthquake. Many others remained behind hoping to find another place near the coast that was more stable. Don't your archives tell what happened?"

"A lot of the material was destroyed under the old Schoolmen," Dovella said.

"Ah!" said Narina. "That would likely be the second group of Technols who left. Well, really they were expelled because of their fanaticism. Anyway, the ones who remained built a number of villages and small farm settles. Later, they were joined by others ... both Hill Folk and Fisher Folk." She let out a bitter laugh. "Fortunately, there are no Plains People there."

"And what's your magic?" Dovella asked.

Narina reddened. "I don't have any. And among the Fisher Folk, those with no magic don't count. *Numbs*, they call us. That's why I was hoping to find some new songs. I had hoped it would be a way to gain some ... recognition for my family."

"Are you sure you don't have any?" Dovella asked. "I've heard you play."

The young Fisher woman shrugged. "If I have it's never been recognized and I wouldn't know how to use it. There is a separation between those who have magic — they call themselves the Gods-touched and say that they alone have been given the gift — and those who do not. If you belong to the forgotten ones, as my people do, you are forbidden even to claim that you have magic. And if you actually *do* have magic and practise it, you are taken before the courts and accused of witchcraft."

"Perhaps you'll discover it if we keep up with the exercises Dovella taught us," Vebelle said.

"Perhaps," Narina said, but she didn't sound convinced.

"I'm surprised your people let you travel so far on your own," Vebelle said.

Narina reddened. "I was with five others," she said, "only ... we got separated." She tightened her lips and looked away.

There's more to that story, Dovella reflected, but clearly Narina wasn't ready to reveal the rest just yet. Seeing that Narina had said as much as she was going to, Dovella told them her own story.

Each day one of the prisoners was taken to Fvlad, who tried to pry information from them. "It angers him that he cannot delve into our minds," Narina said, "especially as he doesn't know why it isn't possible. He seems to think that each of us has the power to shut him out." She smiled at Vebelle who was, as usual, slumped down in one corner. "He has no idea that it's Vebelle who shields."

Dovella looked over at the young Giant girl. "And it drains her," she said.

"Perhaps what you are teaching us will help take off some of the burden," Narina said.

But would it be enough? Dovella wondered. Was she strong enough to keep Fvlad out of her mind? And if he broke her — if he learned about Village defences, if he learned about the damage to Village solidarity caused by the New Schoolers — what harm might it do her people?

Eleven

WHEN THE GUARD CAME FOR DOVELLA, SHE SET HER OWN shields as Vrillian had taught her. Knowing that Fvlad must be very strong, she was happy to have help from Vebelle, but she wanted to do as much as she could for herself.

She was taken to the least damaged of the buildings, the only one in any state of repair. The charred outer walls had been patched with new wood and the roof covered with a kind of thatch. The sorcerer sat in the sole chair, the rest of the room bare except for a small, rough-hewn table and the rug under his feet. His pale, thin hair was dishevelled and he looked haggard — the skin under his eyes puckered and dark. Yet he shimmered with power and his fatigue didn't mask the enmity in his eyes. "I hope you are comfortable." His twisted smile made Dovella shudder.

Yes, she thought, just as a forest cat might hope its prey is comfortable. "I was more comfortable where I was."

Fvlad glared at her, clearly displeased by the sharpness of her tone. "And you're more comfortable now than you will be if you don't co-operate." His dark eyes seemed to bore into her and she fought to maintain her shield. "What kind of healing powers do you have?" Dovella forced herself to shrug nonchalantly. "I know a bit about herbs."

"Why were you in the Forester village? You are clearly of Village blood."

"To learn more about herbs," she replied.

He studied her for a moment. "You will tell me the truth eventually," he said. "It will be better for you if you make it sooner rather than later. I *will* take the Village. It is the will of Machia that we turn the idolaters of the Village to her worship." He smiled again. "And you *will* help me. You think to defy me, but no one defies me for long."

Dovella would have feared him less had he ranted, as most New Schoolers did, but his calm voice sent a quiver up the nape of her neck. She wanted to look away, for his eyes were as malevolent as Jael had said, but she was determined not to show weakness. When she made no reply, Fvlad stared at her and once again she felt him trying to scan her mind. When he had no success, he smiled again, a thin, brittle slit across his face. "You still think to resist me. Well, I can be patient ... for a little while. It will make breaking apart your shields all the more pleasurable."

She didn't dare even try to *probe* his mind, for that might reveal that she knew about such power, but with the development of her sight she could see that his mind was like a bog, dark and destructive, sucking life from anything that came near, and his body was riddled with ... not an illness, no, but some kind of deranged energy that defied her understanding.

He rapped on the table and the young woman, Maleem, came in with her mother to escort Dovella back to the cage. Maleem was rough, as always, but Gzofie held Dovella's arm more gently. Dovella didn't have the gift of empathy, but she sensed that Gzofie was not comfortable with keeping prisoners, nor with how they were treated.

As they walked, Dovella decided to see if she could pry

into the younger woman's mind. She knew from Vrillian that this was considered an unclean use of the power, but they'd tried to do it to her, so why shouldn't she do the same if she could?

Clearly Maleem was angry and perhaps because of this she was careless. In any case, Dovella picked up the thought that some of the people wanted to move their camp because they were afraid that the Forester girl who had betrayed Dovella would eventually betray them as well.

Dovella swallowed hard. Although Rhahol had implied that Mandira had betrayed her, although Dovella *knew* it in herself, it was still a wrench to have further confirmation.

As they walked, Dovella reached out to one of the dogs. What if she sent a picture of ... of some small animal in the bush. Would it leave its post to look for food? If so, she might one day be able to use that diversion in order to escape.

Remembering how she had joined with the mind of Calisa's kitten, Dovella took a deep breath, sent the picture of a hare in the bushes and was pleased to see the dog she'd concentrated on turn sharply and race toward the edge of camp, ignoring the calls of the guards. But one of the Plains People must have sent a mind call of some sort, something that hurt, for the poor creature yelped and came slinking back to its duty.

She'd have to find another way, something that would not end in punishment for the animal. But what? And even if she could send a dog to Jael's village with a message, how would she "picture" such a call? Perhaps she could make an image of the path Rhahol had followed to bring her here. Her shoulders slumped. Even if she could do all this, how would the dog get the message to Jael's mind?

Once she was back inside the cage, she was relieved to see that Vebelle was not so exhausted as she had been when Narina returned. The Giant girl looked at her with a speculative gaze but said nothing.

Dovella had scarcely settled in when Gzofie came running toward the cage, her greying hair streaming out behind her. She was sobbing as she unlocked the door. "Please," she said, coming up to Dovella. "Please, help my son. I know you've no cause to do anything for us, but ... please."

"You don't owe them any help," Narina said.

Clutching the ends of the long sashes tied around her waist, Gzofie turned toward her. "No," she replied. "And I would not try force."

"They can make it go ill for the rest of us if she refuses though," Vebelle said.

"I would not," Gzofie said. "And I told no one I was coming here."

"I will come," Dovella said. True, she had no cause to help them, but she was a healer. It would be poor thanks to the unnamed gods for her gift if she used it only for those she liked.

She raced alongside Gzofie to a hut where she found a young man with a twisted arm. He held it tightly against his body. When Dovella gently moved it, she saw a long gash in his side.

"I tripped," he said, "and fell on my knife." He gazed at her, expressionless.

"I have no herbs or healing oils," she told Gzofie, "but I can clean the wound and bind it." She saw that there was a small brazier in the centre of the room on which sat a pan with water, so part of the preparations had already been made.

"I have some healing oil," Gzofie said, "but I don't know if it's the same as you use."

Dovella stared up at her. "Why don't you have a healer with you?"

Gzofie reddened. "Before we left, I was given some oil and herbs," she said, clearly not wanting to answer the question. "I have things for minor ailments, but I've little skill with a wound such as this." She went to a small chest at the side of the room and took out a vial of oil and a box filled with packets of herbs.

The young woman, Maleem, ran into the hut and stopped short when she saw Dovella. "What is she doing here?"

"She's a healer."

Maleem glared at her mother. "She's a *Villager*. How can you take help from her?"

"I'll take help from anyone if it will save Ramis."

"And how do you know she'll help? Maybe she will make it worse."

"She will not," Gzofie's voice was strained but sharp. "A healer —"

"I can't believe you would accept help from such as her." Maleem looked from one to the other, her eyes burning into them. "She's an abomination."

Even though he was grimacing with pain, Ramis looked up at Maleem with a frown. "From what I heard, you didn't think the Outlander Brakase was an abomination and he has the same blood as she does."

Without answering, Maleem stormed from the room, her shoes rapping against the wooden floor.

"I'm sorry about Maleem," Gzofie said, handing Dovella the vial and the box. "She's bedazzled by Fvlad's promises."

Ramis said nothing but glanced at his mother, then looked back at Dovella. "Why would you help me?"

"Because I'm a healer. I wouldn't withhold help even from such as you."

"What do you mean by that?" Though weak, his voice was sharp.

"People who come to burn out innocent homesteaders, who terrorize and kill anyone who doesn't follow them, who steal what is not theirs."

"We haven't burned anything!"

"No? Who burned this place then?"

"The New Schoolers of *your* people."

"But clearly for the benefit of *your* people. On the orders of *your* leader."

Ramis clamped his lips together, but he and Gzofie glanced at each other with a question in their eyes.

Taking a cloth, Dovella dipped it in the hot water and gently cleaned the wound. Ramis bit his lip but made no sound. Dare she use healing energy? Dovella asked herself. She wasn't sure if Ramis would be able to sense what she was doing and she didn't want Fvlad to know about her healing power, didn't want him to know anything of what she could do. Still, the wound was deep and if she didn't bring healing energy to it, the oil wouldn't be enough. Taking a deep breath, she poured some of the oil on her fingers and touched the edge of the wound. If he sensed anything, perhaps she could convince him that it was some power in the oils and that she didn't know what it was.

As she began to gently draw in the hurt and transform it, Ramis opened his eyes and gazed at her for a moment, then closed them again. She was sure that he had felt something.

The question was: would he tell?

When she'd finished, she bound the wound and gave Gzofie instructions on how to tend it. She hoped she wouldn't be called again.

That evening, Gzofie brought their meal and it was much improved from what the prisoners had received previously. When she brought in the pot of food, she smiled shyly at Dovella and nodded as if to assure her that all was well with Ramis.

Each time they were taken to the exercise grounds, Dovella practised communicating with the dogs. Not to get them to do anything, but just to send calming thoughts, pictures of her feeding them and scratching them under their chins. Occasionally one would come up to her and she would pat it on the head, but only for a moment. It wouldn't do for the guards to see them being too friendly.

Despite her caution, however, one of them noticed. "The dogs like her," he said. "That's not good."

"What's the harm? They still guard her.'"

"Yes, but what if she can reach them? She could bring them down on us." He shook his head. "I think it was a mistake to keep her here."

Maleem was passing when he spoke these words. She turned on him. "Are you questioning our leader's decisions?"

The man turned pale. "No. No. But if she has the mind —"

"Mind power is a Plains gift! How can you even think a *Villager* might be able to use it? That is blasphemy."

A few days later, when they were exercising, Dovella caught sight of a man she recognized as one of Havkad's followers, loyal to the New School. Ancel was his name. Did he still believe that Fvlad was working on Havkad's behalf, or was he, like Master Trader Rancer, a traitor who had been in league with Fvlad all along?

As Dovella performed her exercises, she edged closer to where the man stood talking to Rhahol, so that she could listen to them.

"Everything is arranged," Ancel was saying. "At the next Council meeting, we will go in and capture all the councillors when they are assembled. With them in hand, it won't be long before our people will be able to take over Security Hall and release all the prisoners. And once the New School is in control, you can come in with your people and take over."

Dovella felt her pulse quicken. She *had* to escape! Pandil needed to know what they had planned. Needed to know that Rancer was working with the Plains People.

*

Pandil sat in her office preparing for the trial of Bissel's son. Her attempts at convincing Govan he should co-operate had failed and though she knew she could truth-read his mind — and would if that was the only way — she was loath to do so until she had tried everything else. Delving into minds to find the truth did no harm to the person probed, but the practice came too near the immoral mind plundering employed by the old Plains People. It took great effort and skill to find the truth without digging into the deeper, private parts of the mind. The one time she had done it, Pandil had been left feeling soiled though, in truth, part of that had been due to the filth of the mind she had probed.

Earlier that morning, Drase had come in with some information received from his cousin, a Forester woman who kept close to Ancel — one of Havkad's henchmen — in order to gain information. She had confirmed the information Pandil had received from her redbird about the involvement of Bokise and her uncle Bissel. "Havkad is little more than an empty shell," Drase had told her, "but he still commands the loyalty of many New Schoolers. But Ancel is leaning toward the Plains renegades hoping, no doubt, to take Havkad's place."

Pandil looked down at the notes on her desk and shook her head. There could be no doubt about Govan's guilt, but would the New Schoolers have enough influence to sway the jurors to acquit him? She didn't think so but, as Drase had said, Havkad still had his supporters, as had been made clear in the riot that led to his escape.

She buried her face in her hands. As if she didn't have enough here to worry about, she couldn't keep her mind off Dovella's capture. She could still see the look on Jael's ashen face when he came tearing into her office to bring the news.

Gasping for breath, he had stood before her. "Dovella," he'd said, hardly able to speak. "She's been captured." He spoke the words as if they would choke him. "She went out with one of our women to gather herbs and —"

"Slow down," Pandil had told him. She'd taken him by the arm and led him into the office, poured a cup of water. "There's nothing we can do before you've told it clearly."

But there hadn't been much to tell: only that Dovella had been taken by the Plains People. "I'll find her," he'd promised. "I won't stop till I find her."

Pandil hadn't doubted his words, still didn't. Meanwhile,

she'd had to tell Avella and Safir, and Avella was still not fully recovered from the beating she had received. She'd taken the news hard, of course, but even so it was Jael's stricken look that haunted Pandil. And there was nothing she could do except go on with the challenges facing her here.

Later, Pandil looked around the crowded room, packed with New Schoolers, of course, come to see that Govan was given a fair trial. The Master of Law shifted her squat body on the bench and glared at Pandil with her piggy eyes. Master Eilert usually refused to speak to Pandil, but today she would have to, if she were to defend Govan.

As apprentice to Avella, young Carpace was also there, looking troubled. Her faith had been sorely tried, but she was still a New School believer. And yet, Pandil thought, she aspires to be Master Engineer one day, something that would be impossible for a woman under New School law. Pandil was suspicious about the true loyalties of Master Bokise given her Plains heritage, but Carpace and Master Eilert were both Villagers of old blood; and as far as Carpace was concerned, Pandil believed her to be loyal to the Village. So how could she still hold with New School teachings? It was incomprehensible.

Apart from the Master of Law who would defend Govan, the only other councillors present were Bokise, Granzie and Avella. Master Granzie, as usual, wore his robe open at the front to display the rich colours and fabric that he favoured for his tunics. Granzie was one of the more fervent New School followers, but with his distaste for violence, it would be interesting to see how he would react to the accusations against Govan.

Govan, himself, was defiant. "My father had nothing to do with my actions," he declared. As if anyone would believe that he would undertake so bold an action without Bissel's approval. "The Plains People are my people," he went on. "They were unjustly expelled from their land and it is only right that it should be returned to them."

"And is it only 'right' that you should kidnap a Village healer?"

"My people needed him. We have people injured by Villagers —"

"Because they attacked Villagers," Pandil snapped.

But he ignored her interruption and continued, "— and we have a right to have healers to tend them and others that get hurt."

"And how will others be hurt?" Pandil asked. "Are you planning other attacks on innocent Villagers?"

Govan opened his mouth, then swallowed hard and glared at her. Pandil threw a glance at Master Bokise who was frowning. Clearly she was displeased that he had made any mention of further injuries, hinting as it did of plans for more fighting.

Pandil looked toward a group of New School leaders. "You can't make me believe you didn't know this was going on."

Bake Master Hovel stood up. "I did not." He had taken young Carpace into his home when she'd broken with her family, and Pandil believed him to be a good man at heart. But would he stand against his fellow New Schoolers in this?

"I say again that violence is not part of New School teaching," Hovel said.

Lencoln, the blacksmith, stood up beside him. "Havkad preached it, I know, but I have never condoned it. Nor have most of my brothers in the New School."

"And yet you've done nothing to stop it," Pandil said.

"I thought Govan was the one on trial," Master Eilert said. "Not the New School."

"But we should be on trial." Carpace stepped forward. Her face bore patches of a greenish-blue hue, witness to the beating she had suffered at the hands of other New Schoolers, and her arm was still in a sling. It was clear that she was in pain, but she faced the New School leaders anyway. "Even if we didn't take part in the attacks, we took no action to prevent them. And someone among us must have known what was planned."

"But how could we speak against our brothers of the New School? We owe them our loyalty." Hovel looked around at the others.

"But isn't our first duty to the unnamed gods?" Carpace asked.

"Yes, but —"

Carpace gazed steadily at Hovel. "If it is true that New School teaching is against violence, then by using violence, they blaspheme against the gods."

"Sit down!" someone roared. "You should be silent!"

A fist slammed on the table and all eyes turned toward Councillor Granzie. "Let her speak," he said, his voice soft, but commanding. "If you can show her words to be false, do so. *After* she has spoken."

Pandil turned toward him, startled by his behaviour. Although he had always spoken against New School violence, she'd never seen him react so strongly to the foulheads' attempts at silencing their critics. Clearly, he was not the fop she had always thought him to be. Perhaps ... just perhaps ...

he was someone she could rely on.

There was some light muttering that under his glare became silence. He nodded toward the young engineering apprentice to continue.

"Those who twist New School teaching are enemies of the unnamed gods and must be renounced," Carpace went on, her voice gaining strength as she spoke. "Otherwise, we are ourselves guilty before the gods: blasphemers and as guilty as they are." She looked around calmly but Pandil could see how tightly her hands were clenched. "If we do not, then we lie when we say violence is not our way. Why then should others believe us, if we pervert our own religion?"

"A fair question," Granzie said.

Finally Bake Master Hovel let out a deep sigh. "We are well corrected," he said. "It is hard to give up those near us, but we must decide. If we are true followers of the unnamed gods and the teachings of the Founders, we must stand firm against those who do violence. Otherwise, as Carpace says, we stand as liars before all. And more important, we stand guilty before our gods."

There was little to be said after that. Govan had already admitted to being a party to the capture of Elder Master Faris as well as being part of the group who had led the attack to free Havkad. The jury had no choice but to find him guilty.

After judgement, the room cleared quickly — the New School adherents no doubt eager to discuss what Carpace had said, and others to celebrate the conviction. Only Councillor Granzie remained.

He quirked an eyebrow when Pandil approached him. "I surprised you."

"Yes. You have always seemed such a ... keen supporter

of the New School."

"*Rabid*, you wanted to say," he replied with a wry smile. "Well, and so I am. But of *true* Founder ways, not of Havkad's perversions. The Founders were wise people, Master Pandil. They didn't shut out women from positions of leadership. They used law to settle differences, not cudgels. Most New Schoolers know little about true Founder ways, and Havkad's sycophants didn't care to learn."

He lifted his hand to one side of his forehead then gave it a little twist, as if doffing a hat. "And if the laws, as you once pointed out, were more stringent then than they are now, well, the times were more difficult. But had the Founders been determined that we should forever follow those laws, they would not have made provision to have them changed."

Granzie rose and captured her gaze. "Yes, Master Pandil, I would that we returned to Founder wisdom. But Havkad and his lackeys know little and care less about what those ways were. You want to defeat that way of thinking. And so do I."

"And yet, you would have seen me put out of office had Havkad not shown his hand and been defeated."

Granzie smiled. "There was never any danger of that, Master Pandil. You have more support than you know, even if it is not always evident." Making a little bow, he turned and walked to the door.

Pandil could only stare. By the Goddess, how the man surprised her! Almost as much as ... but no. Granzie could not be her redbird. And yet, once the idea had taken hold, she could not shake it loose.

*

Jael was nearly exhausted for he had been working night and day. His people were counting on him, so he couldn't neglect his training. With the threat from the Plains People, everyone would need the skills of a *shagine* — his own people and the Villagers as well. He had to be ready.

Still, he couldn't give up his search for Dovella. He shook his head, remembering how Mandira had run into the village that morning, breathless, her tawny hair all atangle from the wind. Wringing her hands, she gasped out the words, telling how she and Dovella had gone to look for some special herbs, how they had been attacked by someone who'd taken Dovella prisoner. Her story hadn't seemed believable to Jael. He'd seen how Mandira had behaved toward Dovella, so why would she offer to show her where an herb field was?

"Why would she ask you rather than Vrillian?"

She jutted out her chin. "She wanted to surprise him by doing something on her own."

Jael could believe that of Dovella, but he still didn't think she would have turned to Mandira for help. He hadn't exactly said this, but she must have sensed it, because she stormed away, crying that it wasn't fair for him to blame her.

As she ran off, her brother confronted Jael. "Why do you blame Mandira?"

"I didn't say I blamed her."

"You didn't have to *say* anything," Kriat replied, "It's clear from the way you acted that you hold her responsible. Those Villagers should never have come here, and the girl is not one of us, so why should she receive training denied our own people?"

"Is that what this is about? Because Vrillian said Mandira wasn't ready for training, but worked with Dovella instead?"

Kriat smirked. "Did you think it was about you?"

Jael held his gaze and the young man looked away. His face hard, Kriat repeated, "She didn't belong here."

"So Mandira betrayed her." Jael's voice was harsh.

"No! You've no reason to think that." Kriat clenched his fists. "You'd better not accuse her of that or you'll face challenge."

"I'm not the one who brought it up."

"I'm just warning you."

As the days passed, Jael spent hours out searching for some trace of Dovella, and Kriat's criticism became more heated.

"You are wasting time looking for her, time you should be spending with Vrillian. And I'm not the only one who thinks so. Our people need you, but you don't care. You're too busy searching for a *Villager*."

"The Villagers are our friends."

"What have they ever done for us? Just look around you. Our people are divided, and all because of you."

"No," Jael said softly. "Not because of *me*."

But Mandira's brother wasn't the only one who held him to be at fault. Others came to him, pointing out that this was a critical time in his training, that he would be needed in future conflicts, that it wasn't right for him to put his people at risk. Even his mother, who'd never been fully in favour of his training with the *shagines*, chided him gently for neglecting his work.

Not Vrillian, or Tostare, of course. They worried about the time he was losing from his studies; he could see that. But neither tried to persuade him to give up his search, and others of his friends often went with him as did Drase and

Maidel. But he knew they could all feel how the village was suffering from the conflict. The *seraise* was shattered and he didn't know how to heal that.

Clearly Elder Master Faris felt the tension for he broached the possibility that he should probably return home. "I know that no one can be spared to go with me, but perhaps Drase and Maidel can take me when next they go to make their reports to Pandil."

"No," Vrillian said. His face was drawn and Jael was sure he was also spending time searching for traces of Dovella in his own way. "It shames me, shames our village that you should feel unwelcome. You are our guest, as was Dovella. It is our duty to look for her."

Perhaps, after all, Mandira felt some responsibility for the division in the settle — or thought that she should pretend that this was the case — for she approached Jael. "Please, Jael. I'm sorry about what happened with Dovella, but truly I couldn't help it. I thought if I took her to some rare herbs it would make up for not welcoming her as I should have."

But something in Jael couldn't accept Mandira's words, even though his doubt worsened the ill feelings. When it became clear that he hadn't absolved her, Mandira no longer tried to hide her anger. "You're killing yourself, and for what? She's nothing but a *Villager*. And the Plains People are *our* people. We should be joining them, not planning to fight against them."

"It seems you have joined them already," Jael said. "What did they give you for her?"

"What I was denied here — teaching." Her lips curved into a twisted smile. "I'm being taught things that matter. You have no idea what they can do. But I know, and I'm learning how to do them too." She laughed, but it was a harsh, mocking sound. "Go tell, if you like. No one will believe you. They know that you are against me and will believe that you lie because of anger."

"Not for long," Jael said. "They'll see you for what you are." He walked away, leaving Mandira sputtering in rage. She was wrong. If he accused her, Vrillian and Tostare would believe him, but if she were found guilty because of his accusation, the split in the village would only worsen and their *seraise* might never recover. No, he must let her be, let the village quarrel be; he must find Dovella.

And so, night after night, he rode through the surrounding forest looking for a trace, any trace. And found none.

Twelve

TIME IN THE CAGE PASSED SLOWLY. ALL THREE PRISONERS did as much physical exercise as space allowed to keep themselves supple enough for the real training that they practised in the exercise yard. Dovella also spent a good bit of time practising her meditation and the mind drills Vrillian had set for her. It wasn't always easy to concentrate with the others around, even when Vebelle and Narina tried to meditate with her. But even with all this, the hours crept by, so they often talked about their lives and families, things they had done, things they still wanted to do. Dovella thought that was all that gave them hope.

Today, Narina asked Vebelle about her father. "I thought the Giants never came from behind their shield, so how did he and your mother meet?"

"From what little my mother told me, my father chafed at the restriction. And he was curious." Vebelle smiled. "He was young. Anyway, he met my mother when she was hunting. They talked and I suppose they liked each other. They planned to meet again. Eventually, he asked her to marry him and she agreed as long as he promised to let her return to her people once each moon."

"I'm surprised his people agreed to it," Dovella said. "From what I've been told, the Plains People were the Giants' worst tormentors."

"I suppose his parents were indulgent and, perhaps, important enough not to be challenged. In any case, that's what happened. When my mother returned to her village for a visit some moons later and told her parents she was with child, they took her away. The entire settlement moved. Mother never saw my father again."

"He didn't come after you?" Dovella found it hard to believe that a Giant would give up his child so easily.

"Mother had not told him about me. She wanted to tell her mother first. Some blessing, or something like that, from one's mother was important."

"But why would they move away?" Narina asked. "Wouldn't you have served as a bridge between the Giants and your mother's people?"

"I don't think they were interested in a bridge. I believe they thought I might have some special power they could use. I was a 'gift' to their leader, a man not unlike Fvlad, only not so powerful. But, as it turned out, I had little power. Or, if I did, no one knew how to train me. Anyway, I was a great disappointment." Vebelle looked around. "So, you see, I don't know who my father was. And, unless I get away from Fvlad, I never will."

"Nor will I ever get back to my people," Narina said.

"You *will*," Dovella insisted. "Somehow, we will get away."

"Even if one of us *could* escape," Vebelle said, "where would we go for help?"

"Dovella knows people who live nearby," Narina said. "She'd have the best chance of getting help."

Vebelle said, "I could help hide you, Dovella. I could hide all of us, but I wouldn't be able to help us escape without weapons."

"A diversion," Dovella suggested. "While we are training, you two can begin a quarrel. If it looks like a real fight, they'll try to break it up. Vebelle can then shield me while I slip away."

It would give her a good chance, but much as Dovella wanted to escape and deliver her information about Rancer to Pandil, she knew the others had to be ready for the consequences of helping her. "You'll be punished when they discover that I've escaped."

"As long as you get away, I'm willing," Vebelle said.

"And if you're caught — what then?" Narina asked. "I think it's a good idea, mind, but we need to plan for all possibilities."

"I'll say I felt sick. Went to look for herbs." Not that anyone was likely to believe her, but she had seen collitflower growing and if she grabbed a few flowers ... well, at least it gave a story that might protect the others. "I'll do it today."

As Dovella had made friends with the dogs, it wasn't that difficult to slip away. Knowing the herbs would be useful if she were caught, she'd taken the few moments needed to strip a few blossoms and leaves from some collitflower plants before she raced off. She preferred collitflower dried and made into tea, but the leaves would help relax her when she finally reached a place where she could sit and try to reach Jael's mind.

She relished the touch of sunshine on her cheeks as she raced through the forest. How different it felt from the unfiltered sun that beat down on the cage and exercise yard. Her boots beat out a rhythm on the forest floor as she jogged through the tangled undergrowth. There was no trail as such, but there'd been enough people out hunting in the forest that she was able to find the occasional trampled path. Above her a bird sang as if it were as happy about her escape as she was.

When it looked as if she'd succeeded, Dovella let out a sigh of relief, but just as she paused to catch her breath, Ramis appeared on the path in front of her. She glared at him, daring him to mishandle her, but he only shook his head. "I won't hurt you and I won't tell, but I can't let you go."

He nodded toward the handful of collitflower petals and leaves clutched in her hand. "I'll tell them I asked you to come show me some herbs," he said. "What are those good for?"

"They are relaxing herbs."

Ramis smiled. "And who would need to relax more than I do after my injury?" He held out his hand for the herbs.

Dovella hesitated. She might be able to get away from him. Although he carried a knife, having a withered arm, surely he wouldn't be able to fight very well. But the knife hidden in her boot was no match for his weapon; besides, it would take too long to reach it. Worse still, she knew from others that he was a sorcerer and she didn't want to give him an excuse to use his dark magic on her. She smiled wryly at that thought. Here she was dreading a sorcerous attack when less than a moon pass since, she had scoffed at Master Pandil for believing such a thing possible.

"I'm sorry," Ramis said, "but I have to take you back."

Dovella bit her lips together, determined not to cry out her frustration, and handed him the herbs she had gathered. As they returned to camp, he collected several more handfuls of the flowers and leaves and put them in a pouch.

When they rejoined the others, the guard named Lofel

came running up. "You caught her then?"

Ramis looked surprised. "Caught? I asked her to go with me to gather some herbs." He patted his pouch. "Didn't the others tell you?"

"They didn't give us a chance," Vebelle said, sounding outraged. Dovella could see the disappointment on her face. Clearly, she had believed that Dovella would be successful.

Lofel looked from Dovella to Ramis. She could tell that the big guard didn't believe the story, but with Ramis telling it, he had no excuse to punish anyone.

She followed Ramis to the part of the house allotted to his family and watched as he spread out the herbs. The room was cramped, but tidy. In each corner personal belongings were stacked beside a pallet and one wall had a tapestry in shades of green, showing an altar. Other than the table and two rough benches, the room was bare.

"What do I do?" Ramis asked.

"You really want to know?"

"That's why I took you into the forest, isn't it? If you want the story to be accepted, you must show me what to do."

Dovella gazed at him for a moment. He had seemed to be a devout follower of Fvlad. Had her willingness to heal him caused him to help her? Or had what she said about the burning of the farms made him question his leader?

She went over to the table and began to sort the leaves from the petals. "You'll need something to spread them on," she said. "Then put them in the sun and wait until they are dry."

He nodded. "And then you'll show me what to do with them."

She continued sorting, not wanting to make a promise she

would surely break if she had the chance. Why it bothered her to think of breaking a promise to one of her captors she didn't know; she knew only that she'd rather not do so.

"Why are you helping me?" she asked.

"Because I can't do anything more. I've thought about what you said and I see that we have been misled. Have let ourselves be misled. Well, to be honest I've suspected it for a while, but didn't want to admit it. I'd let all of you go if I could, but then the punishment would come my way. Not personally — I could protect myself." He glanced down at his withered arm. "I am as good a sorcerer as Fvlad. But my family ... I fear I could not protect them. And that's the only reason I am staying."

He joined in the sorting, and she was surprised at how well he worked with only one arm. "When we began this trip, I was as fervent a believer as Maleem. But ..." His gaze caught hers and he faltered for a moment. "But since we've arrived, I've begun to wonder. You've made me look more closely at what is happening and I see that most of what Fvlad told us was false. He said the Villagers ... that you were all decadent. Idolaters. He told nothing of his own duplicity in dealing with the New Schoolers. Nothing of putting people in cages."

"Nothing of burning farms and killing the farmers?"

"We were told it was the New Schoolers themselves who were responsible."

"And who controls the New Schoolers?"

Ramis stopped his work and walked over to peer out the door, shaking his head as if that would dislodge the sight. He ran fingers through his hair. "Fvlad said nothing about these burned-out homesteads. And, until we had arrived, nothing of the manufactured drought. I once believed that he spoke for Machia, but now I see he speaks only for himself, for his own twisted dream. But Maleem doesn't see that. Can't see it." It was almost as if he talked to himself rather than her. Then he sighed heavily and rejoined Dovella at the table. "And so I've decided to stay against the day when her eyes are opened and I can help her."

"What does Fvlad plan to do with us?"

"That I don't know. I think at first it was just a matter of pride, that he had prisoners. But with you ... " Ramis studied her. He wasn't trying to pry into her mind, but it seemed as if he were trying to see something. He shook his head again. "Fvlad talks about a prophecy and I think you are important to it."

"What kind of prophecy?"

Ramis let out a soft snort. "Fvlad has been very careful not to let anyone know exactly what it says, but it seems to have to do with those who have more than one gift and how they will bring down the shield of the Giants. Fvlad knows that you are a healer and that you must have some of the gift of the Technols if you work with the machine. Now you've shown that you can shield your mind. With so many gifts ... well, that's as much as I know."

Perhaps she'd made a mistake in shielding her mind so well, but, had she not done so, Fvlad might well have gleaned some knowledge from her. From the traitors, he would already have gained information about the Village, but she didn't want him to learn from her about Jael's settle or about her studies with Vrillian. She didn't want him to learn anything.

When they finished sorting the herbs and setting them to dry, Ramis thanked her and took her back to the cage. He looked apologetic when he opened the door, but he locked her in all the same.

Narina and Vebelle looked at her with bleak faces.

"I almost made it," she said. "I don't intend to give up. The next chance I get, I'll try again."

*

Maleem hesitated as she tied the white sash around her waist. Would she ever wear several, as her mother did? She slammed the lid on the chest that held her things. No, she didn't want to think about children, for that made her think of Brakase and she didn't want to think about the handsome Outlander, didn't want to think of how his dark eyes had warmed her. Not until he and his people had proved themselves as true friends.

She glanced again at the chest, then hurried from the room. She'd be late taking food to the prisoners. Not that she cared if they had to wait, but Fvlad insisted that they had to be treated well. Especially that Villager girl, though Maleem couldn't see why *she* was so special.

Maleem shoved the dish of stew across the floor of the cage and watched as part of it slopped over on to the floor. She was sorry about the waste but she resented having to feed them. Her people had little enough food for themselves. The prisoners were nothing but a drain on food supplies. But they *could* be useful — they could provide the energy Fvlad needed for his work. She didn't understand why he hadn't drained it already. Oh, she knew he thought they might be of help, either as hostages or as sources of information. Well, they'd provided no information and that was another thing she couldn't understand. They weren't supposed to be able to resist a Plains mind probe. Only Plains People had that power. So how were they doing it? Well, if Fvlad wouldn't tap their power, she'd find a way to do it for him.

She stomped back into her family's small hut where she found her mother tending Ramis' wound. And that was another thing. That girl should never have been allowed to touch him. Maleem walked over and examined the wound.

"See," she said. "It was little more than a scratch. I don't know why you had to humiliate us by bringing that *Village* girl in here."

"It was a lot more than a scratch," Gzofie said.

"Then how can it have healed so quickly?" She smirked. "I guess she has some kind of magical healing power."

Gzofie hesitated and Ramis broke in. "I'm sure it was just that she knew which herbs to use.

"Yes," Gzofie agreed. "If you know the proper herbs, it works better." She turned back to wrap the wound.

Maleem snorted. "You must know as much about herbs as she does. You could have done it."

"Maybe so," Gzofie agreed. "But I was too afraid."

"And it still has a ways to go before it's completely healed," Ramis said. He pushed himself to his feet and grimaced.

"So you'll be able to get out of work a while longer." Ramis wasn't of much more use than Havkad. True, he was a good hunter, or had been until he'd injured himself. And he had a strong gift for sorcery — stronger than that of their father. But he'd done nothing with it, except fight that stupid battle that had left him with a withered arm.

"No. I'm just getting ready to leave. They are sending me to look after Havkad." Ramis walked over and picked up a satchel.

Maleem snorted. "What do they think he's going to do: go off and win a great battle? And you're going to stop him?"

Ramis stopped at the door and glared at her. "True, he's too weak to be of any danger, but he's half demented, so somebody has to make sure he doesn't wander away."

"Maybe it would be best if he did."

"Why don't you favour Fvlad with your advice?" Ramis asked. "He's coming this way." He went out to meet the sorcerer.

Maleem stood at the door and listened as Fvlad gave Ramis his instructions. "Just make sure Havkad doesn't wander off and that no one frees him. He's of no further use to us, but he still has followers in the Village. If he were taken back there, they might blame sorcery for his condition and we could lose some of those who have been helping us for his sake." Fvlad clapped Ramis on the shoulder. "You are strong enough to hold them off. I'm counting on you."

After Ramis and the sorcerer strode away, Maleem slumped down into a chair. Ramis still had Fvlad's trust and he didn't deserve it. He and Gzofie were not true followers; if they were they wouldn't try to cover up for Dovella. Ramis was healed, or almost anyway, and that girl had done it; but for some reason, they wanted Maleem to think otherwise.

"Why are you protecting her?" she asked her mother. "Don't you know that if she has some kind of healing gift she'd be useful to Fvlad?"

"Fvlad has been told she's a healer," Gzofie said. "But so far, except for Ramis, there's been no need for her help. In any case, you can't force her to use her gift."

"I can make her wish she'd used it."

Gzofie whirled around and stared at her. "Why are you so

angry with that girl?" she asked. "She's done you no harm."

"She refuses to help Fvlad," Maleem snarled. "All the prisoners refuse. Information, power — they deny him everything. They are an insult to him. To Machia. And Dovella *was* trying to get away, I don't care what Ramis said."

Maleem rose and stormed from the room. It was time to get the girl and take her to Fvlad. She wondered if she should tell him about Ramis's healing. Perhaps not. Perhaps she'd deal with the girl on her own.

She called Lofel to go with her to the prisoners' cage. Maybe she should suggest that Gzofie not be allowed to help look after them any longer. Her mother was far too sympathetic. You couldn't let yourself care about them, Maleem thought; otherwise it wasn't possible to do your duty.

Fvlad was slumped back in his chair when she arrived with Dovella, but he straightened immediately. Maleem smiled. Of course, he wouldn't let that girl see how fatigued he was. But Maleem knew. She was glad that Lofel was waiting outside. It wasn't good for Fvlad's people to see the sorcerer as being weak. Others might get the same kind of idea Ramis had. No matter how fair he spoke, Ramis was not to be trusted. Despite Fvlad's show of trust, he must understand this; maybe that was why he let no one but Maleem see how exhausted he was. She felt proud, knowing that Fvlad trusted her above all others. That must be why he had brought her back from Barte's farm: he needed her.

As there was only one chair in the room, Dovella had to stand. Fvlad stared at her but didn't speak. Maleem could see beads of sweat form on his brow and knew he was straining to break through the girl's shields. It wasn't fair! The girl shouldn't be able to resist. Even if Fvlad was tired from all the sorcery he'd had to perform, he ought to have been able to break through. Dovella must have some help, Maleem thought. But who? Surely Ramis wouldn't help her. Or would he? They were friendlier than Maleem liked.

After a few moments, Fvlad flung out his hand, signalling that they should take Dovella away. Maleem looked at her sharply, noticed a smile the girl was trying to hide. She'd give her something to smile about. She took Dovella's arm and roughly yanked her toward the door. Dovella snatched her arm away and glared at Maleem, then began to walk on her own. When Lofel joined them, Maleem grabbed Dovella's arm again.

When they reached the cage, she pushed Dovella in, hoping she would stumble, but the others were there to catch her fall. Maleem suddenly turned away, squeezed her eyes tight in a momentary pang of shame at her own behaviour. She didn't want to be rough with the girl; it gave her no pleasure. But it wasn't right that Fvlad should be so weary.

When Fvlad called a meeting around the fire that evening, his face was ashen and the hand that lay in his lap trembled. Maleem wanted to scream at them, curse them as the Fisher girl cursed everyone who passed her. We've given up so much to find a new home, she thought, but without him to lead us, we have no hope. Couldn't the others see how much he needed them to give him more energy?

But, of course, they could not. He was careful to hide it from them. Maleem had done all she could to help, had drawn as much from the earth as she could and directed it toward him. He must have known what she'd done, but he'd said nothing. Still, she could see from the way he treated her that he was grateful.

Fvlad scrutinized the others. "I should be able to break these prisoners." His voice was soft, but Maleem heard the fury.

"But I need power for that," he said. "I've worked for all of you. Making and keeping this drought takes power, more and more power. Some of you help and gladly, but others do not. You must share in the burden if you hope to reap the rewards. You *must* give me the power, all of you. The Village will soon be ours for the taking, but you must deserve it." He looked around, and when he spoke next, his voice sliced through the air. "Or perhaps I will decide to share it with only those who have paid their part of the price."

Maleem noticed many were nodding but Gzofie stood, arms folded across her chest. Others too seemed unmoved.

"There are too many of you who are not dedicated," Fvlad went on. "Well, it is time to make choices. There is no room here for anyone who is not truly with us, anyone who is not willing to share the burden."

Maleem saw her father nod vigorously and felt herself grow cold. She had seen Rhahol with one of the field women. Would he put her mother aside and take a field wife? And what would become of Gzofie then?

She felt a surge of anger toward Dovella. Gzofie had been more supportive of Fvlad before *she* arrived. Even Ramis had changed. Maleem knew he coveted power, resented Fvlad for being stronger. No doubt he rejoiced to see Fvlad so weak. Or would have, had he not been sent to guard that wretched Havkad who'd been so useless to them. She didn't see why Fvlad didn't take *his* energy. Havkad was of no use for anything else.

That Village healer must surely know something that would help them, but she kept her secrets. Maleem clenched her fists in frustration. Fvlad needed to find out what power Dovella had and where she got it. But to do that, *he* needed more power. Maleem had to help him.

Plains women could draw and channel power, even if they couldn't shape it. Perhaps she could draw it from Dovella.

*

Jael studied the sky. Soon it would be too dark to do much searching, but he hated to give up. He glanced over at Drase and Maidel. They wouldn't mind continuing the search, but the others from his village — especially Kriat— were sure to insist on returning home; they'd complained about even coming on the search. But just as he was about to turn his horse, he noticed a thin thread of smoke rising above the trees. "Look," he said, pointing.

"There used to be a small farm beyond that stand of trees," Drase said. "Burned out like the others in this area. Let's see who's there."

Jael, Maidel and one other young man from his village veered left; Drase took Kriat and staked out the other side so they could cut off anyone who might try to escape. Impatiently, Jael waited for Drase's whistle. When it came, he urged his horse forward.

There was only one guard outside the hut and Drase had him tied up before Jael had bounded from his horse. Inside, they found Havkad and a young man with a withered arm.

Jael looked at Havkad and shook his head in wonder. Havkad glared back at Jael, but it was clear from his slumped shoulders and drawn features that he could do nothing more. He heaved his squat body up from the chair and pointed at Jael, then dropped his arm and fell back down into his seat.

The young man sitting with him looked from Jael to Drase, then surveyed the others who had gathered in the hut. "Don't come near me," he said. "Let me go and I'll tell you a thing."

Kriat snorted his contempt, but Jael held up a hand. He sensed that the guard had some power, and wanted to see what he had to say. "Who are you?"

"My name is Ramis. I'm part of a group that —"

"I know what you are here for," Jael said. "Can you tell us where Dovella is?"

"I can, but I won't."

"Then you'll come."

Ramis shook his head. "I can help her or harm her. But even if I won't tell you where she is, I can tell you other things." He nodded at Havkad. "He was a dupe. All of them were. After Fvlad helps them overthrow the Village leaders, he plans to take control for the Plains People." He gave a little laugh. "And your own people helped him. It was Master Trader Rancer who brought Fvlad here. Bissel and Master Bokise supported him. They are all in on it."

"All the New Schoolers?" Jael hadn't believed in what they were trying to do, but he'd thought them sincere.

"No, just those. The others who knew about him thought that Fvlad was just helping them. Stupid not to ask why he was so willing to help, but I suppose they didn't want to know. They wanted only what he could do for them." Again Ramis let his eyes wander over the group of men facing him. "And I'll tell you another thing, for my freedom."

"If it's worth anything," Jael said.

"Your word?"

"My word."

"There's a traitor in your steading, as well. Dovella was brought to us by a young woman, and —"

"No!" screamed Mandira's brother. "No!"

Ramis jerked his head around and looked at Kriat. It was almost as if he felt the grief in Kriat's cry. "Yes," he said softly. "So far she hasn't betrayed the way into your settle, but someone is trying to persuade her even to that."

Jael had known that Mandira was a traitor, she had stated so to him boldly enough herself, but it still gave him a stab of pain to see how it affected Kriat.

"You aren't going to let him go!" Kriat took a step forward, but Drase grabbed his arm.

"It was a bargain," Jael said. "As little as we might like the news, it was important." He nodded toward Ramis. "You may go."

By now Havkad had been constrained, and Jael consulted with Drase and Maidel. The news about the treachery of Trader Rancer, Master Bokise and Bissel needed to be taken to Pandil along with Havkad. "But I want to see if I can follow Ramis," Jael said. "I promised to let him go, but I made no promise beyond that."

Drase nodded. "I doubt that Havkad can gather any power for another attack on Pandil, but if so, I can handle him. You do what you must."

Jael looked at Mandira's brother. "You'll want to go to your home —"

"And tell of my sister's shame." Kriat's voice broke. "I'm sorry. I can't do that. And I won't go with you. But I'll go with Drase and Maidel to the Village. Perhaps I can be of use there."

Jael reined in his horse and closed his eyes. He had lost Ramis's trail. He'd sensed that the young man had some power, but it hadn't occurred to him that Ramis would be able to shield himself so securely. Cursing softly at his failure, he turned his horse toward home. Well, there was another way. As much as he hated to humiliate Mandira before their people, he had to do it. She could lead him to Dovella, and she must be forced to do so.

Mandira, however, still refused to admit her guilt publicly, even after Jael related to those assembled what Ramis had said. "Your brother heard him."

She smirked and looked around. "So where is my brother? Why doesn't he tell what he heard?"

"Because he has the grace to be ashamed."

She blanched at those words and there rose a muttering among those who listened, but she jutted out her chin. "Or you sent him off somewhere so he couldn't say you lie."

Jael took in the faces all around. Though they frowned, no one would meet his eyes. They knew he was telling the truth, but they didn't *want* that knowledge and they blamed him for forcing them to face it. Maybe they even blamed him for what happened.

"Everyone knows I am not lying."

"The Villager girl is not our problem," someone said.

"She was a guest!" he shouted.

"Mandira is one of us." It was said softly, but with force and people began to drop away. Even his mother, though her eyes were sad, turned away.

Jael looked around at the few who were left, Mandira and her family among them. "I'll find her," he said.

"Your duty is here," Mandira screamed. "She's done enough damage to this village. Now you desert your duty."

"At least I haven't deserted honour."

Mandira jerked her head back and glared, but her mouth trembled.

Jael remounted his horse and rode away. "I won't be back until I find her."

"Go in peace," Vrillian said, his voice heavy. "You must find her. For all our sakes."

As Jael rode through the still night, he thought of what his life might have been like if the Plains People had remained far away. He and Dovella would not have had so much to separate them. But, easy as it was to blame the Plains People and the New Schoolers for all the trouble, he knew that his own people were to be blamed as well, for valuing one of their own above what was right.

Yes, he knew that his people, *all* people, needed the skills he was learning from the *shagines,* and he knew he was letting them down by not giving his training his full effort. These thoughts nagged at him constantly. But he also knew that they needed Dovella.

Anyone could make war and destroy, but few could heal and even fewer could heal as Dovella did. She was important in other ways as well. Remembering what Vrillian had said about Dovella, Jael knew that his teacher believed her to be important in ways that as yet couldn't be fathomed.

Thirteen

ALTHOUGH IT WAS A PLEASANTLY WARM DAY, THE SUN beating down on the roof of the cage made for sweltering conditions, and the prisoners received none of the light breeze that rippled through the branches of the trees at the edge of the camp. They kept as clean as they could, but even so the cage stank; they all stank. Her sweat-sodden tunic sticking to her back, Dovella paced the cage, chewing on a fingernail. If Plais hadn't been so obstinate in refusing her the opportunity to go through the Rites, she might have stayed in the Village and studied; then none of this would have happened. She knew that between what her father had taught her and the opening of her senses by the Khanti-Lafta, the Guild would have been satisfied that she knew what she was doing. True, she needed more training in using her new sight, but she could have learned that there. Plais was the one who had stood in her way and all because of something that happened years before, something that had nothing to do with her. She beat her fists against the bars, even knowing that her anger was fruitless — and unfair.

Whatever else he might have done, Plais wasn't responsible for the rest of the danger faced by her and her people. He wasn't responsible for the New School lust for power or for the determination of the Plains People to take over the

Village, nor could he be blamed for the treachery of Master Trader Rancer and Master Bokise. And had Dovella not been brought here, perhaps no one would have known of this treason. And they still wouldn't know unless she could escape. She felt her eyes well up as she pictured all those who would die. All those who had died.

She slumped down in one corner and rested her head against her knees. Caught in this cage as she was, the knowledge was of no use. She was so tired of all this worry, she just wanted to rest; but she couldn't rest, not when her people would soon be attacked — killed or enslaved by Fvlad and his followers.

Still, what more could she do? She'd failed to get away yesterday. Dovella was grateful that Ramis had not told the truth about her attempt to escape, glad the others hadn't suffered because of her; but she couldn't let it go at that. She had to try again. Knowing what they were planning for the Village, she couldn't give up. But how would she ever get another chance?

In one corner, Narina strummed softly on her harp. Again, Dovella wondered if there was some magic in the Fisher girl's playing. Narina had said she had no magic and perhaps she didn't, but all three of them became more relaxed when she played. Perhaps, music itself was a kind of magic.

"I'm surprised they let you keep your harp," she had remarked the first time Narina played.

"They give it no importance," Narina had replied. "And maybe they hoped it might keep me more docile," she added with a mischievous grin.

Remembering that, Dovella smiled. It was hard to think of Narina as being docile, the way she cursed the guards each time she saw them; as she did now, when they came to take the prisoners to their exercise.

While they trained, Dovella "listened" as Vebelle had taught her. It hadn't been easy to concentrate on her fighting skills and listen at the same time, but with practice she'd reached a point where she could fight well enough and still pick up much of what the guards were saying, even at some distance. Perhaps she was in their minds. Again she heard them talk about a prophecy, but clearly they didn't know what it meant; they knew only that Fvlad was angry about something.

Dovella saw them glance in her direction and turned hurriedly away. She didn't know if they were aware of her listening or not, but she didn't want to give them any reason to suspect that she was. When they resumed their conversation, she began to listen again and heard them wonder what role she was to play. That was something she would have liked to know herself.

She saw Fvlad striding along with two men, gesturing angrily. Rancer and Bissel. She *had* to get this information to Pandil. No matter what it cost, she had to escape. She exchanged glances with Vebelle and it was almost as if the girl knew what was on her mind, for she smiled and nodded. But then, Dovella thought, Vebelle wouldn't have to read Dovella's mind to know that she was always looking for a chance to escape. They'd talked about it often enough, and both Vebelle and Narina had insisted she should try again if ever she got a chance, not matter what the cost to them.

They had almost finished their time in the exercise yard when the rain came. Dovella lifted her face to let the raindrops wash away the sweat and grime. It had been so long since she'd seen a proper rain that she scarcely remembered how it felt. No wonder Fvlad was so gaunt, if he was controlling the weather. What an enormous amount of energy it must demand to create and maintain a drought for so long: to shape the clouds so that they brought the rain he needed but kept it away from others. And he'd have been fighting against the efforts of Vrillian and his fellow *shagines*. It was staggering to think how much power was at Fvlad's command — and how he squandered it. And for what? Only to gain more power for himself.

Thanks to the rain, there was now enough water for the prisoners to bathe and wash their clothes — and welcome that would be. Apart from the stink, their clothes were stiff from sweat and dirt. The prisoners were herded to the side of the camp where a couple of troughs had been set up. Each had been allotted a soft tunic, a pair of trews and a set of undergarments to change into after they bathed. The things they were given were all well worn but at least they were clean and, having been stored with sweet herbs, smelled fragrant. For now.

The water was cold, but it still felt good even if the troughs weren't big enough for a true bath. While the prisoners were occupied, the guards began conversing among themselves and Dovella caught Vebelle's eye and motioned with her head toward the forest. The Giant girl nodded and began to work a kind of shielding magic that would distract the guards and keep them from noticing Dovella's absence. Quickly, Dovella quietened the dogs and slipped into the forest.

She raced through the undergrowth, pulling free of the twigs and brambles that snagged at her clothes and slapped her arms and face. Mud splashed up against the leg of her trews. This time surely she would succeed. She must. The rain still fell, but now it was little more than mist. And then she was back into the drought-ridden part of the forest and sunshine.

Hearing the pounding of footsteps, she picked up speed and had almost reached the deep forest when a hand grabbed her arm. Spinning around, she faced Maleem and Lofel. "No!" Dovella screamed, trying to pull away. She'd been so close to succeeding! Blinded by tears of anguish, she fought the urge to strike out. They would show no mercy if she did, she was sure, and she had to retain the ability to escape when she got another chance. And she was determined to get ... or make ... another chance. She would never give up.

"Gathering herbs again?" Maleem leaned over, gasping for breath. Straightening up, she said, "That story won't work this time. Ramis is away, so he can't say he sent you."

She and the guard herded Dovella back to the cage, handling her more gently than was usually the case with Maleem. Perhaps the girl was afraid the guard would report any mistreatment to Fvlad, who seemed intent on keeping Dovella safe.

After Lofel left, Maleem remained outside the cage and stared at Dovella. "Why do the others help you when they know it's futile? And don't you care that they will pay for assisting you?"

"Wouldn't you try to escape? Wouldn't your people help you?"

"But no one is hurting you here. You're treated much better than the ones who work the fields."

Dovella couldn't believe that the girl was so naive. "I'm a prisoner!"

Maleem stepped back as if Dovella had struck her. "But ... we had to take you. We need you. I don't know what it is, but you have something Fvlad needs. You owe us your help."

"I owe you nothing! You can't think anyone would accept such imprisonment willingly."

"All we want is our home." Maleem seemed almost in tears. Dovella wondered if Ramis had been talking to her, wondered if she was having doubts.

"*My* home." Dovella's voice cut through the air. "The homes of the Outlanders."

"This used to be our home; it could be again. It *should* be. If your people would acknowledge our right to live here, we wouldn't have to hurt anyone."

"No? What about the people who lived right here?" Dovella gestured toward the burned-out buildings. "These people were hurt — their homes burned and many of them killed."

"We didn't do that!"

"It was done for you."

Maleem stared at her, then looked away, her face hardening. "That's a lie. And we have a right to a home too."

"You had a home. Why did you leave it?"

"We had to. People there wouldn't ... they wouldn't listen to Fvlad. He had to find us another home."

"*Take* another home, you mean. Because your own people didn't want to be his slaves either, you came to take our homes. And kill wantonly."

"No. I don't believe you." Maleem turned back to Dovella and glared at her. "I *don't* believe you."

*

Pandil had eaten her noon meal with Avella and Safir and now the three of them made their way through the Village; Avella and Pandil were on their way to Council while Safir was heading to Healer's Hall. Before separating, they stopped briefly and Master Plais joined them.

"I heard that Dovella had been captured by Plains People. What nonsense is this?"

"Not nonsense, though I'm sure everyone would like it to be," Pandil said. "Plains People have gathered in various farms and settlements. My information is that they are behind a lot of the New School trouble."

The thin healer snorted. "Legends!" he said. "Surely you don't believe —"

"I believe my daughter has been captured by them, and all because she had to leave the Village to get training," Avella said, her voice breaking. "She was put into danger —"

"It's not my fault." Plais cut in.

"Then whose fault is it?"

"Please, Avella." Gently, Safir laid a hand on her arm. "It's done."

Pandil could see from the set of his jaw that Safir too held Plais responsible, but he had to be careful how he spoke to the Master Healer.

Plais tightened his lips and turned away from Avella.

To steer the discussion away from Dovella, Pandil broke in to relate what she had heard. "There is a group of Plains People with designs on the Village. I have this from several sources. They are led by a sorcerer named Fvlad, but although he was at one time housed with Bissel, he keeps moving."

Plais swallowed hard and shook his head. "If you say so, Master Pandil. I would never doubt your word, but this is ...

this is so hard to believe. Plains People and sorcery, this is all the stuff of old Edlena tales."

"Surely you can't doubt sorcery after what you saw Havkad attempt?" Avella's voice was cold.

Plais looked back at her then looked down at his clasped hands. "No. And I know that your coma had to be caused by something more than your injury. But all this is too much to grasp." He turned to Pandil. "Do others know?"

"I've warned them, but I don't know how many believed me. I can only hope that the warning will at least put them on their guard."

After Council meeting, Pandil sat at her desk and rubbed the back of her neck. Sometimes she wished she'd stayed in the Outlands, working with Drase. The training had been hard and the conditions often uncomfortable, but the forest had been peaceful. And she'd been working with people she could trust, not like here where she had to be wary of many of her colleagues. At times like this, she wished she could leave these burdens and return, but with the threat to the Village, with Dovella still missing, Pandil had no choice. She had to go on working, trying to protect her people.

Pandil had just reached to turn out the light on her desk, when the door was flung open. She looked up to see Drase and Maidel push Havkad inside. He was dishevelled and hollow-eyed, and his shoulders slumped. Had he been anyone else, she would have felt some compassion for him perhaps, but after he'd brought such a threat to the Village, she could feel nothing but contempt.

Havkad's eyes were dull, but had lost none of their old malice. He looked at her and smirked. "My people released me before," he said. "They'll do so again. The power of the gods is with me."

"It was the powers of force and treachery that freed you," Maidel said.

"And once the New School followers learn about how you sold them out," Drase snarled, "they will use those powers against you." The tall Outlander looked as if he were about ready to throttle his prisoner.

Pandil turned sharply and Havkad threw his head back. "I've done nothing of the sort."

"No? What kind of bargain did you make with Fvlad?"

Havkad puffed out his chest, looking almost like her old adversary before his botched attempt at attacking her with sorcery. "Ask rather what bargain he made with me. Once we New Schoolers have taken our rightful place in the Village, we will help them find vacant land on which to make their home. And why not? They are our brothers, brought to Edlena by the unnamed gods, just as we were."

"But that's not what Fvlad has planned." Drase glowered at the prisoner, gave a little snort of disgust and turned to Pandil. "He was guarded by one of the Plains People, a young man named Ramis. He supported the story we've been told — after the New Schoolers take over the Village, Fvlad and his people will take over the New School. Once in control of the Village, they will use our people as field hands."

"No! They wouldn't. He promised —"

"Yes," Drase said. "And, what's more, it was Master Trader Rancer who invited them here. And he has been fully supported by Master Bokise and her uncle, Bissel."

Havkad faltered, then sat heavily in a chair across from Pandil's desk. "No," he said. "No."

Maidel took Havkad's arm and drew him from the chair to lead him away to a cell. "I'll make sure he's more securely guarded than last time."

After they left, Drase told Pandil what more he had learned from Ramis.

"I wish you had brought him."

"We wanted to, but Jael had promised to let him go if he gave us worthwhile information. Besides that, he was hoping he could trail him to find out where they are keeping Dovella and the other prisoners."

Pandil sighed. "I can understand why Jael let him go, but I could have used Ramis here. Without his testimony, I have nothing."

Fourteen

IN THE CORNER OF HER FAMILY'S SMALL ROOM, MALEEM lay curled up on her pallet, a spread pulled over her head, trying to drive out the words that kept echoing in her mind. What Dovella had told her couldn't be true; she'd only said it to make Maleem doubt. Fvlad had promised that the Plains People would be welcomed by most Villagers and that only those few who denied the gods would oppose them.

"They fight among themselves," he'd said, "killing their own and burning their homes. We will bring peace. We will bring Machia."

It was true that he had created the drought to help the New Schoolers gain power, but surely he wouldn't have told them to burn homes. Maleem bit on her fist and blinked away tears. No, the New Schoolers had done that to force people to support them. And even if Fvlad had known about the burning, well, her people *deserved* a place. And if a price had to be paid ...

Too great a price. That was what her oldest brother had said when he'd refused to come with them. Pharvin had said lots of other things too, but she hadn't wanted to listen to him when he'd renounced Fvlad's teachings — *couldn't* listen.

Ever since she could remember, Maleem had been taught that Fvlad was the spokesperson for Machia. To listen to him was to listen to Her; to deny him was to deny Her. Maleem's stomach clenched at the very thought of this being false, for that would make everything she had believed a sham and ... ugly.

Now, it appeared that Ramis also doubted Fvlad. Or, maybe, it was just that he wanted to sow discord. She was sure that Ramis coveted Fvlad's power, for why else would he have lost his fervour? She hugged her knees closer to her chest. How she wished that Pharvin were here. Maybe she could make him see the truth ... or he could help her know what was true.

Only she knew what Pharvin would say — and she could not accept it. She *must* have faith. And as long as she accepted that Fvlad's word was the word of Machia, then Maleem had no choice but to follow him all the way. That meant taking the Village any way they could. No matter the cost.

Even now Fvlad and the others were gathering at Bissel's farm to make final plans for helping the New Schoolers take over Village Council. The New Schoolers had a lot of support on Council already, but some of the councillors would need swaying by Fvlad's sorcery — or to be persuaded in some other way. Fvlad would work his sorcery from Bissel's farm, but he would need more power. And no one seemed to be willing to make the sacrifice. Maleem went very still. *Sacrifice.* Perhaps that was the answer.

Quickly, Maleem rose and raced across the camp, closing her eyes to the charred, hastily repaired buildings. What happened here had nothing to do with her people; they were just taking refuge here. Reaching the far side of the little settle, she stood quietly as the priest prayed in preparation for the evening service.

It grieved her that they had nothing better than this makeshift altar, but Machia understood that they hadn't the materials to make the altar She deserved; once they were settled, Machia would have the finest altar anywhere.

When the priest had finished his prayer, Maleem ran up to him and burst out, "A sacrifice."

Bratan turned, his face puzzled.

"Fvlad has said he needs more power and we could raise that for him with a great sacrifice."

Bratan stepped away from her and shook his head vigorously. "No, Maleem. A great sacrifice ... that must be carefully thought out, the hunt specially prepared for and blessed. Besides, this is not the time of year for a great sacrifice."

Perhaps Bratan didn't want Fvlad to succeed either, Maleem thought, a bitter taste rising in her throat. Perhaps he, like Ramis, was jealous of Fvlad's leadership and power. Trying to disguise her rising anger, she spoke calmly. "Maybe the great sacrifice is called for in times of need even if it isn't the season for it."

"No," the priest repeated. "It is too serious an undertaking. And Fvlad has not called for a sacrifice."

Maleem nodded, as if in agreement, but went away determined to carry out her plan. She caught Lofel just as he was preparing to join the others who were going to gather at Bissel's house. His hair glowed golden in the late afternoon sunlight.

When he saw her approaching, Lofel smiled as he always did. Perhaps he still hoped that she would respond favourably to his offer of marriage. Although he continued to chide her about her behaviour with Brakase, his eyes showed that his love was unchanged.

The tall man listened as she laid out her idea and for a moment she thought she might have convinced him. "I could get away to hunt," he said, "and join the others later."

"You have no need to hunt," she said. "We have a sacrifice here."

"Here?"

"Dovella. She must have great power to be able to resist Fvlad. Think how much power she could give him."

Lofel stopped and stared down at her, horror etched on his face. "Have you lost all reason?"

"We won't harm her. Just a little blood, that's all."

Why did everyone thwart her attempts to help? It seemed that no one was still faithful to Fvlad.

"Don't even think it, Maleem. It's wrong." Lofel studied her carefully, then placed his hand on her shoulder. "You know Fvlad has said she isn't to be harmed, that he has plans for her. If you do this, there will be no limit to his anger."

When she made no answer, he said, "You are a fool if you go through with this abomination."

Watching as he stalked away, Maleem hugged her arms against her chest. At least he wasn't going to try to stop her. She would find a way, even if she had to do it herself. And maybe she'd take more than a little blood; maybe she'd take it all. After all, whatever she did, she would have to pay for her actions when Fvlad returned. But that didn't matter. Once before, she had paid the price for helping her people. She could do it again. And when Fvlad saw that Maleem had bought his success, he would have to agree that she had been right.

Too great a price. She could hear Pharvin's words again and shook her head. What he had said wasn't right. It *must* not be right. Too much depended on its *not* being right.

*

As the afternoon wore on, the encampment grew quiet. The men must have left for their meeting at Bissel's house, Dovella thought. She gripped the bars and tried to shake them, even though she knew it was of no use. Even Narina's soft playing could not soothe her helpless anger. She watched over her shoulder as the young Fisher woman bent over her instrument. Did she feel as desolate as Dovella did? Dovella turned away to look out at the burned-out farm. At least she was still alive. What had happened to the people who had once lived here?

From the edge of the camp came the sound of singing, but Dovella shut her ears to it. It was beautiful, or might have been, if praise of such a goddess as the Plains People worshipped could be called beautiful. For her, it could not.

She went to her corner and tried to meditate. The last time she'd returned from questioning, she'd thanked Vebelle for helping her shield her mind against Fvlad's probes. Vebelle had smiled. "I didn't help you," she said. "You haven't needed my help for some time."

"But how is that possible?'

"I don't know," Vebelle had replied, "but it seems you are stronger than you think."

If that was true, Dovella thought, then she needed to spend as much time as possible exercising the skills Vrillian had taught her. Eventually, she would find a way to use them to escape. She had to.

A short while later, she saw Maleem coming toward them. Dovella pounded the bars of the cage, but the young woman wouldn't meet her eyes.

As she unlocked the cage, Maleem said, "Fvlad wants you."

It was unusual for Maleem to come alone, and at first, Dovella refused to go with her. "I thought Fvlad had left for Bissel's farm. Why would he have returned for me?"

Maleem's eyes widened.

Dovella faltered for a moment. Perhaps it had been a mistake to let Maleem know that she was aware of the sorcerer's plan, but what harm could it do at this point?

"He's not gone yet," Maleem replied, but she averted her eyes when she said it.

She was lying, Dovella thought. So what was the girl up to? Then an idea formed. With the camp almost deserted and Maleem on her own, perhaps it would be possible to disable the girl and make good an escape. She caught Vebelle's gaze and the young Giant nodded.

Maleem didn't lead Dovella to the hut where Fvlad usually met her. Instead she took Dovella to a place near the edge of the camp and led her up to an altar. Really, it was only a broad stump, just over waist high, covered with a black cloth. In the centre lay a knife with a red haft and curved blade. Just beyond rose the forest and the way to freedom if Dovella could get away.

While she was still staring at the altar, Maleem shifted her grip on Dovella's arm and twisted it behind her, then reached over for the knife. "We need your blood," Maleem said, her voice unsteady. "Fvlad needs your blood."

Maleem tried to force her prisoner to the ground in front

of the altar, but Dovella twisted away from her and knocked the knife from her hand. Maleem kicked but Dovella jumped out of her reach. Clearly enraged, Maleem screamed and threw herself forward, fingers outstretched as if she would claw Dovella's face. Crossing her arms between Maleem's, then flinging them outward, Dovella knocked her attacker's hands away, slammed the heel of her hand against the girl's jaw and scraped the side of her boot down Maleem's shin. Grabbing Maleem's arm, Dovella jerked it around behind her, kicked against the back of her knee and pushed her to the ground. Pulling loose the sash from around the girl's waist, Dovella used it to bind Maleem's wrists.

Grateful that the Plains People didn't train their women to be fighters, Dovella crouched down with one knee on Maleem's back and pushed the girl's face down against the ground. "Be quiet," she snarled as Maleem tried to call out.

Maleem struggled and Dovella took hold of her hair, thinking to pull up the girl's head and slam it into the dirt, but she stopped herself. No, she would not let Maleem's cruelty infect her.

Still, Maleem tried to get free, but Dovella held her fast. The sash binding her wrists wouldn't be enough to hold her — Dovella needed something to bind the girl's legs as well, and to cover her mouth. The cloth on the altar, she thought; she'd have to cut it into strips. She reached up and pulled away the cloth, then grabbed the knife. At that moment, she heard footsteps and looked up to see Gzofie running toward them.

"Please, don't kill my daughter," the woman cried out.

Dovella paused, knife raised. "She was going to kill me."

"Oh!" Gzofie lowered her eyes. "I ... she was wrong. And

it was wrong to capture you and keep you here, I know. But please don't kill her."

After a pause, Dovella said, "I never intended to kill her. I was just going to cut the cloth so I could bind her." She glared at Gzofie. "But I won't go back to the cage. I won't! If I have to ..."

But even as she spoke, Dovella knew she couldn't kill Maleem, not like this. Had it happened while they were fighting, evenly matched, perhaps she could have done so if that had been the only way to save her own life — but not with the girl lying here face down in the dirt.

"I'll help you. Here." Gzofie pulled off all the sashes from around her waist and tossed them to Dovella. Without making any acknowledgement, Dovella tied a sash about Maleem's mouth so that she couldn't call out, then securely bound her ankles and looped a second sash around her wrists.

"I'll lead you —"

"*All* of us," Dovella said.

Gzofie paused for a minute, then nodded. "I'll get the others." She raced away.

Dovella waited, knife to the ready. If Gzofie betrayed her, what would she do? She couldn't just kill Maleem. She hoped that Gzofie wouldn't know that.

Then she saw Gzofie and the other prisoners running toward her.

"What about her?" Narina pointed to Maleem. "If someone comes by and sees her, they'll be after us." She nodded toward Gzofie. "And how do we know this one won't betray us once her daughter is no longer in danger?"

"Because I'm going with you," Gzofie said. "I have to. I can't stay here, not after this."

"She's right," Dovella said.

"We can hide Maleem in the bushes just outside the camp," Gzofie said. "She'll be discovered soon, but we'll be well away by then."

"I can shield us," Vebelle said.

"And I can help," Gzofie said. "I haven't been taught to shape the power, but I can raise it and transfer it to you. And I can help shield."

After they had concealed Maleem's struggling form behind a clump of bushes, they raced into the forest to put as much distance as possible between them and the camp. When they were well away, Dovella slowed the pace for she knew they'd tire too soon if they kept going that fast.

It was growing dark and given that bright Lucella no longer shone in the sky, they had to take greater care not to stumble on roots or get tangled in the underbrush that crowded the narrow paths worn into the forest floor. Having missed the evening meal, they were hungry and thirsty. Still, no one complained. Besides, Dovella had another worry. Although she knew that she could find the way back to the edge of Jael's village, she didn't know how she was to gain entry. She would not be able to see past the illusion that concealed the entrance. She gave herself a little shake. We have to get there first, she thought. Already she could hear the distant pounding of horses' hooves coming behind them.

Fifteen

MALEEM SQUIRMED AGAINST HER BONDS UNTIL HER wrists felt raw, but try as she might she couldn't untie herself. She rested for a moment and her mind flooded with rage at having failed. And then came fear.

What punishment would she have to endure this time? Not only had she defiled herself by handling the knife — the sacrificial knife at that — but because of her arrogance and disobedience she'd allowed all the prisoners to go free as well. It wasn't her fault alone, of course. Gzofie had helped. A hot fury surged through Maleem. How could her mother have betrayed everything they believed in?

Everything I *believed in.* Her mother hadn't believed in Fvlad for a long time, if ever she had. Still, Gzofie wouldn't have had a chance to intervene if Maleem hadn't thought she knew best. However much she might try to argue otherwise, Maleem knew that she alone bore the blame — which made her rage all the more.

She renewed her struggle to free herself, fuming. If only she'd been taught how to fight, that *Village* girl would never have been able to overpower her, but Maleem had been denied such training, just as she'd been denied the right to use a knife. Quickly, she buried that burning resentment; she must not think such things.

The dirt and small stones ground into her flesh and the underbrush tore at her hair and clothing. Being a woman, she'd never been taught the mind speech either, so there was no way to reach out to anyone to call them to help her. Tears of anger and despair flowed down her cheeks, soaking the sash that bound her mouth.

From a distance she heard her name called and writhed in frustration that she couldn't respond. All she was able to do was roll away from where she'd been concealed behind the bushes and hope that someone would come along and see her. Her face was scratched and her arms chafed by the dirt and pebbles she'd scuttled her way over. Closer now, the call. Then the light from a lantern.

Maleem!

He'd seen her: Ramis had found her!

Kneeling, her brother put down the lantern and quickly removed the tie from her mouth. Maleem spilled out her story as he released her from her other bonds; she could hardly speak through the tears of anger and relief. At least, she told part of her story — she didn't tell him how the escape had come about until he rocked back on his heels and gazed at her with a quizzical expression.

"You want me to believe that Mother just went to the cage and let them go? For no reason?" His eyes mocked her.

Maleem felt her cheeks burn. "All right, it was my fault! I shouldn't have taken Dovella to the altar alone."

"The altar!" Ramis paled. "You shouldn't have taken her at all. Maleem, what were you thinking? And on Machia's judgement night, at that." He pressed his lips together and glared at her.

"I was *thinking* that Fvlad needed the power," she stormed.

"When they gather tomorrow night to move in on the Village Council, he'll need power. Managing the drought, keeping the camp hidden, trying to break through the shields of the prisoners: it takes power, and no one will give him the power he needs."

"I cannot believe you would murder —"

"*Sacrifice!* It was to be a sacrifice to Machia." Again, Maleem fought against tears as she spoke. The priest Bratan, then Lofel, and now Ramis — why could no one see what needed to be done?

"No, Maleem," he said softly. "It would have been murder. And a murder for Fvlad, not Machia. It's not the same."

Maleem looked away. "Whatever it was, it would have brought Fvlad the power to succeed; it would have gained us the Village." She could not believe she was wrong. She *would* not believe it.

Once he had freed Maleem, Ramis paused. "I'll help you find them," he said, "but I want your word that you won't do anything so foolish again."

"I promise," Maleem said. But *she* would decide what was foolish.

Still, she followed him as he raced back to the stables and together they saddled horses. "We should rouse others to go with us," she said.

"Do you really want all the camp to know what you've done?" Ramis mounted his horse without looking at her.

She got on the roan mare he'd chosen for her, gathered the reins and rode up beside him. "How can the two of us bring back four?"

"There will be three of us with Mother to help."

"Mother helped them escape."

Now he did look at her and his eyes were dark with fury. "To save you from your foolishness. Now, come or stay." And with that, he rode away.

Without further words, she followed, still trying to re-assure herself that what she'd done — had tried to do — had been right. But she could not scrub out of her mind the expression she'd seen on Ramis's face, the same expression she'd seen on the faces of Lofel and Gzofie. They had looked at her as if seeing a monster.

*

At the sound of the pursuing hoof beats, Dovella's group went still. It was only then she remembered that she'd shoved the altar knife into her belt. What good it would do she didn't know, but she was glad to have it. She'd not be taken without a fight.

"They won't see us," Gzofie whispered. "It's too dark and, in any case, the shield is solid. If we are all very quiet, they will pass by."

"Mother!" Ramis's voice rang out. "Mother, you don't have to go with them. You can let them go and come home."

Dovella felt her throat throb and her mouth was dry. She wiped damp palms against the legs of her trews.

Ramis's call was followed by Maleem's hissing voice, "You never meant to take them back."

"No, I didn't," he said. "I only came for Mother." Again, his voice called out, "Mother!"

The horses stopped. Was he seeking them with some kind of sorcery? Dovella held her breath, wondering if Gzofie would betray them. They would be evenly matched in numbers and

Dovella had a knife, but Ramis had sorcery. And he would be armed as well. What she had been taught would be as nothing against his power.

But Gzofie didn't move. Dovella let out her pent up sigh.

When the sound of the horses faded, Gzofie said, "It isn't that I don't trust Ramis, but your Villagers may be more easily convinced if someone from our people can give witness. If left unopposed, Fvlad will lead our folk to ruin, as well as yours."

Dovella reached out to touch Gzofie's arm, though she knew that gave little comfort. She understood it was difficult for Gzofie to go against her people and she felt a wave of admiration that the Plains woman would stand for what was right, even against her own family. After waiting a few heartbeats, Dovella led them on through the forest, all the while trying to reach Jael's mind.

Gzofie was lagging a bit and Vebelle tugged on Dovella's arm. "We could all use a rest," she said.

"As I recall, there's a small stream just a little ways on. We can get something to drink and wash our faces. Perhaps that will help."

Silently, they moved on, more slowly now, and when they reached the stream, Gzofie sank heavily to the ground.

"Are you all right?" Dovella asked. "We can rest a while."

"Only for a while," Gzofie said. "We need to make haste. Don't worry. Just give me a breath or two and I'll find the strength."

Dovella splashed the cool water on her face and drank deeply. Then she settled back and tried once again to reach Jael.

Then all of a sudden, she heard, "*Dovella?*"

Dovella. The call rang out in her mind.

Crouched in the darkness, Dovella felt her heart speed up. She held herself still and the others followed her lead. Could it be ... ? She dared not hope. It might well be Ramis trying to draw her out.

Hoofbeats approached slowly and again came a voice, more insistent now. "*Dovella?*"

Jael! There was no mistaking it. Standing up to look, Dovella saw Jael sitting on a horse only a few feet away. She sent out to Jael's mind as she had been taught and felt the connection.

"Here," she cried out, her voice ragged with relief. She turned back. "Vebelle —" But before she could finish her sentence, Vebelle had dropped the concealing shield so that Jael could see them.

He leapt down from his horse and raced toward them, drew Dovella into his arms and pulled her against his chest. She could feel the beat of his heart against hers, feel his ragged breath against her hair. "I've been so worried. I've searched — I don't think I could have stood it if I had lost you."

Dovella reached up to touch his cheek, smiled. "You found me." She could be content to rest here forever, she thought, but as much as she welcomed the safety of his arms, she pulled away. "We've got to get to the Village!"

"We will," he said, "but first, who are these people?"

Quickly, she made introductions. "But there isn't time for this. Rancer and Bokise are traitors, and Fvlad means to attack —"

The words tumbled out, but before she could finish, Jael said, "Be easy. Pandil knows about Rancer and Bokise, but yes, we should go at once. Only, we need to get horses first. Come. We are close to our village."

Holding firmly to Dovella's hand, he led them through the protective shield. "You know the way to the village from here," he said. "I'll ride ahead and make preparations." He tightened his grasp on her hand for a moment and held it against his cheek, then released it, mounted his horse and rode away.

Hurrying her steps, Dovella led her companions into Jael's village. When they arrived, they found that a ceremony was underway before the altar.

Gzofie stopped short and stared. "Machia," she whispered. "I didn't know She was still honoured here."

Vrillian and Mandira stood before the altar. Vrillian's white hair shone in the candle light. Mandira was further away from the light, so all Dovella could see was the paleness of her features.

"You have been accused of leading Dovella into captivity by the Plains People," Vrillian said. "There is discord in the village because of this treachery, even more because of your denial. The *seraise* of the people is shattered and if we are to survive, we must be reconciled."

Mandira stood head held high, arms crossed over her chest.

Vrillian touched her hand and said more gently, "That can only come to pass if you tell the truth before Machia. This is Her night of judgement and healing. Give Her your anger and disappointment. Let Her transform it to peace and hope."

"I've done nothing!" Mandira said. "False witness —" But before she could say anything more her body went into a spasm.

Seeing Mandira in anguish, Dovella started forward but Gzofie took her arm. "This is not something you can heal," Gzofie said, her voice soft but firm. "The girl must do this herself. She has lied before Machia."

"Is Machia so cruel?"

"It isn't Machia who does this to her," Vebelle said. "The girl does it to herself. She knows that she has lied, knows she has betrayed her people, knows she is responsible for the discord in the village. Machia will not tolerate a lie before Her altar."

Gzofie studied the young Giant. Clearly, she was surprised to hear Vebelle speak in this manner.

"When the girl gives up all this to Machia," Vebelle went on, "she will be well. If she doesn't — there is nothing anyone can do for her."

"We had been told that Machia was no longer honoured here," Gzofie said. Then she let out a bitter laugh. "One of many lies," she said, and turned her attention back to the altar.

Still Mandira refused to confess and, after a short time, her parents and brother came forward. Others of the village joined them, including Jael's mother. "We confess that we have added to the friction by not admitting to what we knew must be true," Mandira's mother said.

As they placed their hands on the altar, she went on. "I give my complicity in this to Machia and promise to take responsibility for Mandira. I will do my best to bring her to truth."

"And so will I," the others said, one by one. Taking Mandira's arms, her parents led her gently away, their supporters following them.

Other villagers come forward, admitting to their part in the disharmony caused by accepting Mandira's treachery and lies, among them Jael's mother.

To one side Jael stood and watched, his face like stone.

Sixteen

WHEN THE LAST PERSON HAD PASSED BY THE ALTAR, VRILLIAN bowed his head and made a quiet prayer. Jael had not moved from his position, though several people glanced at him, doubtless wondering if he would be reconciled with Mandira. When Vrillian had finished his prayer, Jael spun away from the altar and raced off in the direction of the stables.

Vrillian turned and hurried straight toward Dovella and her group. How he'd known they were there, she couldn't guess, but as he hastened in their direction, he opened his arms, ready to embrace her. "Dovella, it does my heart good to see you." He enclosed her in his arms and she surrendered to the strength and comfort he offered.

After a moment, he released her and studied her companions, a question in his eyes. Before she'd finished introducing them, Elder Master Faris and others had gathered. Dovella found herself passed from person to person as they hugged her and welcomed her back. Not all, of course. Although a few called out their welcome, she still felt that they blamed her for all that had happened to split the harmony of their village.

She told bits of her story when questioned, but she was too eager to be away to want to talk now. Looking around anxiously, she saw Jael approaching with horses and several of his friends.

"Let's go," he said.

Dovella and her companions mounted the horses he had made ready, and together they set out. She was surprised to see that Elder Master Faris was among the riders, for she had thought he'd remain with Vrillian. She had so many questions she wanted to ask, and no doubt he did as well, but it was difficult to talk as they raced along the road to the Village. They used ways that Jael seemed to think would be safe from attack, but Gzofie and Vebelle rode with him in front of the group. Perhaps they were helping him shield the riders.

It was nearing dawn when the group reached a small farm belonging to an Outlander Jael trusted. "I'll take a couple of men and ride on to the Village," he said, "to find Pandil and tell her what's going on."

"Best I come with you," Gzofie said. "I can witness to things you have not seen."

After a pause, he nodded. Looking at the others, he said, "Rest here. You can come into the Village later. By then, Pandil will have decided what to do."

Dovella was reluctant to wait, but Master Faris said, "It's as well that no one sees too many people ride in at such an hour. Besides, Dovella, you've had quite an ordeal. You and your friends need to restore yourselves."

"It's been hard for Gzofie too."

Gzofie came up to her. "It speaks well of your heart that you should worry about me, but I was not kept in a cage ... at least not as you were. It is little enough atonement for me to push myself a bit more."

Dovella and her friends were happy to have a rest, for they were fatigued and hungry. The Outlander family welcomed them, set out freshly baked bread, a platter of cheese and a bowl of sweet, red okerberries. After they had eaten, they took turns telling their hosts the story of their escape. As they were talking, a grey and white kitten wandered in. It gave a little mew, then walked over and climbed into Dovella's lap. She stroked its silky back and felt her tension dissolve.

Weary beyond all measure now, the travellers welcomed the blankets on offer and found a place to rest. At least, her two fellow prisoners did. Tired as she was, Dovella found it impossible to sleep. Instead she sat with Master Faris and told him more of what had happened while she had been in captivity.

When she mentioned the prophecy, Faris looked at her sharply. "Vrillian spoke of that," he said. "He doesn't know exactly what the prophecy says either, but he thinks it has something to do with those who have multiple gifts — as you do. He's been quite worried about you." Faris reached out to give her hand a little squeeze. "Prophecies are tricky things though, and easy to misinterpret, so we'll concern ourselves about that another time."

Another time. But unless they defeated Fvlad's attack, there might not be another time.

"Now," Master Faris went on, "once we are in the Village and Pandil has everything sorted out, I'm going to take you before the Guild. You are more than ready to work on your own as a healer and I will see that you are accepted."

Dovella looked down at the sleeping kitten. "Master Plais won't like it."

"No, he won't. But he'll learn to live with it."

But would that be enough? Dovella wondered. Could *she* bear working for a Master Healer who accepted her only because he had no choice? The thought of that possibility no longer gave her the satisfaction it once had.

There was a stirring in the blankets and Vebelle got up and joined them. She bit on her lip, then turned to Dovella. "When we were prisoners, you talked about meeting a Giant during your time with the Hill Folk ."

Dovella smiled. "Yes."

"I didn't even dream of asking before, when it seemed there was no hope that we'd ever get away, but do you think the Hill Folk might help me find my people among the Giants?" Vebelle looked away. "Would *you* help me?"

"Of course, I'll help if I can. Do you know anything at all about your father?"

Vebelle shook her head. "It's as I told you. Although my mother lived among the Giants for a short while, she never talked much about them. I don't know if she was trying to be protective of them or if it was because she regretted marrying my father." Dovella could hear the ache in her friend's voice. "Before she got ill," Vebelle went on, "Mother asked her people to let us go back to the old settle where they had lived when she met my father, but they refused. Then, when she died, I suppose they'd decided that I was of no use."

Dovella reached out and clasped Vebelle's hand. Because she was as tall as any of them, they had all forgotten that she was still little more than a child.

"You know you could have a home with me. Or in Jael's village."

A wistful expression flew across Vebelle's face. "But I wouldn't belong there any more than I belonged among the Plains People." She gave a little snort. "Maybe I won't belong among the Giants either."

"I don't know," Dovella said, "but if not, I'm sure the Hill

Folk would make a place for you and you would never feel that you don't belong there."

Dovella smiled as she said these words. It was hard to believe that she'd ever hated and feared the Hill Folk. Of course, it hadn't been them she'd hated; it had been the false picture she'd been given of them. After she'd met them, after she'd opened her mind to the idea that what she had been taught had been wrong, she'd been able to see them as they truly were. That's where she and Maleem had been so different, Dovella reflected, for Maleem could not open her mind to the idea of being wrong.

*

In Healer's Hall, Pandil sat at the side of Carpace's bed stroking the girl's hand. Shortly after her outburst at Govan's trial, Avella's young engineering apprentice had been harshly beaten once again by foulheads from the New School.

Plais only shook his head sadly when Pandil asked how the young woman fared.

"What have they done to you?" Pandil whispered, little expecting a reply.

Carpace opened her eyes. "No more than I expected." The words were faint and clearly uttered with pain.

"They had threatened you? Why didn't you tell me?"

"... Couldn't protect me forever." Carpace drew in a jagged breath, tried to smile. "Maybe others will see now ... maybe do ..."

"After this, anyone who opposes them will be more afraid than ever to speak out."

"... Cowards wouldn't. But others ... will know we spoke true. Surely, when they ..."

"Don't spend your breath, child." Pandil gave the young woman's hand a squeeze. Perhaps it comforted Carpace to think that what she'd done would instill courage into others, but Pandil feared that this outrage would make others even less willing to oppose New School intimidation.

Hearing a sound at the door, Pandil looked around and saw Bake Master Hovel standing there, tears welling in his eyes. He'd taken Carpace in, stood as a father to her when her own father had disowned her for opposing his violence.

Hovel came in and knelt by the bed. "It grieves my heart more than I can say to see you come to this," he said. "You are a brave girl."

"... Only my duty ..." Carpace said, struggling to get out the words, "... to my gods and my people ... To myself."

If only others would do the same, Pandil thought, we could defeat the evil that threatens us.

"Rest," Hovel said. "Rest and be well." He struggled to his feet and stumbled out of the room.

Master Healer Plais came closer to the bed and studied the young woman. His face was drawn and his dark eyes weary. He'd been working with Carpace for hours and Pandil knew he must be exhausted.

Gently, he touched Carpace's forehead and the girl's eyes closed. "There's little more I can do," he said, "but sleep will at least give her some relief." After a moment, he turned to Pandil. "Could Dovella have helped her?"

Pandil started and stared at him, at a loss for what to say.

"I know there is something," he said, "something about her healing gift that has been kept hidden."

"I believe she could have helped," Pandil said.

"Blessed gods," he said and sank down into a chair.

Despite the anger she'd felt toward him in the past, Pandil could only pity him now, for she saw the devastation in his face. "We'd have needed Dovella to go to the *shagines* eventually," she said. "We know nothing of the mind healing they have mastered."

He smiled weakly and ran a trembling hand over his knees. "Thank you for trying to make me feel better, but what you say changes nothing." He looked up at Pandil. "But, don't you see, Dovella's just like ... she's just the kind of healer who would have given too much of herself, given all. I only wanted to protect her and those like her. I never meant ..." He threw his hands up to cover his mouth and looked up at the ceiling. "What have I done?"

Pandil had just arisen from bed when she heard the pounding at her door. Wondering what could be amiss that someone would be coming for her before she'd broken her fast, she rushed to answer. There stood Jael and a stranger, a Plains woman from the looks of her. Before Pandil could speak, Jael was motioning for her to let him and his companion come in.

Quickly, he introduced Gzofie and laid out for Pandil what had occurred, but before she could express her relief at Dovella's escape, he was giving the news of the planned attack.

"We'd had some word of that," she said, "but —"

"But now we have someone from the Plains People who can bear witness to what is going on," he told her. "Gzofie will confirm it. But we have to be ready. They plan to attack tonight at Council."

"The sorcerer will come here?"

"No." Gzofie spoke for the first time. "He'll work from Bissel's farm."

"I'll want you at Council," Pandil told Jael. "You're the only one who can stand against this man."

"I'll be there," he said, "and by mid-morning, Vrillian and Tostare will be here too."

"Good." That was welcome news, but Pandil knew there was still much to do. "We have to get word out to those we know we can trust, especially among the New Schoolers."

"Do we know anyone among them that we can trust?"

"I think I know of at least one," Pandil said. "I'll leave the others in his hands."

Pandil was pretty sure by now that Master Granzie was her redbird, but in any case, she didn't have time to leave a thread and hope her informant would be in touch before she needed to take action about the threat posed by Fvlad and his Plains warriors. Even if she was wrong and it wasn't him, from what Granzie had said at their last meeting, Pandil believed that, although he was a fervent follower of the New School, he still had the best interest of the Village at heart. Quickly, she flung on her uniform and returned to her guests.

"There's food in the cupboard," she said. "Eat and rest. I'm going to seek out Master Granzie."

"Granzie?" Jael frowned.

"I think he'll help," Pandil said. "In any case, we need someone the New Schoolers will listen to."

*

Dovella had managed to sleep for a short while, but when she opened her eyes and saw that her friends were awake as well, she was eager to go on to the Village. They made a quick meal of bread, sliced vesson, cheese and berries, then prepared to set out. Just before she mounted her horse, their hostess came out carrying the kitten. "I believe you formed an attachment to this little one," she said to Dovella. "Would you like to have her?"

"Oh, may I?" Then Dovella remembered her manners. "Are you sure your children won't mind?"

The Outlander woman smiled. "We have several others and I've been wondering where I might find a good home for this one."

"Thank you." Dovella took the kitten and cradled it against her chest.

"You'll need something to carry it in," the woman said. She must have assumed that Dovella would accept the gift, for one of the children came bearing a small basket. After securing this to the front of the saddle and placing the kitten in it, Dovella thanked her hostess again, then mounted, and her group set out for the Village.

It had rained lightly while they slept, and now the grass glistened in the sunlight. The wind shook drops of water from the trees, which sprinkled them as they rode. After such a long drought, the moisture felt good against Dovella's cheeks. The way was smooth and they covered ground quickly.

When they arrived at the Village stables, Elder Master Faris said, "Dovella, you'll want to see your parents and assure them that you are safe. Go, and take Vebelle and Narina with you. We'll see to your horses."

"But I should —"

"Go," the ostler echoed. He limped forward and took hold of the reins. "And you too, Master Faris. There are plenty of us to see to the horses."

"My thanks," Dovella replied. Part of her thought that she should protest more, but she was anxious to see Avella and Safir. Accompanied by the Elder Master and her two friends, she set off for home.

Amidst the hugs and expressions of thanks and relief from Avella and Safir, there was a flurry of words back and forth as Dovella introduced her friends, presented the kitten and told her parents what had befallen her since she had left the Village.

When she had done, Avella told her about what had happened to Carpace.

"Plais says she is beyond his help," Safir said.

"Is she beyond mine?" Dovella asked.

Safir paused for a moment. "I don't know," he said.

"Then I must go at once and do what I can," Dovella replied, "no matter what Plais says about me being barred from Healer's Hall."

"I'll come with you," Master Faris said. "I can reason with him if he tries to make trouble."

"I don't think he will," Safir said. "He is too disturbed by Carpace's condition."

When Dovella and Elder Master Faris entered Carpace's room, Master Plais looked up. His face was even more drawn and haggard than usual. To Dovella's astonishment, he rose and motioned her to the bed, then stumbled into the hallway, head bowed. Faris followed him.

Dovella sat by the bed and scanned Carpace's body,

taking note of the battered muscles, organs and broken bones. Dovella remembered how she'd once been suspicious of Carpace for being a New Schooler; but from what Avella had told her, Carpace had stood up for the true values of the New School and denounced what was being done falsely in the name of her beliefs. She had tried to convince others. And this was how she was repaid.

Well, even if Carpace had been an enemy, Dovella would have tried to help her. Given the young woman's courage, there was all the more cause to try to save her. Dovella reached out and laid her hands upon Carpace, filling the young woman's body with healing energy.

There was so much to be done. Dovella sensed that Faris and Plais were watching her through the doorway. Judging her. She knew she had to be careful, for in trying to save Carpace, it would be far too easy to drain herself. Even if it didn't kill her, it would be cause for Plais to claim that he'd been right to exclude women from Healer's Hall. She monitored the energy as it drained from her body and when she deemed that she'd given all she could safely give, Dovella withdrew from the bond and sat back.

"There's still a lot to be done," she said, "but I believe she will mend."

Silently, Plais came up and looked down at Carpace, felt her forehead. Then he nodded. "Thanks be to the gods that you arrived in time." Now for the first time he looked Dovella in the eyes. "I give thanks also that you are home safely."

Then with a short nod, he left. Now what, she wondered, was she to make of that? She looked at Elder Master Faris who only smiled.

Seventeen

G RANZIE WOULD LIKELY STILL BE LOLLING ABED, PANDIL
thought as she knocked on his door; but she'd scarcely let
the knocker fall before the door opened and he welcomed her
with a wry smile. He stood aside for her to enter and the smile
faded as she told what she had learned from Jael and Gzofie.
His lips pressed together into a grim line. "I might doubt the
Plains woman," he said, "but not if Jael brings witness from
Dovella herself."

"They plan to attack Council tonight with sorcery and
bring in their warriors to subdue any opposition."

"Then we must attack first." Granzie motioned for her to
follow him and led her to a small breakfast room. He gestured
to a chair and, when she'd seated herself, poured her a cup of
tea, and sat down across from her.

Given the flamboyance with which Granzie usually
dressed, Pandil was surprised at the simplicity of the room.
The tapestries were lovely but in muted shades of blue and
green, not the garish reds and golds she would have expected,
and his dishes were plain pottery.

Until recently, Pandil had thought that Granzie's clothes
and affected manner were unsuccessful attempts to divert
attention from his shallowness; the look on his face now
convinced her that what his showiness had been meant to

conceal was something else entirely. Were his anger directed at her, his hard eyes would have her preparing to face a formidable enemy.

"And how do you suggest we do that?" she asked. "I have my security forces, yes, but they are too few to do much against Plains warriors."

"Then supplement them with loyal Outlanders and Villagers."

Pandil snorted. "And how am I to know which ones are loyal? Even if they are not followers of Fvlad, you know well that a lot of them are in Havkad's camp. Many an Outlander settle was burned out by other Outlanders — on New School account."

Granzie reddened but his expression remained unchanged. "Because they were deceived by Havkad's lies."

Pandil found it interesting that he should say "they" rather than "we," but before she had time to consider it further, he went on, "But now that you can prove that it was a Plains plot to take over the Village, I tell you, they will follow you."

"So what do I do?" Pandil asked.

Granzie took a sip of tea, his eyes closed. Then, he looked at her and smiled. "I will ask for a little more trust from you," he said. "Let me bring in the New Schoolers who have not been seduced by Havkad's promise of an easy victory. Meanwhile, you gather the Village forces. We will go at once to Bissel's farm and confront the Plains People there."

Pandil rested her head in her hands for a moment. So many things could go amiss, and what if she'd been wrong to trust Granzie? She raised her head and met his gaze. She couldn't see that she had any choice. "I'll have my people at the south gate two hours after the nooning."

"And I'll have mine." He smiled. "Or, perhaps I should say *your* people, for you will lead."

*

After returning home to refresh herself, Dovella returned to Healer's Hall, this time accompanied by Vebelle and Narina. As she worked again on healing Carpace's battered organs, she felt hands on her shoulder and then a surge of new energy flooded through her. *Vebelle*. Dovella had never known that two people could work together in that manner, the one raising energy and channelling it to the other who used it. Of course, she thought wryly, until recently she'd not known about raising energy at all and probably would have rejected the notion entirely.

When Dovella had done all she thought Carpace could handle for the time being, she drew her hands away and looked up at her friend. "My thanks," she said. "You helped me do more than I could have possibly done alone."

Vebelle touched her arm. "I'll help any time I can."

While Dovella worked, Narina had taken out her harp and played softly. Now, Dovella watched Carpace as the music enfolded her and sensed something in her patient responding. "And you say you have no magic," Dovella said.

Narina looked up. "I haven't."

"Well, whatever you're doing, it's helping her. It is a crime that you were not taught about your gift."

"I've always been told I had no gift." Narina shrugged and turned back to her harp. "And even if I could weave spells with my music, I'd never be allowed to do so."

"That makes no sense," Vebelle said.

"It's the old story," Dovella said, remembering her conversation with Elder Master Faris about the old Schoolmen. "Some people take the power for themselves and deny it to others, no matter the cost. No matter the waste."

The sun had passed its high point and a light wind rose as Dovella and Pandil's mixed group of defenders paused a short distance from Bissel's farm. Half of the security forces from the Village had remained behind with Maidel, as Pandil had been unwilling to leave the people there unprotected in case she'd misjudged the danger. Or misjudged Granzie. Would he truly fight his fellow New Schoolers, or was he luring them into a trap? When Dovella had voiced that doubt, Pandil said, "It's a possibility. But trusting him is the best chance we have." Dovella knew this was true but it was hard to imagine a dandy like Granzie being of much use in a fight, let alone leading one.

Dovella looked around now at the gathered forces. Alongside Pandil's security force were other Villagers, among them one of the councillors and also the knife maker. And Safir. Dovella hated to see her father taking part in another fight, knowing how it hurt him to deal injury to anyone.

Beside Dovella rode Narina and Vebelle, who had insisted that they could help as well. When Pandil expressed a doubt, concerned for their safety, the two girls looked at each other and smiled. "We can fight, Master Pandil," Vebelle said.

"It was hard when we were prisoners," Narina added. "There were too many of them. But with you, with all these others, we can help."

Gzofie too, had joined the group, though she refused a knife. "A bow and arrow," she said. "I'm a fair shot."

It would be hard for her, Dovella knew, to fight her own people, and once again she admired the woman. Would I have so much courage? she wondered.

Jael, Drase and the other Foresters were gathered at one side of the little army, among them the *shagines*, Vrillian and Tostare. Dovella hoped they would be strong enough to contain the sorcerer.

When Dovella spotted Granzie and his followers, she felt a jolt of surprise. She was used to seeing him dressed in fine materials of brilliant colours, but here he was in sober tarvelcloth. Now they would find out whether he was to be trusted.

There were many New Schoolers with him, as he had promised. The Outlander, Barte, was there, his hands knotted into fists. Bake Master Hovel nervously patted the neck of his mount, while the blacksmith stoically stared ahead, his axe resting lightly in front of him on the saddle.

Granzie caught Pandil's eye and nodded. She returned the nod. Loose strands of hair blowing about his face, Jael rode up beside Pandil.

As the group neared Bissel's farm, Dovella saw a lone rider approaching.

Drawing to a halt, Jael said, "It's Ramis." His voice held a note of surprise.

The young man rode toward them slowly, his withered arm held close to his body. "I'm here to help," he called.

Dovella watched Jael who was studying Ramis. She heard a horse move from behind, and saw Gzofie ride up to Jael. "He will help us," Dovella heard her say.

When Jael nodded, Ramis turned his horse and waited

for the others to move up beside him.

Once they were all together, Granzie turned to Pandil. "My people know that you lead this battle. They also know it is our battle as well."

"Thank you," Pandil replied. She looked about her, then lifted her hand and slashed it downward, signalling the troop to set off.

Dovella rode with her friends, wondering where the battle would take place, for she saw no sign of the enemy. Then, as they approached Bissel's steading, Fvlad's fighters poured out from the house and other farm buildings and Pandil drew her force to a halt. There was silence for a long moment, then a muttering grew amongst some of Fvlad's fighters as they began to recognize the New Schoolers in Pandil's army. Brakase blanched when he spotted his father. He whipped around wildly. Clearly confused, other Outlanders and Villagers loyal to the New School also held back. Trader Rancer was nowhere to be seen nor was Master Bokise, but Bissel was there. Pandil studied the crowd, then nodded to Granzie. He urged his mount forward and stood in his stirrups to address the opposing force.

"We have been betrayed! The Plains People are not here to help us but themselves," Granzie shouted. "Villagers, New Schoolers! Stand with us!"

There was louder muttering among the men gathered with the Plains People, and then Lencoln added his call. "It's true!" Though firm, the blacksmith's voice was filled with sadness. Dovella had once seen him as a New School enemy, but she pitied him now.

Pandil's fighters slid off their mounts, preparing to fight afoot, though Tostare, Vrillian and Ramis remained on their horses. Jael hesitated, no doubt torn as to whether he should remain with the *shagines*. After the space of a breath, he joined the other fighters on the ground, keeping always as close as possible to Pandil. Dovella smothered the brief pang she felt at noticing this. It was only right that he should be with Pandil, she thought. As Security Master, Pandil was the one in most danger — an obvious target. The Plains People would know that without her, the Villagers would quickly fall into disarray.

There followed such a melee that Dovella could scarcely be aware of anything but her own fighting. She fought with fist and boot and her short cudgel, and she had a knife strapped to her waist. Pent-up anger fuelled by the exhilaration of battle strengthened her arm as she slashed at the enemy attackers. Most of them were good fighters, but she more than held her own.

Dovella was vaguely aware of arrows flying, of knives and swords flashing in the late afternoon sunlight. She caught a glimpse now and again of her friends, who kept close to her. All around her was the clash of metal, the crack of fist on bone, the screams of pain and cries of anger. Once, when there was a breath-long lull, she found herself beside Granzie. He fought with a ferocious but deliberate skill she could scarcely believe of him, long legs slashing out, one after the other, while one hand wielded a knife and the other chopped at an opponent's jaw. Just beyond Granzie, the blacksmith wielded his axe as easily as if it had been a twig and she caught sight of Ramis swinging a cudgel with his good arm. Then a glowering, bloody face came at her and she was swept once more into the fray.

Suddenly, Barte was beside her with his son Brakase facing

them from the other side, and for a heartbeat Dovella faltered, but then Barte broke the moment. He gave his son a clout and yelled at him, "Face it, boy! We've been fed a lie." Brakase dropped his weapon and stared at his father as if in a daze.

Then a howl arose as Fvlad came out from Bissel's farmhouse, his white hair whipping about his head. Pulsing with thick dark energy, he raised his arms and scanned the battlefield as he strode forward. When he caught sight of Dovella, he froze.

Dovella could now see clearly the movement of energy as Fvlad gathered it to himself from the surging bodies around him. Once pulled into his hands, the energy turned dark and malevolent. And Dovella was afraid.

Although focused on Fvlad, Dovella was conscious of the others who had gathered around to protect her from the fighters while she faced Fvlad. No doubt they too saw that Fvlad meant to attack her. She felt a sudden inflow of energy, from the *shagines,* she sensed, or from Gzofie or Vebelle. Dovella welcomed it, as much for the encouragement it gave as for the power it massed. But she could not help her fear surfacing at the sight of the solid waves of twisted evil energy surging toward her.

As she braced herself, she remembered the woodcat that had threatened her in Jael's settle. Just such energy had swirled around it and she had been able to push it away. She would try the same thing here.

Dovella shielded her mind as Vrillian had taught her and prepared to receive the blow. She felt a shock as the blast of energy hit her outstretched hands, but she stayed focused and before it could travel up her arms she sent a pulse of energy to meet it, hurling it back. She watched Fvlad step backward as he saw it coming, his face contorted with surprise and rage. And perhaps just a touch of fear. Only a touch, but it was enough to make him hesitate, give her time to prepare for the next strike. It would be fiercer, but with this first success, her confidence rose.

Another surge of energy filled her and she recognized Vrillian's touch, quickly added to by Tostare. Suddenly, with a jolt of fear she realized what was happening: the accumulated energy of her allies was being funnelled through her alone. Dovella didn't know why the *shagines* had chosen to let her do battle for them all, but she suppressed her fear of failure and accepted that this had to be her fight. Perhaps she was the only one who could ward Fvlad off in this way. Or, perhaps, they felt that defeat at the hands of such a young Village woman would convince the Plains People that Fvlad was not a worthy leader, that he was not as powerful as they had believed.

And so, with their help, she withstood wave upon wave of the filthy energy Fvlad blasted at her relentlessly. She could feel herself tiring, for fighting such as this was new to her. At the same time, her battle instincts rose as she countered his assaults and followed them with attacks of her own. With each bolt of energy that hit him, Fvlad's face grew ever darker.

And then, out of the corner of her eye she saw, appalled, that Jael had fallen and a Plains warrior was raising a cudgel, ready to crush him. "No," she screamed, rushing forward. Overwhelmed by fear for Jael, she dropped her guard for an instant, all Fvlad needed to break free and race for his horse.

Assailed from all sides, Jael's attacker backed away. As Dovella ran toward him, Jael sat up and began rubbing his knee. Her throat clogged with tears of relief, Dovella knelt by his side.

"Only a twisted knee," he said.

"I thought you'd been ..."

"I got careless." He blushed and looked away.

He'd been distracted by his concern for her, Dovella thought. She wanted to embrace him, wanted to feel the comforting beat of his heart, but knowing others were watching, she only touched his knee, sending healing energy.

"Thank you," he said, clutching her hand with a smile. "It's much better." He looked around. "Now that Fvlad is running away, I think the others will lose heart."

As Dovella watched Fvlad gain his horse, she noticed that Ramis was already giving chase.

"I'll follow," Jael called out to Pandil. "Ramis may need help."

Dovella wanted to shout that she would ride after Ramis too, but she knew that Jael would be the best person to go. Somehow, she had held Fvlad off, yes, but Jael had more experience. Besides, she was needed here on the battlefield to attend the wounded. There were many.

Hugging her arms tightly against her chest, Dovella looked back at the place where Fvlad had stood. She began to tremble. Now that it was over, she had to give thought to what had happened: she had faced a powerful sorcerer, had felt the onslaught of his rage and power — and had held him at bay. How was this possible? *What have I become?* She was scarcely aware of Vrillian taking her hand.

"Child, I cannot believe how you fought off his attack. But look how you shake! Are you sure you have not taken an injury?"

Not injured, and yet she was not who she had been when

she rode to this battle. Aware of people staring, she said, "I'm sorry I failed."

"Failed? How can you think such a thing?'

"I let him escape."

"No one could have expected more of you," Vrillian said. "Indeed, no one could have expected as much."

And yet, they must have, she thought, or else why had they let her fight him? And the accusing stares: were they because she had failed or because she had revealed such magical powers? "He still got away," she said, and turned away to tend the wounded.

*

Pandil felt as if the world would stop when she saw the sorcerer focus his attack on Dovella. But there was nothing she could do to help the girl fight sorcery, and the brief lull in fighting that accompanied his first onslaught didn't last long. Pandil had to concentrate on her own fight and keep concern for Dovella from her mind, for such a distraction would surely be fatal. Still, she fought filled with heavy dread. What would she say to Avella if the girl fell? Pandil glanced quickly around, caught sight of Safir. Saw that he too had resumed fighting. Was it because he knew he could give Dovella no assistance, or had he more faith in his daughter? No time to ponder either way, for a Plains man was coming at her with a knife.

By then, Trader Rancer and Master Bokise had appeared and joined the fight, but when a tremendous wail rose from the battlefield as Fvlad broke away and fled, the battle was as good as over. Most of the Outlanders and Villagers who still stood with the Plains People dropped their weapons, hands held high in surrender. The remainder simply gathered to one side and watched the last individual fights come to their conclusions. Rancer and Bokise tried to rally the New Schoolers who were with Pandil to desert her and join them, but with Granzie, Lencoln, Hovel and even Barte shouting at the same men to stand fast, the final dissenters were quickly subdued.

Surrounded by Villagers and Outlanders, Pandil climbed up on a large rock and waited for quiet. As the hubbub settled into an expectant hum, she addressed herself to the vanquished in a strong voice that carried across the field.

"Trader Rancer invited the Plains People here — not to help the New Schoolers, but to take the Village for himself and the Plains People. His treachery was fully supported by Master Bokise and her uncle, Bissel."

"Lies!" someone shouted. "The sorcerer was going to help us."

Gzofie strode forward, gesturing to Pandil, who helped her climb up on the rock. Standing beside Pandil, the Plains woman shouted, "Not lies!" She looked at the New Schoolers who stood together, their faces proclaiming their confusion. "You, Barte, you and Brakase know me," she called out. "You visited our camp and know I was in Fvlad's company. I tell you, everything Master Pandil says is true. Fvlad was going to take the Village for himself — for us. Young Dovella was captured and kept in a cage, as were her friends here. They can witness also."

"What they did was never for you," Narina shouted, her voice carrying above the muttering of the crowd.

"You are dupes. All of you," Bissel called out, still defiant.

"You think it's over. *We* are Plains People."

"You think Fvlad considers you a man of the Plains People?" Gzofie shouted. "*Mongrels!* That's what he called you. Your moment of triumph would have been short-lived."

"I don't care what he called us," Rancer said. "We *are* Plains People and we *will* take back that which is ours."

"The Village was never *yours!*" Councillor Granzie snarled as he strode forward.

Rancer did not speak, but Bissel continued his harangue. "We are not defeated," he cried out, both fists raised in the air. "Fvlad will return. We *will* have the Village."

Bake Master Hovel came up to join Pandil. He was limping, but waved away offers of help. "We were deceived by Havkad," he shouted, "who was himself deceived by Trader Rancer and Fvlad." His voice softened, but still carried to the crowd. "But, my brothers and sisters, even worse was that we deceived ourselves. We claimed that we were against violence, but we turned our eyes away when our own people did violence. We cannot claim innocence for the burning of Outlander farms, the killing of Outlanders and Foresters, even if we didn't sanction it. We didn't know because we didn't want to know, didn't want to make a choice between our brother New Schoolers and what was right. Young Carpace spoke out and has paid dearly for her courage. Now I say, we *must* choose. I choose the Village. I choose the true teachings of the New School."

He stood quietly for a moment, looking around, meeting the eyes of his fellow New Schoolers, then raised his hand high above his head. "Who will choose with me?"

Pandil watched as people bowed their heads and, one by one, raised their hands. It was not a reconciliation exactly, but at least things would be quiet while they gathered up the injured and buried the dead. She stepped down from her rock, suddenly tired.

"May I go now?" Gzofie asked. "Fvlad will surely head straight back to the camp and I'm worried about my daughter."

Pandil hesitated. What if they needed her to witness further? But she could see the worry in Gzofie's eyes, and the woman had helped far more than one might reasonably have expected. Pandil nodded her permission and the Plains woman made her way to the edge of the crowd as did several Outlanders. They mounted their horses and raced away.

Pandil turned her attention to the Plains People they'd captured. She must decide what to do with them. And there was still the worry about the escaped sorcerer. Quickly, she and her supporters rounded up the prisoners. After expressing her thanks and taking leave of Vrillian and his people who were preparing to return home, Pandil and her force set out for the Village. When the prisoners had been secured there, she returned to her office and found Granzie propped up against a wall, his arms crossed, a triumphant smile on his lips. As she drew closer, she noted the pattern on the hilt of his dagger. "It was you," she said. "You saved me in the park that day."

He nodded. "I, or one of my people, always kept you in sight when you were on your own," he said. "You are much too valuable to the Village to let anything happen to you."

"And now?"

He laughed. "Never more valuable than now. I hope that, between us, we can bring the Village back into some kind of harmony."

Pandil nodded. She would not fool herself that the danger

was past. But, later, perhaps those New Schoolers who could think for themselves would work with Granzie and other Villagers to defeat whatever threat was still posed by the Plains People. She had come to trust Granzie despite his being a New Schooler. But even if there was still much work for the future, she relished this victory, this moment of peace.

Eighteen

MALEEM KNELT BEFORE THE BLOOD-SPLASHED ALTAR, weeping softly in the dying sunlight. Ramis had left for Bissel's farm. No doubt he'd be fighting against Fvlad when the sorcerer attacked the Village Council, but there was nothing she could do about that. All she could do was plead with Machia to aid in the battle her people would fight this night. Maleem saw that the blood had ceased to flow from her arm. It was not a life sacrificed, as she had intended, but she hoped that there was enough blood shed to open Machia's ear. Her cheeks stained with tears, Maleem prayed for forgiveness for the arrogance that had caused her to let the prisoners escape.

At the sound of hoofbeats, she raised her head, then stumbled to her feet when she saw Fvlad riding toward her. Puffs of dust rose around him as the horse's hooves struck dry earth. What was amiss? Fvlad should be at Bissel's farm preparing for the attack against the Village Council.

She took a step toward him but he raised a hand, signalling her to stay where she was. As he drew near, he swung down from the saddle.

"How did the prisoners escape?" he demanded, as he rushed toward her.

She felt her mouth go dry. How could she confess what she had done?

"They gave warning of our plans and the Villagers struck before we were prepared. And that girl from the Village, *she* defied me. Was able to defy me." His face twisted and his hands clenched. His black look of rage made Maleem tremble. She knew she deserved his anger, knew she had shamed herself by her actions, but hard as it was to meet his eyes, she would not look away.

"It was my fault," she confessed.

His face hardened further. "What did you do?"

"I ... I wanted to help you," she said. "I brought Dovella here. I thought a sacrifice would help, would give you power."

"Here? You were going to sacrifice her? Fool! Have you any idea what we would have lost?" His voice rose to a pitch as he stared at her, his eyes growing even colder. He raised his hand as if to strike her, then slammed it down on the altar. "What, because of your foolishness, we *have* lost?"

Maleem shrank away, wiped her damp palms on her tunic. She bowed her head and fought to control her ragged breathing. Was it too late? she wondered. She could make amends by being the great sacrifice herself. Perhaps her life would give Fvlad the power he needed to defeat the Villagers and gain a home for her people after all.

"But surely with enough power —" She looked up.

He studied her for a long moment, as if weighing her offer, then smiled and lifted his hand again, this time in the gesture the priest used when passing Machia's blessing. "You are a true daughter of Machia," he said. "Yes, with power, I can escape."

Maleem threw a hand up to her mouth, unable to conceal her horror on hearing his words. "*Escape?*" She took a step away.

"I must rebuild our forces to carry on the fight. Surely, you can see that." He spoke softly, smiled as if at a favoured child.

Maleem shook her head as if to deny the words. She didn't want to die, but she would have offered herself willingly to give Fvlad the power to fulfill his promise to Machia. But to help him break his vow to the Goddess, to abandon Maleem and the rest of his people, leaving them to the mercy of the Villagers — how could he ask such a thing? Maleem felt as if the world were crumbling beneath her.

"No!" she cried out. "Surely you won't desert us."

He drew back his hand as if to strike her, but instead reached down and drew a knife from his belt. "You have lost me the best chance I had to defeat the Giants." His words sent her mind reeling.

"The Giants? But I thought the Village —" Maleem shook her head again as if to dislodge the thought that was forming. She felt her throat close. What did the Giants have to do with anything? They were enemies, yes, but she'd thought it was for the good of their people that Fvlad had been gathering power. Her knees weakened, and she supported herself against the altar. Now, she saw how wrong she'd been! Fvlad had never cared about the people, never worked his sorcery to find them a home. It had always been about his own ambitions, his desire to find the Giants, to gain more power. *For himself.* She fell to her knees, sobbing. How could she have been so grossly deceived?

"The Giants are the cause of all our defeats. *They* were the ones to first deny us what was rightfully ours. Then the others of our brother settlers turned against us. Jealous, Maleem! They wanted what *we* had. Wanted to deny us. Once I have brought down the shield of the Giants, no one will be able to stop us. The girl was the key, the many-gifted one, but thanks to you, I've lost her. Lost everything!"

Fvlad took a step toward Maleem. "You owe me the chance to start again. You owe it to Machia to help me."

Maleem lowered her head, cringing as she awaited his blow, but the sound of horses' hooves made them turn away from one another. Ramis! A spark of hope leapt in Maleem's heart as he raced toward them.

Ramis slid from his horse even as it was moving, and shouted, "Get away from her!"

Behind him came another rider whom she didn't know: a Forester from the looks of him.

"She stole my chance," Fvlad cried out. "She owes me —"

"She owes you nothing!" Ramis shouted.

"And *you*." Fvlad spat out the words. "You are a worse traitor than she. You fought with the defilers. You defied *me!*"

"Move away from her!"

Fvlad laughed. "Or what? Do you truly think to stand against me, boy?"

Ramis mocked his laugh. "You ran away from an untrained girl."

"I didn't run from her," Fvlad snarled. "I left because my people failed me. The battle was lost by them."

The rider dismounted and walked up to stand beside Ramis. He and Ramis exchanged glances and Maleem could see the Forester would aid her brother should he need it. Ramis smiled at his companion and shook his head, but his hand trembled.

"I'll fight you if I have to," Ramis said. "I'll not let you harm my sister."

Maleem stared, seeing him with new eyes. He would fight for *her*? Ramis was strong but surely he knew that, even with help, he could not defeat the sorcerer. Fvlad would kill him. Yet Ramis was willing to risk that to protect her. She wept anew at how she had misjudged her brother.

In a single swift motion, Fvlad faced her, knife raised. But within the instant, a flash of light hit his hand and he cried out in rage and pain. He whirled into a fighter's stance, glowering at Ramis.

Other riders came now, among them her mother and several others: folk of Village blood and some of the mongrels. They gathered behind Ramis and the young Forester.

Fvlad pointed a trembling finger at Ramis. "You only want to rob me of my power. You pretended to follow me, but you've always been jealous."

Ramis laughed. "I've no need of your power. I never have had. I stayed only for my sister and Mother. Now, step away."

Others of the Plains women and children who'd remained at the camp gathered in small knots watching; there were also a few men who must have escaped from the fighting.

Maleem shook with dread as she felt Fvlad gather his energy and direct it at Ramis. She watched Fvlad's face as the strain etched ever deeper the lines of fatigue that had so troubled her over the past few weeks. For a moment he faltered and steadied himself by grabbing the edge of the altar. He took a deep breath and once more gathered his power.

Fvlad glanced over at Maleem. "Raise some energy for me," he commanded. "I must leave here to carry on my work. Your folly was my defeat. Now you must redeem yourself."

Maleem shuddered. Everything she'd done, everything she'd believed — it had all been a sham. To raise energy for him — that was all he'd ever valued her for. She felt as if she were seeing clearly for the first time, and what she saw horrified her.

"Do it!" he snarled.

She buried her face in her hands and sobbed. There was no way she could undo what she had done, but she would not give Fvlad her blood, nor would she raise power for him. Never again.

She *would* raise it for Ramis. Placing her hands on the ground she began to draw strength, set a path to send it to her brother, but before she could do so, Fvlad hurled himself between them and tried to seize the power.

No! Maleem snatched the power away ... or tried to. What followed then she couldn't understand. There was an exchange of flashing light and then Fvlad *disappeared*. At least, part of him disappeared and reappeared in a series of terrible jolts. The crowd watched, eyes wide with the horror at the sight as Fvlad twisted and writhed. A terrible wail shattered the stillness and the smell of burning flesh hung in the air. Many turned away, shaking as if they shared whatever agony Fvlad might be experiencing. It seemed as if he were being torn between here and nowhere. Then, with another piercing scream, he materialized completely and toppled into the dust.

Maleem gazed at his still form for a moment, then — filled with a gaping nothingness — she doubled over into the dirt before the altar and her world disappeared.

*

Jael watched, still caught up in the horror of what he'd witnessed, as Gzofie raced to her daughter's side, Ramis hard on her heels. Gzofie drew the girl into her arms and screamed up into the sky, but though she breathed, Maleem was senseless to all around her. Jael joined them and stood quietly. He'd never seen anyone hit with such an enormous backlash of power and was at a loss as to how he could help.

Laying Maleem gently on the ground, Gzofie went to gaze down at Fvlad's lifeless body. She kicked some dirt on it, then stood before the altar. Raising her hands, she cried out, "Machia! I call on you to witness what has happened here. Hold my daughter guiltless in this death." Placing her hands on the altar, she said, "I give you my rage against all those who brought us to this pass. I give you my weakness in not standing up for you. Take from me what you will, but I ask that you will bring peace to my child." Then Gzofie went again to her daughter's side, drew the girl into her arms and rocked her gently as if she were a baby.

Jael heard Ramis draw a sharp breath. "I was afraid she was going to curse his spirit." He looked up at Jael, his face pale. "A mother's curse at Machia's altar is a dreadful thing."

"He deserved a curse," Jael said.

"Yes, but my mother does not deserve to bear the cost of such a curse."

Jael reached down and took Ramis's arm, motioned for him to come away. Speaking softly, he said, "What happened there? I've never seen anything like it. Fvlad ... was he actually ..." Jael had heard tales of how the Giants could step from one place to another, travelling through nothingness. Taking the Giants' Path it was called. But even the *shagines* believed it was only stuff of legend. And, in any case, he'd never heard of anyone but the Giants being able to do it, even in childrens' woodtales.

Ramis nodded. "Fvlad guarded his knowledge jealously. He is the only one among us who knew the secret." As he spoke, a howling wind arose and the sky blackened.

"We'd best seek cover," Ramis said. "Fvlad has been controlling the weather for two years, just one of the reasons he needed so much power. I dread to think what chaos will surely come upon us now the weather has finally been set loose."

Without delay, Jael joined others to gather the horses into shelter while Ramis and his mother moved Maleem. He'd scarcely led the last horse under cover when the deluge came. He raced for the small house he'd seen Ramis enter and was already soaked through when he reached the door.

Ramis handed him some clothing. "It won't fit very well," he said, "but at least it's dry."

Quickly Jael changed into the dry garments and joined Ramis and Gzofie at the table, where Gzofie had placed a cup of steaming tea for him. "Is there nothing you can do to control the storm?" Jael asked.

Ramis shook his head. "That was another piece of knowledge Fvlad kept to himself. I'd help if I could ..." He shrugged.

Jael sipped his tea and studied the young man. "You *can* help," he said. "My *shagines* have been fighting the drought with some success. They could teach you and you could add your power to ours. It would mean delaying your departure, but —"

"We can do that," Gzofie broke in. She placed her hand on Ramis's shoulder. "It is little enough to make up for what has been done in our name. Besides, it will take some time for us to get everything ready to go. And we need to see if Master Pandil will release those of our people she captured."

"Why would she do that?" Ramis asked.

"Why would she want to keep them? They would ever be a sharp stone in her boot. If we promise to leave, to take them with us, that would be better for her."

"Gzofie is right," Jael said. "There is little enough room to keep prisoners, yet Pandil can scarcely set them free. Still, if she could be assured that you'd leave, it would relieve her of the burden. If you will come with me to help with the weather, I'll send someone to discuss the matter with Pandil. Meanwhile, Gzofie can make preparations here for your journey."

Ramis looked at his mother. "Will you be all right here? On your own?"

Gzofie smiled. "Not completely on my own. There are others here besides our own folk and by now even our people will have understood the madness of what we have done. When the rain lets up, go with Jael and do what you can to right some of the wrong Fvlad has done."

The rain continued to rage, sheets of water falling around the house while the wind sent the trees swaying. Low branches pounded the roof. From time to time, streaks of lightning lit up the sky and a deep roaring thunder seemed almost to shake the house. Finally, the rain eased and the air was tinged with green.

Jael glanced up at the sky. "I think we can make it before the next storm," he said.

The two young men rode through wide puddles, water from trees dripping down onto their necks, scarcely talking as they hastened on their way to beat the next storm. As they neared his settle, Jael pulled his mount to a halt and his companion stopped beside him.

"Are you sure your people will want me?" Ramis asked. "I've been thinking and ..."

"You can help us," Jael said. "That's enough. Only ..." He paused, wondering how to phrase it. "We ask visitors to bind their eyes before they pass through the shield." Jael let out a little laugh. "Useless in your case, I expect. No doubt you would be able to see right through it."

Ramis smiled. "Perhaps, if I tried, but I won't. Still, whether I could or not, you shouldn't treat me differently." He edged his horse closer and leaned over so that Jael could tie a scarf around his eyes. They kneed their mounts and continued until they reached the villagers who were keeping watch.

The guards came out from the shelters they'd raised against the storm, eyeing Ramis with frowns until Jael explained their mission. "His help will be welcome," one of the men said.

Jael helped Ramis dismount, then bound the eyes of his horse so it wouldn't be frightened by passing through the shield. Horses that belonged in the settle were used to the illusion, but a horse going through it for the first time often shied.

As they passed through the shield into the village, Jael felt the comfort that always eased him when he returned home.

But if the guards were happy to have Ramis's help, others were not so welcoming. Though no one spoke against Ramis, Jael could feel the eyes of suspicion following them. After they had tended their mounts, Jael led Ramis along the muddy path to Vrillian's small house. The *shagine* welcomed Ramis and insisted that they sit while he brewed a collitflower tea.

"You've had a wet ride and a trying day," he said. "You need something warming inside you."

As they drank their tea, Vrillian told them what had passed at Bissel's farm after Jael left. "It looks as if the Villagers have things pretty well in hand. With Bokise and Rancer exposed, most of the dissidents have come around and Pandil has gained the support of some of the leading New Schoolers, so one can hope they will preach reason to their people."

"And Dovella?"

"Ah," Vrillian said. "She has a great deal to think about."

By the time they'd finished their tea, Tostare had joined them and the two *shagines* listened with sombre faces as Jael told of what had happened at the camp of the Plains People. Clearly, they were astonished at Jael's tale of how Fvlad had almost captured the power raised by Maleem to help him walk the Giants' Path.

"I'm truly sorry for what has befallen your sister," Vrillian said. "Do you think we could help?" He turned to Jael. "Or perhaps, Dovella ..."

"I thank you," Ramis said, "but I believe this is something that must be worked out by Maleem. The backlash damaged her, of course, but I think even more, she was shattered by her final understanding of Fvlad and his true purpose. She needs time to acknowledge her own complicity in his work."

"This ... thing that Fvlad attempted," Vrillian put in, "I've heard of tales of the Giants' Path, but I always thought it was just that — a tale. Had he travelled in this manner before?"

"Many times," Ramis replied. "That's how he was able to do so much mischief here and still keep track of us as we travelled."

"It must have taken enormous energy," Tostare said.

"Yes, that much travel while still maintaining the drought and carrying on his other activities required enormous amounts of power. That's why he demanded so much energy from the rest of us."

Tostare shook his head. "Blessed with so much power, and he squandered it only because of greed for yet more."

Vrillian looked up from his tea, his face drawn. Suddenly he looked like an old man. A tired old man. "Ramis," he said seriously. "Do you think the defeat of Fvlad's forces at Bissel's farm has freed us of this threat? I fear that others may well continue his work."

"Not if I can help it," Ramis said. "I intend to take my people back to the home we left. I doubt we'll find much welcome there, but I hope that, freed of Fvlad's malicious influence, my people will be able to see the wickedness of his plans. From the beginning, the ones who stayed behind refused to take part in Fvlad's madness. It is my intention that you will be completely free of us, if not of the evil we brought."

"And with your help," Jael said, "we have a better chance of correcting the weather patterns and we'll no longer have to work against Fvlad's energy. It will be difficult and take time, but we can do it."

Vrillian nodded and straightened his shoulders. "Yes, and in the meantime, there is much in which we can rejoice. Fvlad's evil is no more and the New School threat to the Village has been contained — at least, for the time being." He turned to Ramis. "And we are thankful that you have come to help us."

The work was intricate and tiring, but thanks to Ramis's great strength, they were able bit by bit to shift and reshape the weather patterns so that the violent rainstorms were of short duration in any one place. Gradually the disturbances were smoothed away and the *shagines* pronounced themselves satisfied that they would be able to bring the weather back to its normal patterns.

A few days later, Vrillian approached Jael with a broad smile. "I have received word from Elder Master Faris that the Village Healer's Guild is meeting and he is standing with Dovella to ask that she be granted membership."

"At least that wrong will be set aright," Jael said.

"We have been invited to the Village to be there with her in her moment of happiness," Vrillian added.

Jael forced a smile. Truly, he was happy for Dovella. She should never have been denied her chance to go through the Rites. But, surely this meant that she would remain to work in the Village, while he had to stay here. Jael stifled a sigh. He and Dovella would be separated again.

Nineteen

DOVELLA PLACED HER HANDS AT THE SMALL OF HER BACK and leaned back against them to ease the ache. Since her return to the Village she had been working long hours at Elder Master Faris's house: preparing herbs, practising healing techniques and mastering the understanding of the body as she could see it with her opened sight. And trying to forget her battle with Fvlad. She had talked of it briefly with Pandil and her father, but once they understood that talking about her use of such magic distressed her, they had abandoned the subject. No one else spoke of what had happened, but she could feel the glances that followed her, assessing and accusing — as if to say that she had used magic, so she must be evil.

Dovella went to the window and looked out. After two years of drought, the earth was parched and baked hard. It took time for it to soak up the water and when the rain beat down so heavily, it damaged the few crops they'd managed to plant. She had heard that Ramis had been helping Jael and the *shagines* and it seemed as if the last couple of storms had been a bit less turbulent, but it would take many moons for the *shagines* to coax the weather back into some normal pattern. Meanwhile, Jael had to stay in his settle.

Not that he would have come to see me anyway, Dovella told herself. Only, remembering how he had held her close the night he'd found her, she thought maybe he would have. She sighed. Jael had his duty just as she had hers, but the brief moments of closeness had made her long for more. Yet she couldn't go back to his settle, not after all that had happened — and he had to stay there to finish his training. But, later, when he was ... she dared not even hope that he would return to the Village. His people needed him. What did *he* think, she wondered, of what she had done? Again, the question arose: *What have I become?*

*

The squeak of wheels and the slight jolts against her spine told Maleem she was moving again. The low cart in which she rested was well padded, but she could feel each bump in the road. Although her thoughts were muddled, her eyes were clear enough that she could see the branches of trees and the brilliant sky above her. Sometimes the sky was almost blinding but squinting up at it was better than gazing at the rump of the horse pulling her cart.

Someone had draped a kind of canopy that sheltered her face from the sun, but the sides of the cart shut off the breeze, so sweat gathered on her brow and ran down her neck. The leaves that blew listlessly in the wind drew her gaze. They looked as limp as she felt.

Somehow, she couldn't control her tongue well enough to form words, but she could hear those who complained loudly about her riding while others had to walk. She wanted to tell them that she'd rather walk, wherever they were going. She felt she ought to know why she was lying in this cart, but she didn't. Sometimes fragments of pictures flashed through her mind, but they carried no meaning, only a feeling of horror that she couldn't understand.

When they stopped again, someone came to her with a bowl of food and the aroma made her mouth water. She looked not at the bowl but at the one who carried it, and knew that this was her brother, Ramis. He helped her sit up straighter, then filled the spoon and lifted it to her lips. Why would Ramis feed her and look at her so tenderly?

"Eat, Maleem," he said, and she opened her mouth. Slowly and with great effort, she chewed the tender bits of meat, while Ramis smiled his encouragement and occasionally murmured, "That's good, Maleem. That's good." Then he was gone and they were moving again.

When next they stopped, it was almost dark. Maleem was lifted from her cart and two women came and took her by the arms. One of them was her mother. As Maleem looked into Gzofie's eyes, the picture shards came together to form a whole and Maleem remembered what had happened.

She blinked her eyes and bit the inside of her lip to keep from crying out her anguish. For a moment, she wished that she had never emerged from the fog that had shrouded her mind. When she had been dazed, she had not had to wonder why she felt like a withered husk. Now, as her mind cleared, she had to relive the death of her faith in Fvlad, had to experience again the moment when she'd been forced to acknowledge that her passion for conquest had been as twisted and foul as his.

Maleem smelled the aroma of vesson stew and once again it was Ramis who fed her, his eyes mirroring the pain she felt. A wave of shame swept through her when she remembered how she had scorned him as one who only wanted power.

How blind she had been! Clearly, he had vast magical power, more than she had ever imagined, and now an authority granted him by those who followed willingly. And, just as clearly, from his drooping shoulders, the latter was one he wielded with no great enthusiasm.

There were, of course, those who would wrest it from him if they could, her father being one. Rhahol had had no choice but to follow along, unless he'd wanted to languish in a Village prison, but he spoke for a group who objected to Ramis leading the people back to their former home.

"We'll not be welcome," Rhahol warned.

"Not if we insist on embracing the madness that Fvlad preached. But we've seen how false that was." Ramis's voice was patient and firm.

"We should stay here," her father went on, "and carry on Fvlad's work. We should bring those godless people to the worship of Machia!"

And truly that was part of what Fvlad had preached, but now Maleem knew how empty that preaching was. She didn't doubt that Fvlad wanted people to bow before Machia, but it was more for his own aggrandizement at bringing about the conquest than for real faith.

Maleem's faith in Machia had not died along with Fvlad, but she was now forced to ask herself how many of the words she had mouthed had been from her own heart and how many had come from Fvlad.

"Do you really think Machia desires slaves at her altar?" Ramis asked. "Or do you think only to make yourself look more faithful by forcing people to bow before Her?" Ramis's voice grew heated. "You are all fools and what's more you defile Her name by making Her nothing more than a slaver."

There was a low grumble from the men, but no one except Maleem's father challenged Ramis. "Fvlad would not have quibbled over words," Rhahol said. "He knew where his duty lay."

"It is Fvlad who brought us to this pass," Gzofie snapped, "and the only duty he followed was that of his own will to gain more power." She often quarrelled with Rhahol in the privacy of their own quarters, but this was the first time she had done so before the entire group.

"He was going to give us a home!" someone shouted, made bold perhaps by hearing a woman speak out.

"We had a home." Clearly, Gzofie was not intimidated. "We were lured away with false promises and lies."

"We could have stayed," the man said. "We didn't have to go on warring. We could live in peace."

"How?" Ramis asked, his voice growing sharper with each objection he countered. "After the burning, the killing and the drought Fvlad brought on them, how could we hope to be accepted in peace?"

"But it was New Schoolers who burned those people out, not us."

"Because of their own rabid beliefs. But they were spurred on by Bissel and Rancer, and that on our behalf."

"But we didn't know!"

"We knew about the drought."

"You are quick enough to judge, but you came willingly enough," Rhahol said.

"To my shame, I did." Maleem heard the weariness and sadness in Ramis's voice and knew he truly felt the shame as keenly as if he had burned out the farms himself. "When we left to come here, I believed Fvlad. I believed in our cause.

But when I saw what had been done to those people, I could no longer believe."

"But you stayed," Rhahol went on.

"I stayed for my mother and my sister." Ramis reached over and touched Maleem's hand. "She believed without question and look at the cost to her of Fvlad's treachery."

Maleem flinched, not from Ramis's touch but from the memory of what her belief had led her to attempt. And what more might she have done? *Too great a cost.* That's what Pharvin had said when she and the others left their home to follow Fvlad on this madness. Pharvin had been talking of the cost to the Villagers and Outlanders, of course. Or had he? Perhaps he had also been thinking of the cost to the *seraise* of the Plains People and to Maleem herself, though he could not have dreamed of the form that cost would take.

Now, as she looked at Ramis, she understood that without having paid that price, she might never have known what a good man her brother was, nor how much he loved her. At least, with the price she had paid, she had come to understand that. This new vision of him would make bearable the deep well of emptiness in which she now existed. She worked to bring a smile to her lips.

Twenty

THE MORNING DOVELLA WAS TO GO BEFORE THE GUILD, she sat in her small room and stared at her mother who stood at the door, a white tunic in her hand. "I had it made moons ago," Avella said, "when I thought you'd be going through the Rites."

"Would it be appropriate to wear it when this isn't really the same as the Rites?"

"But it is a special occasion." Avella's brow creased as she looked at the tunic. "If you wear dark trews instead of white, no one can complain."

No doubt her mother was thinking of Plais, just as Dovella had been earlier. Although Elder Master Faris had been confident that the Guild would accept Dovella, she was still concerned about how Master Plais would react. He had allowed her to help Carpace, but that didn't mean he had changed his mind about welcoming her into the Guild — and if the Guild was forced to decide between them ... It would choose Plais, of course; it had to. That would further divide the Guild. She let out a long sigh. Was she destined to sow discord wherever she went?

"It will be all right," Safir said. Her father had come to the door and put his arm around Avella's waist. "Elder Master Faris is held in great regard, Dovella, especially by Master

Plais. Plais will not speak against you."

But would he speak for her? As long as he didn't oppose her, Dovella thought, she would have to be content.

"I do think though," her father went on, "that it might be best if you didn't wear the medallion the Khanti-Lafta gave you."

He was right, of course. The Guild members were likely to look askance at her coming in with a medallion, as if she were sure she would be approved. Even as if she thought she didn't need their approval. No doubt, they would be wary of her anyway after hearing of her battle with Fvlad. She didn't want to give them more reason to disapprove of her.

She nodded and reached out for the tunic. Soft and sleek, the garment almost slipped from her fingers. Her parents smiled and left, closing the door behind them. Dovella slipped on the tunic, which felt cool against her skin. She combed and braided her dark hair, then pulled on her black trews and boots.

Dovella looked down at the Healer's Medallion which she'd placed on her bed. Vrillian had been kind enough to send along her and Master Faris's packs with a messenger who'd come to report to Pandil on what had happened to the sorcerer. Even if she didn't wear the medallion, Dovella decided, she would at least wear the small Kavella medal given her by the leader of the Hill Folk.

When she walked into the sitting room, she found Vebelle and Narina there with Avella.

"How lovely!" Narina said. "But you should have flowers in your hair."

"Master Plais would think it frivolous," Dovella replied.

"And if it is?" Narina laughed. "No doubt you are right,

but it would be lovely."

"I'm glad we could be here for this," Vebelle said.

"I think we should be on our way," Avella broke in. "We don't want to be late."

Dovella ran her hands nervously along the sides of the tunic. "That would be all Master Plais needs to refuse me the medallion."

"I'm sure everything will go well," Vebelle said. "We'll be waiting to celebrate when it's over."

It had rained earlier that morning, but it had been a gentle rain. Now the sun was shining and the sky clear of clouds. For a moment Dovella wondered if the *shagines* had provided good weather for her, but she brushed that thought aside. It would have been irresponsible to fashion the weather just for her convenience. No, it was a matter of easing it back into its natural pattern and she was blessed with this fair day.

Together they left the apartment and walked toward Healer's Hall where the Guild would be waiting. Even though the grass had not yet returned to full green, when the sun shone everything had a newly washed glow. Along the road many Villagers were standing to cheer her on her way. Had she been here for the Rites, the sides of the road would have been thronged with people cheering on all the candidates. But even as it was, quite a few people must have learned of her appeal to the Guild. She knew most of them, but there were some who were unknown to her. They seemed to know who she was, however, for they shouted out her name. Some even called out thanks to her for restoring the machine. Others only stared.

Pandil was there, dressed in her formal uniform, a black tunic trimmed with red. Maidel and the other apprentices were likewise formally dressed. Drase was dressed as usual, only his dark hair was loose and he wore a red ribbon tied around his arm. A little further away stood Jael and Vrillian. At the sight of Jael, Dovella almost stumbled, but Avella caught her arm and patted her hand.

As they neared the front entrance to Healer's Hall, Avella stepped to the side to stand with two of her apprentices. To Dovella's surprise Carpace was there, sitting upright in a padded chair on low cart. Carpace grinned and waved. Vebelle and Narina left Dovella's side and went to join her.

Master Granzie stood on the other side of the road, with several New School leaders. He was more soberly dressed than usual and the supercilious smirk he'd so often worn in Council was absent. Many of the New Schoolers had fulminated against the medicine of Healer's Hall, but now Granzie and several others cheered.

Dovella climbed the steps alone, her palms sweaty and her mouth dry. At the top, Elder Master Faris awaited her, his blue tunic whipped about his legs by the wind. He smiled and Dovella felt more at ease. He took her arm, walked her into the building and closed the door behind them, shutting out the shouts of her well-wishers.

Faris led her into a room where nine men sat at a long table. Plais was at the centre, dressed in white while the others wore healer's blue. Safir, sitting at the far end, smiled and gave a little nod. Dovella blinked her eyes but didn't return the smile. She was too nervous to smile, and in any case Plais would think she was not being serious enough. At that thought, a smile almost broke through, but she stifled it and kept her face empty of expression.

Elder Master Faris gave a little bow before the men. "I

bring you candidate Dovella," he said. "As you are aware, she missed her opportunity to go through the Rites although it had been her heart's desire for years. She made the sacrifice for us. For me. For each of you. Without her efforts, the machine would not have been repaired and Havkad's plans to take control of Council would have succeeded. Without her latest trials, we would not have received word of what the Plains sorcerer had planned and we would have been overrun."

Dovella felt a flutter in her stomach. Surely, he would not speak of her battle with Fvlad. They would be sure to reject her for being a worker of magic.

"We owe her much," Faris went on, "but that is not why I have brought her before you. I have brought Dovella here because she has a great gift for healing and she has the knowledge and skill to support that gift. I have worked with her and stand here as an Elder Master to ask that she be accepted by the Guild."

There was a silence as the other members looked to Plais. He gazed at Dovella

"What of the medallion you were wearing earlier?" he asked.

Before she could speak, Faris broke in. "Her eyes were opened by the Khanti-Lafta, who offered teaching. But Dovella has chosen to return to us, her own people, for her training. Are we going to refuse her? Are we going to say that others value her more than we do?"

Plais looked away for a moment, licked his lips, then glanced up and down the table. "You have heard Elder Master Faris's words. Who will join me in welcoming Dovella as Healer affirmed, one of our Guild?"

One by one hands were raised, Safir waiting until last. His

smile warmed Dovella and she let out a quiet sigh, felt her shoulders relax. Finally, the moment she'd awaited so long was here! She felt a sudden lightness in her chest even as a rush of tears threatened to flood her eyes. She lifted her chin and blinked hard.

Plais stood and came around the table. He picked up a ribbon with the Healer's Medallion and placed it around her neck. Then he shook her hand and paused for a moment. He licked his lips again as if he were preparing to speak, then turned away in silence. But it seemed to Dovella that his eyes were moist. Disappointment or shame? It didn't matter at this point, at least he had accepted her. One by one the others came to welcome her, Safir folding her into his arms and kissing her brow.

Safir took her arm and led her outside. Tables had been set up and were now laden with hot pies, both sweet and savoury, their spicy aromas perfuming the air. There were also platters of cheese and fruit and pitchers of drink. To one side sat Narina, harp in hand. She grinned at Dovella and struck up a joyous tune.

Avella and Pandil came to hug Dovella and soon she was surrounded by others wishing her well. Once the dancing was underway, her father took her hand and drew her out among the revellers. Across the courtyard she saw Vrillian and Jael. She felt a tightness in her throat as she remembered Jael holding her close when he'd found her in the forest near his village.

At that moment, Jael looked up and smiled. He came toward her holding out his hand and she stepped shyly away from her father to meet him. She felt a giddiness she couldn't put a name to, but she knew it had to do with Jael's arms being around her, knew she didn't want this dance to ever end. They didn't speak as they danced and when the music stopped, he led her away from the dancers.

They looked up to see Vrillian standing discreetly a few steps away from them. Dovella smiled at him and beckoned him to join them. "Blessings, Dovella, on this day of happiness."

"Thank you, Vrillian. It pleases me that you were able to share this day with me."

"I hope we will share many more. You have learned so much, Dovella, in such a short time. But there is still so much more you need to learn. You have great potential. I hope you will return to us to continue your studies."

Suddenly, she had to speak of the thoughts that had been troubling her since the battle. Of all people, Vrillian and Jael might be understanding.

"I don't understand what happened," she said, "or how I was able to fight Fvlad. But I failed and ..."

Jael took her hand and stroked it gently. "How can you think you failed?"

"Because he got away. And because I let him get away, Maleem suffered."

Vrillian looked at her gravely. "Had you destroyed him, he would ever be a hero to Maleem. Because he survived and returned to the camp, she was able to see what he truly was and she was able to be a part of his destruction. You needed only to hold him at bay: *Maleem* needed to be the one who helped defeat him. Never think you failed, Dovella."

"There is so much I need to learn."

"And you will."

At that moment, Elder Master Faris joined them and

Vrillian gave a little bow in his direction. "And you as well, my friend. We have much to learn from one another."

"But how can I return?" Dovella asked. "How can you want me to after all the discord I caused?"

"Though it was centred around you, Dovella, you were not the cause of it," Vrillian said. "All know that, even if some few might not yet admit it. But they will. In any case, what you need to learn is too important to let that hinder you, or us."

"I will think on it," Dovella said.

Vrillian nodded. "Think well," he said.

He and Elder Master Faris left together and Jael drew Dovella to him again, saying quietly, "I hope you will come, Dovella. I would like for us to have some time together, but I cannot come back here to the Village, not until I have finished my training."

"I know," she said. "It is important that there be more *shagines*. But Jael, how can I return? No matter what Vrillian says, I know there are many who blame me for what happened."

Clasping both her hands in his, Jael drew them to his chest. "I know. I love my home, but even for me it is difficult. The *seraise* has been destroyed and I don't know if it can ever be restored. But I know this as well: it cannot be home for me if there is no place for you. Only, perhaps you don't feel ..."

"I do," she said, warmly. "Oh, Jael, I do." She had longed for a moment such as this, but now that it was here, she felt suddenly awkward. How was she to let him know how she felt? "We've had so little time to get to know each other, but I know I want to be where you are."

"Then we'll find a way," he said, cupping her face in his

hands. "When I'm done with my training, I'll come to you. We'll find a place or make a place. But we will be together." He drew her close and kissed her. "I must leave now," he whispered, "but I will come for you when I can."

Safir came up, smiling at Jael, and took Dovella's hand to lead her to dance.

When she looked again, Jael and Vrillian were no longer there.

Everyone danced into the night. She didn't know half the young men who took her by the hand. Drase danced with her twice, as did Granzie and several other Councillors. Even Plais came by and asked for her hand. She could sense that he was torn, wanting to speak but not finding the words.

She was footsore by the end of the evening, but she couldn't remember when she'd last been so happy. After the celebration, tired but content, she walked between her parents back to their apartment. And now she had to think: what was she to do?

After they returned to the apartment, Dovella and her parents sat into the early hours and talked again about all the things that had befallen her since she had left the Village with Drase.

"Like it or not," she said, "I've accepted that I do have a gift for magic. Not just healing, not just my feel for the machine. Vrillian seems to think I may have some of the Fisher Folk magic as well, something to do with music." She hesitated for a moment, then added, "And, though I still can't take in what happened with Fvlad, clearly I have mind magic too."

And what did that mean for her? Dovella could not shut the anxiety out of her mind. She looked up at them, afraid of what she might see, but their eyes held the same love they always had.

"Then you must learn how to use it properly, all of it, for otherwise you might well do harm unwittingly," said Safir.

"Yes, I have to learn. I don't want to leave the Village again, especially not now when I've finally been confirmed, only ... I know that even though Master Plais accepted me, even though he joined in the celebration dance, even though he welcomed my help with Carpace, he still won't be comfortable working with me at the Hall."

"He'll try, Dovella."

"I know, but in some ways it would be cruel. Every time he sees me, he'll be reminded of the past and of how hard he fought to deny me the medallion."

Dovella met her father's dark eyes and smiled. "It gripes me to admit it, but he *is* a good healer. It would be unkind to cause him pain. And ... I no longer want to spite him."

That sudden admission surprised her, but pleased her as well. Safir's sudden smile told her he was happy to hear her words.

Avella gave her a squeeze. "Perhaps it would be a kindness to give him some time. But what will you do?"

"Keep practising what I learned from Vrillian. Like it or not, I have to determine just what magic I do have and how to use it. Understand what it means. And I'll keep learning about healing. Give *Master* Plais time to accept me." This time when Dovella emphasized the healer's title, it was with understanding. With understanding had come respect.

And wait for Jael, she thought; but she did not speak of that.

OTHER GREAT SUMACH PRESS BOOKS
FOR YOUNG ADULTS